"This is a gripping tale that made my heart ache for the oh-so-believable characters. Misty Beller is a new author well worth watching out for."

—Lauraine Snelling, author of THE RED RIVER OF THE NORTH series

"I've long been a Misty Beller fan and her book *Hope's Highest Mountain* didn't disappoint. Misty tells a wonderful tale of adventure and romance as her characters face challenges from the past and present that threaten their ability to deal with the future. My only negative thought is that I'll have to wait much too long for her next book."

—Tracie Peterson, bestselling author

"*Hope's Highest Mountain* is a nonstop mountain adventure. Misty M. Beller takes her characters to the edge of disaster time and time again, while still telling a hope-filled, inspiring story. Readers will be delighted."

—Regina Jennings, author of *The Lieutenant's Bargain*

"With a heart-pounding opening, *Hope's Highest Mountain* keeps a breathless pace, each broken yet beautiful character overcoming their own mountainous hurdles while navigating the epic yet treacherous Montana Rockies. Hope is indeed the shining thread in this first novel of the series, sure to captivate historical fiction fans. Misty M. Beller brings the nineteenth-century American frontier to vivid life!"

—Laura Frantz, Christy Award–winning author of *The Lacemaker*

"The exciting opening captured me in the Montana mountains. I fell in love with the well-developed characters and experienced their highs and lows. Misty is a master storyteller. Her richly evocative word choice bring everything to life. I've loved all her books, and now this one is my favorite."

—Lena Nelson Dooley, author, editor, and speaker

"This Rocky Mountain wilderness story is one of romance, adventure, and survival, and it kept me enthralled. It reminds me of Charles Martin's *The Mountain Between Us*, with the added elements of faith and hope. I couldn't put *Hope's Highest Mountain* down until I'd finished the last page."

—Shelia Stovall, executive director,
Allen County Public Library

# *Hope's*
# HIGHEST MOUNTAIN

# *Hope's* HIGHEST MOUNTAIN

## MISTY M. BELLER

BETHANYHOUSE
a division of Baker Publishing Group
Minneapolis, Minnesota

© 2019 by Misty M. Beller

Published by Bethany House Publishers
11400 Hampshire Avenue South
Bloomington, Minnesota 55438
www.bethanyhouse.com

Bethany House Publishers is a division of
Baker Publishing Group, Grand Rapids, Michigan

Printed in the United States of America

Library of Congress Cataloging-in-Publication Data
Names: Beller, Misty M., author.
Title: Hope's highest mountain / Misty M. Beller.
Description: Bloomington, Minnesota : Bethany House Publishers, 2019. | Series: Hearts of Montana ; 1
Identifiers: LCCN 2019016256| ISBN 9780764234866 (casebound) | ISBN 9780764233463 (trade paper) | ISBN 9781493421701 (ebook)
Subjects: LCSH: Montana—Fiction. | GSAFD: Western stories | Love stories | Christian fiction
Classification: LCC PS3602.E45755 H67 2019 | DDC 813/.6—dc23
LC record available at https://lccn.loc.gov/2019016256

Scripture quotations are from the King James Version of the Bible.

Cover design by Kirk DouPonce, DogEared Design

Author is represented by Books & Such Literary Agency.

19  20  21  22  23  24  25      7  6  5  4  3  2  1

To my editor, Raela Schoenherr,
for believing in me and not giving up
on me until God's perfect timing.
You're an amazing lady,
and I'm blessed to work with you!

If I take the wings of the morning, and dwell in the
uttermost parts of the sea;
Even there shall thy hand lead me, and thy right
hand shall hold me.

Psalm 139:9–10 KJV

# ONE

*My Darling Rachel,*

*You were everything to me. You still are. Don't ever forget that.*

*I saw a beaver today that reminded me of you. The creature paddled to the edge of the river and peered up at me through the water, just like that summer you learned to swim in the Ohio.*

*Your mama could barely pull you from the river to eat and sleep, you loved swimming so much. When you did come home, water dripping from your red curls, you always carried some treasure you'd gathered—smooth river rocks or a pail of tadpoles you planned to keep as pets. That was the summer you earned your nickname, sweet Ducky.*

*Mama didn't care for the title at first, but the name captured your personality so well, I couldn't help myself. Always swimming. Always smiling. My little Ducky.*

*I only wish I would have watched you swim more often instead of spending long days away from you and Mama. So much I missed. If I had it to do over again, I'd have kicked off my shoes and dove into the water with you. Played games to see who could reach the shore first or who could hold their breath the longest. I would have joined in any amusement you thought of, just to spend another marvelous hour with you.*

*I miss you every hour of every day.*

*Papa*

◊⟨═══◦═══⟩◊

OCTOBER 1866
MONTANA TERRITORY

*T*hey say the last man who attempted this died in the doin'. Rest his soul."

A frigid gust of wind ripped around the freight wagon. Ingrid Chastain pulled her cloak tighter around her shoulders. She tucked her chin into her collar, blocking out both the icy air and the images their driver's morbid words conjured. This rugged cliffside might be as perilous as the old man described, but the staggering beauty of the mountains around them caused her chest to pulse, as though she was just now coming alive.

The mules plodded ever upward as the side of the mountain fell away on their left. It seemed a wonder this road could have been carved into the edge of such a jagged cliff. Every difficult step carried them higher, almost eye level with the majestic peaks surrounding them. This land possessed a strength she'd never imagined possible.

"Was the traveler properly prepared for the elements?" Her

attention shifted back to the unlikely pair on the bench seat in the front of the wagon. Father, with his newly purchased fur coat, sat upright and confident beside their driver, a hunched gray-haired man in worn buckskins. Father spoke again, "Any endeavor worth doing can be harmful if not attempted correctly." Of course he would look at the story from the most logical approach.

Ingrid slid a glance at Beulah, their quiet maid, perched across from her. The supplies almost buried Beulah's ample curves but didn't hide her dark gaze swimming with worry. She looked away from Ingrid, down to their pet dog who'd nestled in her lap. Did she regret her determination to accompany Father on this trip of mercy? The gentle maid had been with them as far back as Ingrid could remember and had as tender a heart as any woman alive. When the desperate wire came, begging Father to send smallpox vaccines to an obscure mining town in the Montana Territory, Beulah had insisted on accompanying Ingrid and her father. There would likely be a need for nurses if the smallpox outbreak had spread.

Their driver didn't answer Father's words right away, merely hacked a raucous cough, then spoke to the mules as they climbed upward on the rocky trail. "Git up, boys." He added more encouragement with a flick of the reins. At last, he sent a sideways glance to Father. "I reckon' Angus Jones knew about these mountains as much as anyone. I 'spect he did as well as he could."

A moment of foreboding silence hovered in the air, mingling with the cloud of breath from their driver's words. "We've already passed the spot that did him in."

Father's shoulders relaxed. "Well then, Mr. Sorenson. We'll make it through just fine. I have faith in you, these mules, and especially in our Lord, who has promised to be our Salvation and Deliverer."

Mr. Sorenson didn't respond but hunkered down a little more, his elbows pressing on his legs. He coughed again, a rough bark this time, shooting another white cloud into the air.

"When we camp, I'll prepare a tea that will help your ailment." Father's voice hummed low, the tone he used with his patients.

Their driver leaned forward and flicked the reins on the mules' backs again as the brutal slope steepened. Ahead, the road bent in a switchback as it climbed toward the summit. The choice Mr. Sorenson made to use only a two-mule hitch to pull their substantial load made sense now. The tight turn would be a difficult angle for a longer rig pulled by more animals.

He guided the mules wide to take the turn, and another cough jolted the man's shoulders. He collapsed over with a ragged gasp.

"Sorenson?" Papa's shout came just as the driver dropped the reins. The leather straps bounced unguided against the wooden brace.

Ingrid's heart surged to her throat. She lunged forward, over the bench, scrambling for the leathers. Father grabbed Sorenson, and she slid her willowy frame under his arms as she closed her hands around the thick straps.

A mule let out a blood-curdling bray, and the wagon seemed to hover for a second. Or maybe a long minute.

Then the conveyance slid. The mule cried out again, this time sounding hoarse and strained.

The flap of Father's coat hindered her view of the animals. She clutched harder at the straps in her hands. Though panic stole her breath, she attempted to shake the reins, the way

12

Sorenson had when urging the mules forward. "Git up!" Her voice didn't hold the strong command of their mule-whacker. Only shrill fear.

A loud crack splintered the air.

The wagon slid backward. Her grip tightened on the straps, clutching with every bit of strength. Though the wagon shifted beneath her, the animals hitched to the leathers didn't seem to move. The mules pulled her forward as the wagon slid backward, hauling her up on the bench between her father and their driver.

Father yelled. Someone screamed. Whether a man or woman, she didn't know.

Ingrid pulled the reins even harder, trying to end this madness. Her chest caught a hard blow on the front of the wagon— the footboard. She tried to brace herself against it, not finding purchase with her body.

But she refused to release the reins. Holding tight to the connection with the mules was their only hope of keeping them all from sliding down the side of the mountain.

Arms pulled at her. Or maybe it was the wagon pressing into her chest, wrenching her in two. She fought harder to keep her grip.

For a dizzying moment, she was rolling. Floating. Falling.

Something hard and heavy crashed into her leg. Then . . . blackness.

Micah Bradley forced one foot in front of the other as the icy wind surged along the mountain crag, buffeting his neck beneath his beaver-skin hat. He almost didn't notice the gusts anymore. Not much anyway. Except when the icy fingers snuck under his defenses.

A hoarse cry filled the air, stilling his feet mid-stride.

He strained to hear above the howling gusts. A mountain lion? Or maybe the eerie wail of wind sweeping around the rocks?

There, it came again. A mule?

No wagon train would dare venture through these mountains so near to winter. The first snowstorm appeared to be only hours away.

He plunged forward, angling higher up the mountain as he lengthened his stride. It must be another trapper. Yet something about the cry set the hairs of his nape on end and pressed him forward.

He rounded an outcropping of rocks, bringing the wagon road into view in the distance. A figure shifted on the trail. A man? His heart gave a leap. He'd not seen a person in weeks. He squinted to focus.

Two forms, actually. Animal, not people. One must be the mule he'd heard. Micah lengthened his stride. Where there were mules, there had to be men to handle them.

The animals lingered on the mountain road, waiting. But for what? No man moved around them. At least, none he could see.

Something was wrong. He could feel it in his bones. The same way he used to know his doctoring skills were about to be summoned, even before a pounding knock sounded on his door.

That had all been so many desolate years ago. Too bad the instincts hadn't died along with everything else he'd loved.

# TWO

A mournful bray sliced through the blasts of icy wind. Micah approached the two mules with a slow step and an outstretched arm. The animals stood in the bend of the road in the switchback, harnesses hanging from them, reins and straps dragging behind into the brush along the side of the road.

The mule that cried out stood with its hoof cocked at an odd angle. Broken. He'd seen that twisted look enough to know, even before feeling the bones. The other mule stood on all fours, although the whites of its eyes flashed, as though still recovering from a fright.

Micah's chest tightened as he scanned the area, his gaze drawn over the side of the mountain. Had a wagon tumbled down that treacherous descent? The cliff didn't drop off completely but tapered steeply enough that a hurtling conveyance wouldn't survive the impact at the bottom. Neither would the people inside, unless they jumped off.

He stepped from the trail and grabbed a bush to help him descend the incline. A motion to the side snagged his focus.

Was that . . . blue fabric?

His pulse surged as he scrambled toward it, jumping a rock and sidestepping a scrubby pine.

A woman lay on the rocky ground, her body twisted.

His chest clenched as he slowed to take in the details as he approached, his mind falling into the habit too easily. Her head lay at an angle, but maybe not as much as he'd first thought. The loose strands of her glossy brown hair gave her more of a disheveled look, not that of a broken spinal column.

Dropping to his knees beside her, he pressed two fingers against her slender neck. He'd not seen a woman like this in more months than he could count.

He forced his mind to focus, to shift back into his training. He scanned the rest of her. Arms bundled in a coat, not lying at awkward angles. Legs were hard to tell under all those skirts. She hadn't dressed for the mountains in winter, but more for an eastern ballroom. What was a woman like this doing in the wilderness with a snowstorm coming any minute?

A faint pulse sped under his fingers. Light but quick. Her face was pale, and a bead of sweat glistened across the porcelain skin of her brow. He pressed his hand there. Cold and clammy. A knot formed in his gut.

"Miss?" He patted her cheek with just enough *umph* to pull her to consciousness if she wavered at the edge.

No response.

He stroked her head, running his fingers over every inch. A bump rose near the base of her skull. How long had she been unconscious? Her condition required getting her to a warm shelter, but there might be others who needed him, too.

Shifting away from her head, Micah began a quick fingertip assessment over the rest of her. He'd feel better about doing so if he had her consent before checking her legs, but if a bone needed to be set, she'd thank him later for getting the job done while she couldn't feel the pain.

Before he'd raised the skirts higher than her booted ankles, the unnatural turn of her left leg twisted the knot tighter in his gut. A quick inspection revealed the truth. Her thigh bone had a full break—an excruciatingly painful break, given the amount of swelling already.

He had to set the bone before she moved, preferably before she woke up. But he still needed to look for other survivors. She couldn't be traveling alone, and someone's life may depend on him.

He rose and strode down the mountain, shifting and sliding as he went, bracing himself against brush and rock. It wasn't hard to follow the trail of bent saplings and rumpled bushes. He hoped the thick underbrush had helped slow the careening wagon.

Partway down the slope, the shattered remnants of a conveyance pressed into a cluster of sturdy lodgepole pines. His breathing grew harder, but he forced himself to shuffle down the steepening hill. No one could have survived that crash.

A flash of buckskin snagged his focus, just beside his foot. A leg.

He stumbled forward, then twisted and dropped to his knees beside the man who'd been shielded under a squatty bush. An older fellow with graying hair and a thick beard. The haggard sun-leathered lines of his face and well-worn buckskin carried the look of a man familiar with this territory.

Micah waited a whole minute with his fingers pressed against the patient's neck, shifting in search of a pulsing artery. Nothing.

He straightened the man's arms and gave him a final squeeze

on the shoulder. "Rest in peace. I'll be back to settle you when I can."

He pushed to his feet and another boot caught his glance, only a stride or so behind this man. How many were there?

Micah swallowed the burn in his throat as he stepped toward a stout, well-groomed man. A gash ran from his cheek all the way down his neck, the skin split wide and still oozing blood. Micah avoided the crimson while he focused on finding a pulse somewhere in the man's veins. The gray interspersed through his hair made him appear to be in his middle years. Maybe the woman's father or uncle? His hands weren't work-worn but did have burn marks and calluses in odd places. Interesting.

But the man would never be able to explain the oddity, as his heart no longer beat. Not enough blood left to pump, considering how much had leached into the rocky soil, running down the mountain in a long stream.

Micah looked away, forcing his gaze up to the heavens. Anything to clear his head of other images of blood oozing over pale flesh. Once-delicate skin, marred with the awful pox. Death. No matter how far he ran, he seemed to drag it behind him like a prisoner's ball and chain.

The sky above offered nothing to encourage him. Only the thick gray of coming snow.

He pushed to his feet. There was much to do and very little time left to do it.

The ebony-skinned woman he found mixed in the debris of the wagon held a sweet smile, even in death. A final sweep of the area showed only splintered wood and fragments of supplies. No more bodies.

There had been only one survivor, and he'd best turn his focus on her if he hoped to keep her alive. With a coil of rope,

a blanket, and boards he'd pulled from the wagon, he climbed
the steep slope and knelt beside her. "Ma'am?"

She stirred. A good sign—for her head injury at least.

He brushed his hand across her forehead again. Still cold
and damp. He had to get her warm. She needed a fire and furs
to snuggle under. Both of which he couldn't give her here.

Especially not with the air thick with ice-tinged moisture.
The first flakes would fall any moment, and by the look of the
clouds, a dangerously heavy snow would follow. If only God
would hold off the snow, at least for a few hours.

But the Almighty had stopped doing him favors a long time
ago.

He touched the woman's shoulder. "Ma'am. Your leg is
broken, so I'm going to set the bone. It will be painful, but
it's important I do it right."

No flutter of her dark lashes. No pinch of her brow. Maybe
she'd stay unconscious a little longer.

He inhaled a long breath and set to work. After positioning
her skirts out of the way and slicing through her stockings,
the knot in his chest eased a little to see that the bone hadn't
broken the skin. Her limb had already swollen to almost twice
its size, and the knob raised a handbreadth above the knee
showed exactly where the bone had broken and now pushed
against the inner wall of the skin. Thankfully, the bump was
on the outer side of the leg, so there was less chance he might
nick the femoral artery when he set the bone. Still, he'd have to
watch closely for signs of damage to that critical blood vessel.

He settled himself where he could pull the bone back into
place. Not an easy position for either of them. At least she
wasn't awake to realize it.

With a firm grasp on her ankle, he clenched his jaw and

pulled on the bone, shifting her leg, then easing the limb to the ground as the internal workings pulled the bone back into correct position. He let out a long exhale, then crawled back up to her head.

If possible, her face had lost more color. Since the pain hadn't awakened her, the agony of what he'd just done must have forced her into a deeper sleep. He'd set more broken limbs than he could count in the seven years he'd spent doctoring in Indiana. This kind of intense pain could drive the patient either way. He'd have to work fast to brace her leg and get her back to his camp before she awoke. *If* she awoke. Healing the head injury might prove harder than setting the bone.

Within minutes, he had the limb wrapped in the blanket for comfort, then secured tightly to the boards along the length of her leg. He'd chosen wood that would hang past the end of her foot for good reason. Where the break was located, she'd not be able to bear weight for several weeks. If the brace kept her from pressing her foot against the ground, she'd be less inclined to try.

And there was still a strong chance that trauma this severe— both her head and her leg—might be more than her body could recover from. He might fail this patient. Just like he'd failed his own family. His gaze traveled to her face, which was beautiful, despite the dirt and bruising. So fragile. Like Ella and Rachel . . . His pulse thrummed in his ears, and his chest locked down tight.

*Focus.* He couldn't give up yet. He steadied the shaking in his hands and readjusted her skirts to cover her ankles. Given her other injuries, he really needed to check for bruising in her midsection before he moved her. If she was bleeding inside, waiting to address the damage could seal her fate.

She wore a shirtwaist that tucked into her skirt, not a full dress with buttons in the back. He forced his mind not to play back old memories as he worked through the layers. At least he didn't have to worry about pockmarks in this examination.

No swelling or dark bruising in her lower abdomen, which would signal damage to her vital organs. But an area farther up, just above the base of her ribs, boasted a dark, puffy circle. A broken rib, if he had to guess, which meant he'd have to be careful. Too much jarring could pierce a lung. The last thing she needed.

He readjusted her clothing and wrapped her cloak tighter around her. Moisture beaded on her brow again, intensifying the clammy feel of her skin. Her body seemed unsure whether to turn feverish or give out completely.

Pushing to his feet, Micah turned his focus to the mules. An icy prick of sleet stung his nose, and another his cheek. Time was running out. They had to move to shelter. He strode toward the mules, which now stood with their heads hanging, still in harness.

The uninjured animal looked up when Micah approached, and he stroked the mule's face. Weary brown eyes stared back at him, a little glassy, but no longer showing the whites around the edges.

"It's gonna get better, fella. Soon. It has to." If only his words were true. He patted the mule on the neck as he reached under and unfastened the strap that held the animals together.

Stepping close to the hurt mule, he rubbed the animal's neck to soothe him, then ran his hands down its back, working his way to that rear leg. A closer look at the swollen limb and the way the bottom part of the leg hung at a loose angle told him his suspicions had been right, but he still did his diligence.

The mule balked when his hand neared the injury, jumping sideways and hobbling off on three hooves. Not once did it put weight on the left rear. If it had tried, it likely would have driven the bone right through its flesh.

With a sigh, he turned back to the first mule. "We'll get you tied someplace safe, then take care of your friend here." Taking care of the injured animal entailed a task he did not relish.

The mules looked almost identical. Maybe brothers that had pulled together most of their lives. Working in tandem, knowing the other's movements before each came, feeling and doing everything together. No wonder the healthy mule still looked miserable. Micah knew that feeling. Losing a longtime companion shattered one's heart.

Micah forced a swallow past the lump in his throat. It had to be done. It was the only merciful thing.

He grasped the bridle of the healthy mule and pulled it forward, gathering the rein in a loop. The animal walked two steps, then stopped, turning to its companion. "I know, boy. Say good-bye."

The mule loosed a bray, low and hoarse, as though already mourning.

Micah patted the animal's neck, then pulled it toward a sturdy pine twenty strides off the trail. He tied the rein in several knots, then tested the strength of his work. That should do.

The animal stood with its head high, white showing around its eyes again. Micah stroked the bulge behind its ear. "Stay here a few minutes, then we'll find a way to get that lady to a better place."

Micah inhaled a strengthening breath and turned back to what had to be done. The injured mule still stood with its head down, that back hoof cocked so the toe barely rested on the ground.

Micah turned away and strode toward the edge of the trail where he'd left his rifle. He set his jaw and scooped up the gun, then turned and took aim. The quicker the better.

Just as he was lining up the sight, the wounded mule loosed a pathetic bray, sending a surge of burning up to Micah's eyes. He spread his legs and fixed his finger on the set trigger, moving it into place.

The mule behind him released an ear-splitting answer to his friend. His lifelong companion. His brother.

Micah sighted on the injured mule's side where his heart would be, then pulled the trigger, squeezing his eyes shut as the gun exploded.

# THREE

*A* cry ripped through the air.

Micah whirled to see the healthy mule pulling furiously at the rein that held it to the tree. With a pop, the leather snapped, propelling the animal backward. It landed on its haunches, even as its front legs paddled to spin it around. The mule stumbled to its feet, swaying.

Micah strode toward it. "Hey, boy. Easy." He spread both arms wide, shifting right to approach the wide-eyed mule head-on. If he let the animal get away, they'd really be in a mess. If only he'd taken time to make a halter out of the rope instead of relying on the bridle to hold it secure. Of course the sound of gunfire would make the animal bolt. He should have expected the reaction.

The mule released another piercing bray, then jerked its head sideways, swiveling away from Micah. He could close the distance in a half-dozen strides, if only the mule wouldn't kick him in the approach.

"Easy." He kept his voice to a croon and even managed to hold the tone steady, despite the pounding in his chest.

A step closer, and the mule seemed to bunch tight within itself. Like a mountain lion poised to attack.

Or maybe more like a deer. Either way, not safe to be around. With another hoarse cry, the mule sprung forward, leaping over a low cedar shrub and landing on the road. It sprinted down the mountain trail toward Fort Benton, the place the animal probably considered home.

Micah would never catch him. Not without effort and time. And he had no time to waste.

A woman's life depended on him. Again.

The ache in his gut spread through all his muscles. What was God thinking to saddle him with a woman so wounded? Hadn't he proved himself incapable? Yet he couldn't ignore her. Even though she might have as good a chance at survival on her own as with him.

He sighed and turned toward his patient. That wasn't quite true. But he had his work cut out for him.

Ingrid fought against the grip pulling her toward the furnace. The raging fire already seared her leg. And her head. If only she could think straight, she would get loose and run far away from this inferno.

A hand gripped her shoulder. "Miss?"

She fought to wrench free. To back away from the heat.

*No. Let me go.*

Now hands held both her shoulders. Why did they keep her here? Her leg burned as though the flame had already scorched the skin to ashes. She was going to die if they didn't let her go.

Tiny pellets of ice dotted her face, at odds to the heat all around her. Then a hand brushed her brow. Not like the other hands had gripped her. This one had a different touch. Light. Almost soothing. If only they would pull her away from the heat. Away from the fire eating through her leg . . . pounding through her head.

"Sshh."

Someone whimpered, or maybe that was her own cry. She pressed into that soothing hand, letting herself relish the one touch that eased the agony.

Micah didn't have time to waste sitting here with his hand resting on the woman's forehead. Yet she clutched his wrist, holding him still. Her skin was no longer cold and damp; a fever now raged inside, her body warring against the trauma she'd endured.

He had to get her back to his camp and out of the thickening snowfall. Without a mule to help transport her, his only option was to haul her himself. Even if he could carry this woman the hour's trek back to his camp, his arm under her leg would cause her an unimaginable amount of pain, maybe even shifting the bone so the fractured ends drove through her skin.

That wasn't an option.

He'd need to rig some sort of wagon or sled for her to ride on.

"I'll be back soon." He ignored the squeeze of his chest as he peeled his hand away from the woman's weak grip, then pushed to his feet.

A hike back down to the mangled wagon would give him what he needed.

As he sorted through the wood and scattered supplies, some of the objects began to look eerily familiar. A roll of bandaging had unraveled, wrapping itself in knots around a wad of cloths. A black leather case looked much like a medical kit, but that was likely his mind recalling his former life. Yet when he opened the buckle, several wooden boxes stared up at him. A stethoscope. Vials of medicines, well-padded and held in their own case. The bag contained enough bandages to wrap a broken limb, and even a mortar and pestle. Almost everything he once carried in his own doctor's bag.

He shoved the satchel closed, pushing aside the memories that tried to surface, and moved on to another crate. He had to stay focused on finding a way to transport the injured woman, although he should probably come back for these things after he got her to camp, in case he needed them later.

The well-dressed man must've been a doctor. Had he been planning to hang his shingle in one of the mining towns here in the Territory? Life among all those money-grubbers would have been a rude awakening for a man accustomed to finer things.

The front of the wagon was mutilated, having crashed headlong into the stout trees, but the rear axle and wheels were intact. Much of the wood from the bed had split or splintered, but enough remained in that rear section that a woman could lie with her legs extended, if she bent at the waist. He'd have to figure a way to pull her himself, like a pony cart.

The plan would have to work. There were no other choices in the limited time. A glance at the gray clouds closing in above pressed him into action. Time was almost up.

After he found an ax and cleared the boxes from the rear of the wagon bed, he hacked away the remaining strips of wood that held the back half of the wagon to the front. Sweat dampened his buckskins, but this effort would be nothing compared to trying to get the contraption up the mountain.

When he finally separated the rear section from the rest, he piled on all the blankets he could find, then added another coil of rope. Could he make some of the harness still worn by the poor deceased mule work?

Pushing the cart up the nearly vertical incline proved almost more effort than he had in him. His breath came in gasps. His moccasins slid over the rocky ground, now covered with a thin layer of icy slush. He didn't have time to rest, yet every part of him screamed for at least a moment's relief.

Onward he climbed. His legs burned, the effort pressing through his shoulders and chest and down to the very core of him. Each step more hard-won than the one before.

At last, he eased the cart to the ground beside his patient, who still lay in the same position he'd left her. He dropped to his knees, his lungs fighting for air. Inhaling the biting chill made his chest ache, but he couldn't seem to get enough.

As soon as his legs would hold him again, he pushed to his feet. All he lacked was the harness, then he could get her loaded and be on his way. Another hour with this snowfall and he'd have to build a sled instead of a cart.

As he approached the mule's still form to remove the harness, his stomach churned. Poor animal. Had it ever enjoyed a carefree life? He had to force himself into that distant place he hated but knew all too well. Though he was certain he'd done what the injury required, his training had been to save lives, never to take them. His fingers fumbled as he released the leather buckles and pulled the straps away, then worked to make a smaller version of the yoke for himself.

Finally, with the harness ready, the snow wiped off the cart's bed, and a blanket spread to soften the hard wood, he turned back to the woman. This wouldn't be easy. His stomach churned at the thought of the pain she'd endure.

A thin layer of white covered her cloak and skirts, and her eyes still rested shut, long brown lashes fanning porcelain cheeks. He'd not seen skin that soft in so long. Too long. But he couldn't let himself follow those thoughts now. Her lips moved, as though she was whispering.

Or maybe praying. Perhaps God would hear her prayers and help them both. The Almighty hadn't listened to his petitions in years, but maybe He'd answer this woman's request.

Micah blinked away the sheen that blurred his vision, then dropped to his knees beside her and brushed the snow off her clothing. "Miss, I'm going to move you to a cart. That way I can get you out of this weather."

Her lashes fluttered, then parted, allowing him a glimpse of dark pupils surrounded by honey. Surely pain tinged her eyes, yet she seemed to be studying him.

*I'm a doctor.* The statement almost spilled out of him. She needed reassurance, no doubt. But those three words shouldn't reassure anyone. And they weren't even true. Not anymore.

He clenched his jaw tighter and focused on how best to move her. "Your leg is broken pretty badly, so I think I need to lift from your waist. We'll let your leg follow behind and ease the brace along as we can." He'd have to be careful about her injured rib, too. There was no easy way to go about this.

Her chin bobbed a slight movement, and her eyes pressed shut again, as though she were already bracing for the agony likely to come. "Do it." The words came out in a tiny whisper.

He slipped his fingers under her back, taking care to stay well above the bruising in her midsection. Using both hands, he lifted her enough to work his arm so she almost leaned against his shoulder. This position would be awkward, but he could crawl backward and let his body carry most of her upper weight, leaving at least one of his hands free to help support her braced leg. He couldn't let the limb bounce as it dragged over the terrain.

She'd tensed the moment he touched her but didn't make a sound until he moved the first step backward. Then only a gasp through her teeth. He clenched his own, imagining the pain that must be surging through her damaged limb. Through her entire body.

*Go easy.* One inch at a time. When his shoulder bumped the cart, he let out a breath he hadn't meant to hold. Little by little, he slid her onto the boards, upper body first. "You're going to have to lie on your left side and bend at the waist so your leg fits."

He helped her work into that position with one hand while lifting the splinted leg onto the cart with his other. When they finally had her in place, she let out a slow, achingly long breath.

A lock of hair rested across her cheek, and he brushed it aside. Her soft skin sent a jolting warmth through his work-worn fingers. He pulled his hand back. "That should be the hardest part. Now you get to ride a while." Not that traveling on this old wagon frame would be anything close to a padded carriage bench, but something in him felt the need to keep her spirits up. Knowing her name would help, too.

That tiny pointed chin bobbed again, enough that he caught the slight movement. At least she was trying. And she hadn't complained once. Most people would be curled in a ball, wailing. Maybe she was stronger than she looked.

With a final glance to make sure she was secure, he stood and gathered the harness around him. Regardless of how much he'd accomplished in the past hour, in truth, the worst of the journey still lie ahead.

# FOUR

*I*ngrid gripped the sides of the cart, her fingers digging into the rough wood. If only the splinters poking her skin could distract her from the searing pain in her leg and midsection. Icy snowflakes prickled her face—a welcome chill to offset the flames eating her insides. Every breath intensified the ache, and she focused on taking in shallow bits of air.

For hours the cart bumped and jostled over the rough ground—or at least it felt like hours. The contraption tilted upward at times, then leaned so far down as they descended an incline that only her fingers clamped around the side kept her from rolling out.

If she had enough breath, she would call out to the man pulling the rig. Find out where he was taking her. How much farther. But enduring the blade in her middle and the fire in her leg took all the strength she had. Her vision kept blurring, maybe from the tears stinging her eyes, or maybe she crept toward the edge of unconsciousness.

She couldn't swoon though. The risk was too great that she might roll out of the cart and down the side of this mountain.

Micah strained into his load, the effort burning his midsection all the way down to his legs. Camp wasn't much farther, just over this rise and down into the nook at the base of the mountain. Protected on three sides, it was the best campsite he'd found since the cave at the end of last winter. Nothing like what this woman was accustomed to, but it would have to do for now.

As he crested the ridge, he turned to grab hold of the conveyance to keep it from rushing downhill. The woman lay where he'd placed her, but her eyes squeezed shut and her white-knuckled grip on the wood proved she hadn't dozed off.

"Just a few minutes more."

Her eyelids fluttered open, pain lines grooving their edges. She nodded, and seemed to be taking quick, shallow breaths. Maybe he should let her rest a few moments.

He dropped to his knees beside her, keeping hold of the cart's edge so it didn't tilt. "We'll stop a minute."

She shook her head, an intense, jerky motion. "Just go." She must be eager to finish this torturous ride and cease the jarring.

He pushed back to his feet, his legs protesting at the effort. "If you're sure."

As answer, she squeezed her eyes shut again, preparing for the renewal of torment.

He did his best to avoid stones and shrubs that would jostle the wheels, but a layer of snow had settled over the landscape, making it harder to discern a rock from a clump of winter grass.

To the woman's credit, she cried out only once, when the

cart bumped over a low ledge of rock into a gully at the base of his camp.

"We're almost there," he called over his shoulder.

She didn't answer, and he didn't stop to check to see if she'd passed out. Just dug in for the last uphill slope. He didn't even slow as he reached the edge of the little space he called home, just pulled her toward the brush lean-to that housed his supplies and bedding. The wheels barely missed the ashes of his campfire, and he was able to pull her right next to the sleeping pallet.

Exhaustion washed through him as he straightened, keeping tension on the harness to hold the cart level. "We made it." He sucked in air, ignoring the burn in his lungs from the chill.

They both needed water, but not until after he transferred her to the bed. Otherwise, she might spew the liquid back on him with the pain of moving. He should probably steep a bit of willow bark for her, too.

After shucking the harness, he studied the woman's position relative to the pallet of furs he used as bedding. He'd only need to transfer her a few feet, but that movement would be excruciating for her.

Crouching beside her, he settled a hand on her shoulder. "I'm going to move you to the bedroll under the shelter so you can rest out of the snow. It'll hurt, but I'll be as quick as I can."

Her eyelids fluttered open, and her brown eyes met his for a brief moment. Those orbs held so many shades, giving them a depth that felt like he was looking all the way to her soul. Her dark lashes sank shut again before he could read the emotion there. Certainly pain, but much more.

Pushing aside the distraction, he looked to the rough splint peeking out from under her skirt. "I'm going to move your leg down to the ground first, then I'll lift you."

He did as he promised, and her only response was a squeak as he eased her up from the cart. By the time he laid her on the wolf fur, her face was as pale as the snow powdering her coat. He positioned her injured leg so the foot rested at a natural angle, then rolled a blanket alongside her to hold the limb secure. Finally, he draped the extra buffalo and bearskins over her body to protect her from the cold.

A glance at her face showed her eyes open in narrow slits, her dark pupils watching him.

"More comfortable?" He tucked the edge of the fur around her shoulders.

She nodded, more with her eyes than her head, which must mean her head ached. Not surprising with all she'd been through.

"I don't know your name." He shouldn't force her to talk since the effort probably pained her, but if they were going to be spending a while together, it seemed he should know what to call her.

Her mouth parted—working, as though she was trying to summon moisture. Her lips were bright red and dry. He pressed his hand to her forehead, still feverish. She needed water next.

"Ingrid." The word came out in a rasp, and she cleared her throat. "Ingrid Chastain."

The name sifted through his mind, settling in as though he'd known it for years. The words formed a picture of innocence, purity, and beauty. Exactly as she appeared.

Her eyes opened a bit more, her face tipping so she could

look at him better. Her mouth opened, working for another word. "Yours?"

Heat flushed up his neck. He'd been out in this wilderness so long, he'd lost all decent manners. "Bradley. Dr. Micah Bradley."

Her eyes widened a little more, and his stomach flipped. He hadn't called himself *doctor* in five years and hadn't meant to say it now. He had no right to the title anymore. He'd proven himself far too unworthy.

Turning away, he focused on rekindling the banked fire. Too much snow had fallen, dampening the coals, so he had to start from scratch with flint and dry tinder from his stack.

His cold hands fumbled more than normal, and maybe not just because of the frigid weather. The presence of the woman lying just behind him weighed heavy. Why had he brought her here, thinking he could somehow save her life? Yet, what else could he have done? He couldn't leave her to die on the mountainside. Although death may still be her outcome.

After far too long, he worked the fire hot enough to melt snow. A few more minutes warmed the liquid, and he lowered a cloth pouch of shredded bark from a white willow into the water.

The chatter of tiny animals drew his attention, and he slid a glance to the three chipmunks who'd ventured into camp. They kept themselves several strides away, possibly because of the woman they weren't accustomed to seeing behind him. Her presence didn't cease their steady chirping, though.

He reached for the pouch at his waist and pulled a small handful of oats to toss to them. "I don't have the good stuff today. You'll have to come back later."

They scurried toward the grains, scooping them up like beggars gathering coin. With a few final chirps, his friends scampered away. He'd miss those urchins when they went into hibernation, but maybe the timing was for the best. He now had someone else who needed him a great deal more.

At least for now.

When the tea was finally ready, he carried the tin cup to her. "Try to drink some. This will help with your pain and fever." He brushed his fingers against her cheek. Still warm, but not more than before. A good sign.

Her long lashes flicked upward, her eyes meeting his without searching, as if she knew exactly where to look for him. Lifting her head, she reached for the cup. He didn't release it into her hand but helped guide the mug to her mouth. Her lips were still so chapped; she needed bear grease to protect them from the wind and cold.

After drinking half the liquid in the cup, she sank back against the fur, panting.

"Those broken ribs will be painful for a few weeks. Try not to strain yourself. Sleep is what will help the most for now."

She studied him, fear edging into her eyes for the first time. "Where are the others?"

A boulder formed in his gut. She wasn't strong enough to hear about the others. Some of them were likely kin, or at least good friends.

He looked down, examining the contents of the cup. "See if you can finish this." When he raised the tin to her lips again, she accepted the drink, but her eyes never left his.

He didn't meet her gaze, but her penetrating stare pierced his skin as he kept his focus on the cup.

The fact that he didn't look at her may well frighten her, but the truth couldn't be any better than her wildest fears. All the members of her party were dead, killed in a wagon crash. Not only was she utterly alone in this mountain wilderness, she had at least two broken bones and a fever—which might stem from internal infection or trauma, either of which had the potential to take her life. How much worse could her situation be?

But a slip into despair when she heard about her friends might well be the death of her. She needed to heal a little before facing the news.

She made a noise as she sipped the last of the tea, and he pulled the cup away, analyzing the specks of bark left at the bottom. "That should help you feel better. Sleep now."

As he started to back away, she grabbed his arm, gripping with a strength he'd not have credited her with. "Doctor."

He forced himself to look at her. "Please, call me Micah."

"What of my father? Beulah. Our driver. Where are they?" All hint of pain had fled her eyes, replaced by dark determination.

*No.* This wasn't the time to tell her. She wasn't strong enough yet. He forced his most calming expression. "You should rest now. We can talk later."

"Please." She tightened her grip. "Tell me."

She probably wouldn't rest until she knew. He swallowed, summoning some kind of words that might ease the pain. "I'm sorry. No others survived."

That determination wavered the smallest bit as her red-rimmed eyes shimmered. Her throat worked. "Are you sure?" Her words slipped to a whisper.

This was the part he'd never learned to handle. Especially

not when the mere words conjured a wave of despair that stole his breath. "I checked each of them. I'm sorry."

Her hand slipped from his arm, and he took it in his own, his wind-chapped skin contrasting starkly with her black leather gloves. He had so little to offer this woman. "Miss Chastain. Nothing I can say will ease your loss, but know that I'll do everything in my power to see you well and on your way back to your home."

A gasp pulled his focus back to her face, as much as he didn't want to see the tears there. Her reddened eyes had rounded, fear touching them again. Or . . . maybe not fear.

"The box." She clutched his hand. "Do you have the box?"

He scanned his memory for the container she might be referring to. "I saw several crates around the wagon. Which one do you mean? Some were broken open." And the thought of traipsing back out in the snowfall held no appeal.

"The box of vials. It's about . . ." She released her grip to spread her hands twice as wide as her body. "They were packaged carefully. I have to find that crate." She raised her head as though she planned to stand and hike back to the wagon herself.

He pressed a hand to her shoulder. "I'll find it."

She lay back and studied him. "You will?" Her scrutiny made his neck itch.

But he nodded. "I will."

Finally, she relaxed, her eyes drifting shut as though she could no longer hold them open. Probably the willow tea taking effect. "Thank you."

After tucking the fur around her again, he stood and stepped back. He couldn't help but study her, even as he analyzed her request. Of everything she would fight for after the news he'd just given her, a box of vials seemed almost absurd. Perhaps her mind was slipping from the awful strain she'd been through today, both physically and emotionally.

Sleep would help. If she mentioned the crate again, he would ask more questions. Right now, he had much more pressing matters to attend to.

Matters of life and death.

# FIVE

*M*iss Chastain didn't wake again that day.

A fact that brought him relief for many reasons. Maybe after a solid half day of sleep, she'd be more lucid. Less likely to fixate on crates of medicine or perfumes or whatever filled the vials she'd been so insistent about.

Micah left the camp before sunrise the next morning to check his traps. Part of him craved the solitude. He'd been away from other people for so long, but at times the utter aloneness had brought him to his knees, tearing him from the inside out. Yet that pain was nothing compared to what he'd brought upon his family.

Still, he'd expected himself to be glad for another person's company in his lonely camp, even though the pain kept her nearly unconscious. Why did her presence weigh so heavily on him? Maybe it was simply that she was a woman, and clearly from the civilized portion of the country. Not only that, she was in desperate straits, and her life depended almost solely on him.

Because of that, he couldn't linger overlong on the trail.

If the woman woke, she wouldn't be able to get up without hurting herself. Hopefully she wouldn't try. The more still she stayed, the better her leg would heal. He needed to make that point clear the next time she was coherent.

Only two traps were full, so he reset them, then skinned the beaver and marten before bringing the meat and furs back to camp for preparation. It was always better to leave the remains as far away as possible so the smell of blood didn't attract mountain lions or wolves.

He eyed the lump of furs under the shelter as he stepped into the campsite. Her brown hair bunched around one end of the furs, as though her face was buried underneath, away from the cold. Her silky strands had a grayish-brown shimmer, a unique shade that contrasted with the white-and-gray mottled fur of the wolf skin underneath her.

Turning away, he added more logs to the fire. She needed warm food in her belly. Maybe corncakes with the fresh meat.

As he worked on the meal, his mind turned back to the supplies scattered around the wrecked wagon. He'd be a fool not to return for the foodstuffs. And he should probably ask Miss Chastain if there were belongings important to her. The doctoring supplies may be useful, too, but he may not be able to carry much. At least he could bring back the things that mattered.

At times like this, it would be nice to have a horse. But feeding an animal through the mountain winter was no easy task. He'd long ago decided fending for himself was the only way he could carry on. Bearing responsibility for another person or animal was too much. He'd proven himself incapable.

A moan sounded from behind him, and he turned as the uppermost fur on the pallet shifted. The pelt wrinkled as though an animal had crawled inside, scurrying to find a way out.

Miss Chastain's forehead peeked out at the edge, then her eyes, scanning the world around her. Her gaze widened, as though what she'd thought was a bad dream might actually be true.

How awful that this was her new reality, but he would do his best to make it bearable for her. "Sleep well?"

Her eyes jerked to him, and she pulled the fur tighter over the lower half of her face. The morning air nipped with a sharp cold, probably uncomfortable after her cocoon under the pelts.

She didn't answer, so he settled on his heels. "Not sure how much you remember from yesterday, but I'm Micah Bradley. I found you on the side of a mountain and brought you back here for your wounds to heal." He motioned toward her leg. "You have a break in the distal region of your femoral shaft. Also a cracked rib. When you're well enough, I'll take you back to Fort Benton where you can get a ride home." That would be in the spring when the winter thawed, but he was trying to ease her fears with the summary, not stir them anew.

Her eyes grew cloudy with his words. Moist. She was likely remembering the fate of the others in her party.

He turned back to the pan where the morning meal cooked. "I've some food here. It'd be good if you could eat." The effort would likely distract her.

After scooping a small helping onto his tin plate, he reached for the mug of willow tea he'd been steeping, then shifted to kneel at the woman's side.

Her eyes were red, but at least tears didn't flow down her face. She lowered the covers and pulled a hand out from underneath, then reached to take the plate.

"I'm afraid I don't have a utensil. Sorry." How barbaric he must seem to her. Only a single dented tin plate and cup. No eating fork or serviette. But it was only him, and he'd long since stopped caring about such things.

Thankfully, her gaze was on the food, a hungry glimmer now touching her eyes. It had likely been at least a day since she'd eaten, and her body needed sustenance to heal and keep itself warm.

She positioned the plate on her chest. "Thank you."

He stayed beside her as she took up a corncake and bit, her eyelids dipping low as she appeared to relish the simple fare. She must be accustomed to French pastries and all manner of breakfast meats, much grander than his simple cornmeal, salt, and water.

After she finished the corncake, he raised the cup. "Drink this."

She took the mug from him, steadier than she'd been the day before. After downing half, she sank back against the furs with a long exhale. Her eyes lifted to his for the first time since she'd seen the food. "Thank you. That was . . . divine."

He couldn't bite back a snort. "You're welcome. Eat the other if you can."

He took the cup as she turned her attention to the slab of roasted beaver meat on the plate. Her gloved fingers reached for the food, and she raised it to her mouth, taking a dainty bite. Every movement fluid and very, very feminine.

He swallowed. Ella had been like that. Graceful and delicate, with her pale skin and fiery red hair. Not accustomed to life in the prairie town where her family brought her. It was a wonder she'd married him, a country doctor, instead of returning east for a husband.

Still, he'd done his best to make her thankful for her choice. Had she been? Did she ever regret marrying him? On her deathbed, surely.

He regretted so many things. Keeping her in Indiana instead

of taking her back to Boston where she belonged. The long hours he spent with patients instead of devoting himself to his wife and daughter. They'd both deserved so much better from him.

Especially at the end.

But the one thing he couldn't bring himself to regret was his choice to pursue Ella that very first day. She—and then Rachel, too—had been everything to him. His lone source of light and joy. Even if his world was now darker for their loss, he couldn't regret those few bright years.

"Thank you."

He jerked his focus back to the present as his patient handed over an empty plate. "Oh . . . you're welcome." He started to rise, but almost knocked over the cup, still half-full. "Here, finish this. It'll help with the pain." *And help you sleep*. But he didn't say that last part aloud. No need to tell her outright he'd rather have her asleep than lying here, grieving.

She took the cup from him but didn't raise it to her lips. Her gaze found his. "Did you find the box?"

Heat slid up his neck. "Not yet. I'll need to leave you for several hours. I'm not sure you're well enough for that."

Her eyes turned beseeching. "Please. I need that crate. It's vitally important. People could die."

A shiver ran down his arms, and not from the icy breeze ruffling his hair. At least, not completely. "What do you mean, 'people could die?'" More than had already perished when the wagon crashed? Was this a delusion from her trauma? He studied her face for signs of mental instability.

She strained toward him, clutching the cup with both hands. "We were taking it to Settler's Fort. The contents of that box will save the lives of the people there. I can't lose it." She set the mug on the ground and pushed the covers aside. This time she made it halfway to a sitting position before he stopped her with a hand to her shoulder.

"I'll go. But only if you promise to lie still and let your bones heal." What could possibly be in that box of such import that she was willing to injure herself further? But she'd already lost so much. If the box was that important to her, he could retrieve it.

She eased back down, her gaze wary. Searching. "You'll go now?"

He glanced at the sky. Gray, but not so impending that snow would come before he returned. "I'll go now. Is there anything else you need me to bring back? Clothing? Keepsakes? I can't carry much, but I'll get what I can."

She stared upward at the cover of brush he'd constructed above her, clearly thinking through what had been in the wagon. "My father's Bible. It might be in his doctor's bag." Her eyes developed a thick sheen. "I suppose anything else he might have in his pockets. His watch." She nodded, but didn't look at him. "Thank you."

A lump clogged his throat, and he worked to swallow it down. He'd suspected that might be her father's medical bag. Had he been a good doctor? Surely better than Micah had been. He shoved the thought aside. "All right then." Pushing to his feet, he loaded as much wood as he dared on the fire, then moved a small stack of logs close to her. "Keep the fire as hot as you need it. I should be back in a couple hours, but don't worry if I'm not. There's more meat in this pack, so help yourself. Sleep when you can."

He scanned the area. How could he leave her here, defenseless against any prey that wandered along? "Do you know how to shoot a rifle?"

Her gaze jerked to his. "Do you think I'll need to?"

Pressing his lips together, he eyed his Hawken. The gun's recoil would likely break another of her ribs if she actually had to fire it. If she *could* fire it. But it might save her life in a pinch.

Grabbing the weapon, he dropped to his haunches beside her. "If you have to use it, tuck the stock into your shoulder like this." He positioned the gun at his own shoulder. "Squeeze this rear set trigger before you're ready to fire. When you need to shoot, squeeze this front trigger. Be careful. This rifle has a powerful kick, so don't use it unless you have to."

Her eyes had been wide when he started the short lesson, but now they narrowed with determination. At least she wasn't afraid of the weapon.

She reached for the rifle, but he didn't release his hold as he helped her lay it down beside her bedding. This gun was lighter than most, but still heavy enough to strain her broken ribs.

"I'll be careful."

He stood and inhaled a long breath as he looked around once more. That was the best he could do. After reaching for the last of his breakfast, he touched his hunting knife to ensure it hung at his waist, then started out.

The sooner he accomplished this task, the better.

The crash site was worse than Micah remembered.

The snow blanketing the wreckage gave it a ghostly appearance, as though the scattered debris were flotsam cast about years before. A shipwreck with no survivors.

Save one.

Pushing aside his thoughts, he focused on the job at hand. Food, a crate of medicine vials, and her father's Bible. And if he could carry more, some of the doctoring supplies. He could collect the other belongings from Dr. Chastain's person on his way back up the mountain.

After kicking snow off some of the mounds, he found a piece of splintered wood and used it to clear the icy blankets from the rest of the crates and trunks. Several of the trunks were locked shut, but he found the ax he'd used before and split them open.

When he lifted the first lid, a wad of green velvet fabric sprung out at him. He nearly dropped the cover, then lowered it back in place to protect the delicate items inside from the wind and snow. He hadn't seen anything this luxurious in years, maybe decades.

He hated to touch such dainty things with his grimy buck-skin gloves, but there might be something in there Miss Chastain needed. He should at least look for an extra coat or gloves or the like.

After raising the lid again, he peeled back the green velvet and found a striped fabric, some kind of soft blue cloth, and a bunch of white frilly things. Not one would be suitable for the weather in these mountains, especially with winter now upon them.

He eased the cover shut, then moved on to the next box. He could have spent an hour digging through all the crates and supplies, but he could only carry a few bundles in addition to the crate of vials he found partway through. The case wasn't marked, but Miss Chastain had been right about how well each glass container was packed. Partitioned by wooden dividers, then wrapped in stuffed fabric, not a single bottle had broken. Nothing indicated what the contents were, though. Why hadn't he asked?

He stacked the Bible on the crate, then piled on bags of cornmeal, flour, oats, and salt. Perhaps he should leave a bag or two behind so he could bring the doctor's bag, but food seemed more important.

Far more important.

With the load in hand, he started up the mountain. After climbing only a few steps, a whimpering sound from behind stopped him midstride. He braced his foot on a sturdy rock, then turned, leaning to see past the bulk in his arms.

The noise had a high pitch. Maybe a bird? Not a bird call he'd heard before. More like an injured child. Surely there wasn't someone else from the wagon he'd missed before. Hadn't Miss Chastain spoken of only the three people he'd already discovered?

"Is anyone there?" He strained to hear a response.

A movement farther down the mountain caught his focus. Just a shifting of a snow-covered bush, as though a rabbit hopped deeper into the shelter.

"Hello?" He focused on the bush. That noise sounded again, definitely a whimper. Or . . . more like the whine of a dog. "Here, boy." He took a few steps down the hill, then eased his load onto a rock.

The bush moved again, dusting the ground around it with a fine powder of snow. Micah crept toward the spot, taking a visual sweep of the full area. No other movement warned of danger.

As he neared the bush, the whine sounded once more. Louder this time. Definitely coming from within the scrubby plant. "Come here. I won't hurt you."

When he stepped around the shrub, a shadow moved inside. Or rather, a mass of black fur. "Hey, there." He reached toward the shadow, careful not to come close enough that the animal could strike out and bite him. It looked and sounded like a dog, but that was the last thing he'd expect out here.

Another whimper, and the shadow crept out from its shelter, one black paw at a time.

"There you go. Come on." He crooned the words as a fluffy runt-dog inched toward him. "What are you doin' here?"

The dog finally came close enough to sniff Micah's hand, then he tucked his haunches and sat in the snow. A second later, the little thing hiked its tail back up and stood, legs spread and shivering.

Micah couldn't help a chuckle. "That snow too cold for your backside?" He eased closer and stroked the animal's back. The dog was barely bigger than the spread of his hand, and almost all fur. He didn't seem to mind being touched, so Micah slipped his fingers under the dog's belly and scooped him up, tucking him close to his chest.

The little shadow snuggled close, as though relieved to be safe from his nightmare of the past day. He must belong to Miss Chastain. There couldn't be any other logical reason a pet dog like this would be stranded in the mountains, days from any settlement. And this wasn't exactly the kind of animal a frontiersman kept for companionship.

He tucked the dog into the crook of his arm and started up the mountain. "Time to go back, boy. I know someone who needs you as much as you need her."

# SIX

*M*icah's load was already awkward, but he settled the little dog on top of the crate where it could lean against his chest. The animal burrowed in, relaxing into the ride.

The hike back up and down the mountains strained his muscles almost as much as hauling the cart the day before. But he finally made it, and the sight of camp filled him with the last burst of energy he needed.

Miss Chastain opened her eyes as he set his load beside her. She seemed groggy and turned her head to get a better look at the things he brought. When she saw the dog, her eyes widened and she gasped. "Handsome."

"Found this fellow tucked under a bush near your wagon. Thought he might be a friend of yours."

She reached for the dog. "Of course." The pup scrambled into her arms, licking her chin as she held him close. "I missed you, too." She cooed to the dog, a smile finding her face, lighting her features for the first time since he discovered her on the side of that mountain. She'd been pretty even in her pain, but the smile made her radiant.

He blinked, then straightened and stood. Best he focus on

what needed to be done here. "Did you have any excitement while I was gone?" The rifle still lay where he'd left it.

"All was quiet. Thank you for the crate. The vials inside are safe?"

He turned back to her. "No damage."

"Good." She tucked the dog in beside her, pulling the pelt higher to cover all but his head. "I'll be up tomorrow, then I'll figure out how to get them to Settler's Fort." Her eyes drifted shut, as though she hadn't the strength to keep them open another minute.

His chest tightened. She wouldn't be going anywhere tomorrow. But surely she realized that.

If not, tomorrow his most critical task would be to make her see reason.

Something pressed on Ingrid's chest, pulling her from sleep. She inhaled a deep breath, then groaned as a familiar knife plunged through her ribs.

She opened her eyes, but the blinding light made it hard to do anything but squint. As she struggled for a shallower breath, she pushed at whatever sat atop her chest. Her hand caught a mass of fur as she swatted, and the bundle loosed a high-pitch cry.

A flash of memory washed over her. "Handsome?" Forcing her eyes open, she raised her head, fighting to ignore the pain in her ribs. "I'm sorry, boy. Where are you?"

He stood beside her, back raised and tail tucked between his legs as though still trying to determine why he'd been accosted.

"Come here." She reached for the dog and pulled him close to her side. "This is a better spot for you." Breathing was hard enough with her broken rib; she didn't need more weight smothering her chest, even if the little Bichon weighed less than five pounds, according to Papa's scale in his laboratory.

*Papa.* A fierce burning surged up the back of her throat, stinging her eyes. He couldn't be dead. How could she have forgotten, even for a moment, that the best part of her life was gone?

Papa had been her world. Her friend. Her greatest champion. His work had given her purpose. His dreams had been her own for as long as she could remember.

How could it all be gone? Crushed with that wagon on the side of a mountain. She pulled Handsome closer, tucking him into her shoulder so she could breathe in his puppy scent. At least she still had this gift from her father.

And the vaccines. She had to take the vials to Papa's old medical school friend in Settler's Fort. Smallpox had already killed so many in this massive territory. It had been over a year since Papa received any correspondence from his old college chum, but when Dr. Stanley sent a wire desperate for vaccines to protect the town from a new outbreak in a nearby settlement, they'd had to act fast.

Every day she lay on this pallet of furs was one more day lives might be lost. Papa had given his own life to this cause. She couldn't let his sacrifice be in vain. Nor Beulah's. Not even the kind wagoner who'd agreed to take them through the mountains, even though winter was fast approaching. If only they'd listened to his warnings. Yet, hiring Mr. Sorenson had seemed like the only way to deliver the vaccines—and get themselves there to assist with the doctoring.

All three of them had wanted to be there to help, even Beulah. A fresh wave of grief slipped through her for the faithful maid. Sweet, dutiful Beulah. More friend than employee.

"You're awake."

She sniffed, working to clear her senses before she turned to face her host. She opened her mouth to respond, but emotion still clogged her throat. Instead she nodded and swallowed again.

"How about another cup of tea and a corncake?"

Her stomach gurgled, making the ache of hunger clearly felt. But that tea made her so groggy. It felt like she'd been sleeping for weeks. "Corncake sounds wonderful. But no tea, thank you."

He reached toward the fire, then turned back a moment later, a plate and cup in his hands. "How about water instead? We need to make sure you drink enough. How's the leg feel?"

A surge of pain radiated through her leg and hip, as though he'd touched the limb with his words. She gritted her teeth to keep from crying out.

"Still bad, huh?" He dropped to his knees. "I need to pack it in snow again while you eat. We're fighting the swelling."

A dim memory surfaced of him leaning over her leg, icy wetness freezing her skin, numbing the pain as shivers overtook her body. It was hard to say which was worse—the constant agony of pain, or being so cold and miserable.

But there was one other ache that she was no longer able to deny. She dropped her gaze to the blankets. "I, um, don't suppose you have a chamber pot around here do you?" Heat flamed to her cheeks. This was the last thing she wanted to discuss with anyone, especially a man.

But there was no denying the need, and she wasn't sure she could get herself up to take care of things without help.

"Oh, um . . . yes." He leapt up and strode toward his other shelter where he appeared to keep supplies. Surely he didn't actually have a chamber pot.

He returned with something that looked like a leather pail. The top brim was built with wood, probably to make the sides strong enough to carry water or other heavy items.

He crouched beside her. "We can just slide this under you. Do you think you can sit up?"

She nodded, pushing the blankets down. "I can do it. Thank you for the pail." There was no way she'd allow him to help with the actual task. Not unless the pain grew so bad she passed out. At least then she wouldn't be awake for the mortification.

He nodded and rose to his feet, then stepped back. "I'll just be over here. Call if you need help." Thank the Lord he moved to the far edge of camp and turned away from her.

The pain in her rib felt like it would pierce her insides as she sat up, but her leg was by far the worst when she maneuvered herself to do the rest of what she needed to. It took every bit of restraint she had left not to cry out.

At last she sank back down onto the fur, exhausted, her legs and arms quivering. "You can come now." Her voice came out so weak she wasn't sure he'd heard her.

He must have, though, because he was by her side the next moment. Moving the makeshift chamber pot away, he knelt beside her, touching her forehead, her cheek. "I need to cover your leg with snow now."

She nodded, not bothering to open her eyes. She was too weary to complain about anything.

But as he pulled the furs aside, a cold wind slapped her flesh, rejuvenating her senses. She did her best not to look at the man as he worked, trying to focus on nibbling bite after bite of corncake instead of feeling the breath-stealing ice on her skin.

She had to push aside the unease of a man seeing so much of her leg—any man, but especially this stranger, so far from any other person. He was a doctor. He'd said so, and he seemed to have confidence in his ministrations. She had to believe his words and imagine herself back home, being cared for by Dr. Faulkner.

Certainly she could imagine this man twenty years older, hair heavily salted and deep creases lining his face. He already had the beard to match Papa's medical partner, although the rich black hair that peeked out from his hood showed no gray that she could see. Still, he *was* her doctor. The man God sent to help her through these injuries and on to Settler's Fort.

She'd worked her way through both corncakes on the plate, feeding bits to Handsome as she went, before Dr. Bradley finished packing snow around the injured area.

At last, he stretched the furs back over her. "That should help some. What say I take Shadow here for a walk?" The doctor reached for the dog, who pressed deeper into her neck.

"It's all right, boy. He's a friend." She nudged the animal out of hiding, then lifted him up to the doctor. Their fingers tangled with the dog's fur, and even through her gloves, his touch sent a jolt up her arm. She fought to keep her reaction from showing, dropping her gaze to the dog. "His name is Handsome."

"Handsome?" He took her puppy and held him close to his broad chest, eyeing the dog. "You think so?"

The pair of them—the big, strong mountain-man doctor and the tiny barely grown dog who'd been the runt of his litter—made such an incongruous picture that the sight almost pulled a smile from her. If her world wasn't in shambles, she would have enjoyed the image.

Dr. Bradley pushed to his feet. "We'll return in a little while."

They were gone longer than she expected, and the ice wrapping her leg made it impossible to sleep. Thankfully, it numbed both the limb and the pain, and the longer she lay there, the more her mind seemed to come alive.

She needed to sit up, to stand, to begin to maneuver about. The wood strapped around her leg would be ungainly, and the entire limb still maintained a steady ache even while she lay still. Moving would be torturous. But she had to do it. After all, she'd successfully accomplished the chamber pot on her own.

Propping her elbows underneath her, she levered herself up, not daring a breath until she sat upright. Her ribs jerked in spasms, so she took tiny breaths through her mouth. At last, her body settled, and she could take steady—albeit shallow—breaths.

There. She could sit like a normal person again, although her midsection trembled, so she propped her hand on the ground behind her.

Dr. Bradley ambled back into camp, Handsome trotting along behind him. The pup jerked his feet up with each step, as though the cold hurt his paws. Or maybe he was just too prim to get his fur wet.

As for the man, his brows rose when he took in her position. "Feeling better?"

She forced a smile. "I am. I'd like to get up."

He shook his head before she finished the last word. "You

can't. The bone fragments in your leg are just starting to ad-
here. Movement could separate them again and cause a great
deal of pain." He studied her, as though trying to decipher
why she would want such a thing. "Is there something you
need?"

Her father. Her maid, who'd been more like a sister. A dose
of laudanum for the pain. A rush of responses hovered at the
edge of her lips. But he could give her none of these. No one
ever could, except the last, and by then she'd no longer need it.

She bit back every pointless request and leveled her gaze
on him. "I need to get these vaccinations to Settler's Fort."

He didn't act surprised, just nodded. "As soon as you're
well, I'll deliver you back to Fort Benton, then take the crate
to Settler's Fort."

Now it was her turn to shake her head before he finished
speaking. "They can't wait that long. The people in Settler's
Fort need them now. There's an outbreak nearby. The doctor's
trying to keep it contained until we arrive. Every day matters."

The skin around his dark eyes creased, as though pulling
tight. "What type of outbreak?"

"Smallpox. Dr. Stanley said there have been past outbreaks
in surrounding towns that killed the entire community."

He took a step back, swaying as though she'd struck a blow.
His tanned face paled three shades.

"Are you familiar with smallpox, Dr. Bradley?" His reaction
seemed extreme. Did he fear the disease? Perhaps she should
inoculate him before delivering the vials to Settler's Fort.

"I am." Then he spun on his heel and marched toward a
pack he kept in the other branch-covered shelter. After scooping up something from the case, he strode out of camp.

Silence settled over her. Handsome turned a circle beside

her, then stretched out along the length of her side. "What was that about?" She stroked the dog's side, still watching the rock around which Dr. Bradley had disappeared.

But he didn't return.

*My Darling Rachel,*

*When Mama first told me I would be your papa, I immediately knew I wouldn't be good enough for the job. I knew so little about children because I'd never had brothers or sisters of my own.*

*But then you were born, with your shock of auburn hair. When I took you in my arms, you opened your mouth like a baby fish, staring up at me with all the trust in the world. I knew from that minute I'd do anything necessary for you to be happy and safe, and for you to know you're loved every moment of your life.*

*I pray you were happy. My heart yearns to know you felt loved. For I did love you—I still do—with every breath that fills me.*

*But I failed, my Ducky. My sweet, innocent girl. I didn't keep you safe. Can you ever forgive me?*

*Papa*

Micah bent over the paper, his chest aching, his gut tied in knots. If only the pain would take him. Five years ago, why couldn't he have been the one lying miserable in bed, sores oozing all over his skin, throat swollen shut? Instead, he'd watched the two people who meant everything to him fade away in the grips of the cruelest of diseases.

Suffering the horrors of smallpox was worse than hell could ever be, and he'd sentenced his wife and daughter to the damnation of the disease.

And now . . . with this woman lying in his camp, begging him to take a crate of vaccines to quell a smallpox outbreak . . . was God laughing at him? Sending a sharp kick in the ribs while he lay crumpled on the ground?

Maybe the Almighty thought to test him like Job in the Scriptures, to see how much devastation he could withstand without cursing God. Well, he'd never claimed to be Job, and the Holy Father was doomed to be disappointed in him.

Just like everyone else had been.

# SEVEN

*I*ngrid forced herself to stay awake until Dr. Bradley returned to camp. He might be right about her inability to travel on to Settler's Fort until her leg healed more. Especially since he didn't seem to own a horse, which meant she'd be hobbling the trail on foot.

But he had to agree to go in her stead.

Her stomach gnawed steadily at her backbone, and the murky light of dusk settled over camp by the time the doctor's broad, buckskin-clad shoulders appeared around the boulder. Handsome looked up at the man and gave a yip, his tail wagging back and forth in a slow fan.

The man didn't look at them, just strode to his pack and deposited whatever he'd removed before, then turned to the fire.

"I've been adding wood to it." She motioned toward the blaze.

He nodded, but didn't comment on his absence. Nor did he have to. He wasn't required to check in with her before proceeding through his day. But it would have been nice if he'd mentioned he'd be gone for hours, leaving her alone and defenseless.

*Enough, Ingrid.* She wasn't defenseless with God as her protector. *Forgive me, Lord.*

Dr. Bradley didn't speak as he poured several ingredients in a pot beside the fire, then stirred with steady rotations. Perhaps he preferred such silence, but the quiet hung between them, thick and sticky, like the taffy she used to watch being made in the window of Gilden's Candy Emporium.

Was it her desire to take the crate to Settler's Fort that bothered him? Or the mention of smallpox? He'd maintained a steady argument every time she mentioned delivering the box, but he blanched when she told him the contents of the vials.

Did he fear contracting the sickness? Or did smallpox have anything to do with the reason why an apparently competent doctor would be encamped alone in the mountain wilderness, living like a wandering trapper? She had so many questions for him. If only he would turn and let her start a conversation before the pain forced her back to sleep.

At last he straightened from the fire and glanced toward her.

She worked for a smile. "What are you making?"

"Corn dumplings, but I'm sure it won't be as good as you're used to." His voice held a hint of challenge, as though he expected her to thumb her nose at the fare.

"It smells wonderful." And she was hungry enough to eat anything he put before her.

"Here's some tea you can work on 'til the food's ready." He reached for the cup sitting on a rock near the fire.

"Actually, I wonder if we could talk about how to get these vaccines to Settler's Fort first." She kept her voice as pleasant as possible and took the cup when he extended it. She wasn't about to drink yet, though. This tea could make her sleep for days, and she had to have answers first.

He turned to face her fully, sitting on his heels. "I said I would take them as soon as your leg is healed." His tone was soft, almost tender. No hint of the gruffness that had wrapped his voice a moment before.

"How far to Settler's Fort from here?" She watched his reaction. *Don't anger him by pushing too hard*, she warned herself. He was her only means of survival out here. Her only chance of saving lives from smallpox.

His focus lifted over her shoulder, as though he were calculating the distance. "For a man on foot, three weeks maybe." His brows rose pointedly. "On two *good* feet. A woman limping on walking sticks would be prey to wolves or a mountain lion the first night out." He motioned toward Handsome. "That little shadow would be their first bite."

A shiver slipped through her. He was right, no doubt. "You can go, then."

He shook his head. "I can't leave you here. Those same wolves will strut right into camp and eat their fill of you."

She stiffened her shoulders. "I can fend them off. I'll be safe here."

He didn't look convinced in the slightest. "I'm not leaving until you're well enough to travel."

Worry pressed through her. "How long will that be?"

He scanned the length of her, as though he could see through the fur covering her broken leg. "At least a month until you could ride comfortably in a wagon. Except no wagon will be able to get through the snow by then. Three months before you could ride out on horseback, assuming I can find a horse for you to ride."

Three months? The entire town of Settler's Fort could be dead in three months. Desperation welled within her, clogging her throat and stinging her eyes. "You have to take them. Please."

Micah flinched at the pleading in her voice. He was going to have to take those vaccines to Settler's Fort; there was no way around it. And she was right, lives could be on the line. Waiting three months seemed criminal, a death sentence to the cluster of people who claimed that town as home.

But he couldn't leave Miss Chastain, either.

They were about halfway between Settler's Fort and Fort Benton, the place she'd be able to purchase steamboat fare back to wherever she came from. Perhaps he should take her to Benton first. The river would be frozen soon, so she'd have to find a safe place to stay until spring. Not an easy task among the hordes of men—both white and bronze-skinned—who passed through its gates for trading and all manner of entertainment during the winter. She may well be the only white female there. Not an acceptable situation.

Of course, how much more suitable was it for her to be stranded in a mountain camp with only him and a makeshift branch shelter? Perhaps if he got her to Fort Benton, a family member would come to accompany her home in the spring.

He eyed her. "Miss Chastain, where is your home? The rest of your family?"

Her lips pressed flat, her eyes turning glassy. "Our home is in Boston." She inhaled a deep breath, pulling the little dog closer. "My father is . . . *was* my only remaining family. Except for this fella." She cradled the pup under her chin, sliding her fingers through his fur.

She had no one? How was it possible that an obviously well-to-do woman like herself wasn't surrounded by people who loved her? "What of friends? I can take you to Fort Benton, then go myself to deliver the vaccines to Settler's Fort. You can send for a family friend to retrieve you on the first boat that comes in the spring."

Her face took on a depth of sadness that tightened the ache in his chest. "We have household staff who are like family, as well as my father's colleagues. But I hate to burden any of them." She dropped her gaze, and her throat worked. Perhaps she was trying to regain control of herself, or maybe debating who she would ask to come.

Then she raised her chin, her jaw clearly set. All trace of tears had left her eyes, save the lingering redness. "Settler's Fort is where I need to be. We committed to help Dr. Stanley, and that's what I intend to do. Once smallpox has been eradicated from the area, I'll determine my next course of action." She narrowed her eyes. "Get me to Settler's Fort, please. You'll have my deepest thanks, and I can pay you well."

This woman was a force to be reckoned with. Even mourning the death of her father, the last of her family, she possessed a will of iron and strength to match.

It sounded like the people of Settler's Fort really did need those vaccines. But he couldn't leave her alone and helpless here. That left only one option.

He had to take her with him.

But how? He'd need to give that some thought before he voiced any plans.

He wouldn't take her money, though. That, he knew with certainty. Yet one thing she'd said still lingered in his mind. "How long have you lived in Boston?"

"All my life. Father was the first of his friends to leave the waterfront and build in the West End. We've lived in our little Cambridge Street home as long as I can remember."

Images flittered through his mind. There were no little homes on Cambridge Street in the West End. He knew that well, for his mother had worked in at least a dozen of those mansions, taking in laundry and mending. He'd trotted along with Mum to pick up and deliver, and had always been fascinated by the massive structures and ornate décor.

In one of the houses he'd discovered a library, the walls lined with row upon row of books. Mum had only owned two books: the Bible and a storybook that she'd been using to teach him to read. He couldn't imagine having so many volumes at hand. If he had access to all those books, he'd never do anything but read.

A girl in the home had discovered him in that room, and he'd tried to slip away with a quick apology. He shouldn't have gone in. But she'd not let him leave, instead begging him to play stones in the yard.

He still remembered the way she pleaded, her light freckles and honey-colored braids making her look just like the little sister he'd always wanted. In fact, he could almost see a resemblance between that little girl and the woman lying before him now.

He'd given in to her request, of course. And loved every minute of their game until her father appeared in the yard. When he looked up to see the tall man a few steps away, he'd jumped back and mumbled another apology.

The fellow hadn't let him leave, though, just like his daughter before. He'd joined the game of stones, and the three of them played until the housekeeper came to tell him his mother was ready to leave.

That was possibly the happiest moment from his child-hood. A time he'd felt—just for an hour—like he'd been part of a genuine family. A father who took time to play with him. A sister. A place to belong.

But he hadn't belonged in that place. Not like Miss Chastain did. This woman was elite. Upper crust. Except . . . she didn't act arrogant or ostentatious. Not like those women Mum worked for.

She had a gentle strength. A kindness he'd sensed from the first time they spoke.

And that was what made him want to fulfill her request. That and the fact he owed it to all the people who'd died in his care five years ago. He hadn't been able to save Ella or Rachel, but maybe he could protect the people of Settler's Fort.

Though the journey would be grueling, he had to try.

# EIGHT

*S*leep was scarce that night, coming in bitter cold fragments between worry and a chill wind. Micah tried to make sense of the almost impossible task of bringing Miss Chastain with him on the journey to Settler's Fort.

He was more than willing to rise when the first hint of light spread across the eastern sky. Checking the traps was a simple matter, but he had to force himself to focus on his surroundings, to notice tracks and listen for bird calls or eerie silences. His survival depended on his focus, and he couldn't let the woman lying back at camp on his bed pallet distract him. *Her* survival depended on his focus.

He'd almost accomplished that feat until he neared the brush shelter and his mind formed the image of her sleeping, lying as peaceful as an angel. She'd been exhausted after eating last night, and only a few sips of willow tea helped her fall asleep. He needed to pack more ice around her leg today. The swelling had been greater than he liked when he last checked.

As he approached the leaping fire, a figure beside it snagged his focus. A person? He was still at least thirty strides away, but he dropped his load of meat and skins and sprinted forward. Who could have found their camp?

But as he neared, the blue skirt at the base of the figure became clear. Miss Chastain? A little black animal trotted around at her feet.

His breath came in shallow gasps as he reached her. "What are you doing?"

She leaned heavily against a stick, her broken leg propped to the side since the splint extended a couple inches farther than her boot. When she turned to look at him, his heart stalled.

Her face had paled, a sheen of sweat glistening on her brow and upper lip.

"Let's lay you back down." He stepped close and wrapped his arm around her shoulders. "Just lean into me and I'll slide you back to your blankets."

She obeyed, surprisingly, even though leaning back into his arm required her to trust completely that he'd catch her. As spunky as she'd proven, she must be in so much pain she didn't stop to think.

Doing his best not to stress her broken bones any more than they had been, he shifted her back to the blankets. The dog yapped at him, but he ignored the animal. Fear welled in his chest, stirring up an anger that he couldn't allow to slip out. What reason could there have possibly been, other than an attack on her life, for her to try such a foolish maneuver? That's exactly why he'd been giving her so much willow tea— to keep her from attempting something that would harm her even more.

When he finally had her positioned on the fur pallet, she let out a long, achingly slow breath. Her eyes pressed shut, pain lining her face.

"What in all of America were you thinking? What did you need that would be worth re-breaking your leg for?" He clamped his jaw tight to keep anything else from slipping out.

She squinted at him, like she was fighting a roaring headache on top of everything else. "I have to start moving around. Settler's Fort needs those vaccines. If you won't take them, I will."

Of all the . . . He jerked back, forcing himself to inhale deep breaths. She couldn't be serious. With her leg in the splint, she could have easily lost her balance. If she thought a broken femur was painful, the burns from falling into a blazing fire would be excruciating. And burns that became infected would triple her risk of death, at least.

Deep breaths weren't working to calm the anger inside him. He surged to his feet and spun away from her. How could he keep this woman safe if she wouldn't follow his orders? He stomped toward the edge of camp. He needed to get away until he had settled down.

He *had* planned to take the blasted vaccines to Settler's Fort. She didn't need to risk her life to prove her point.

A niggle of thought forced its way into his awareness. Had he actually told her he planned to deliver her and the vaccines? When she'd said she wanted to go with him to Settler's Fort instead of returning home through Fort Benton, had he specifically agreed to that plan? He'd been so lost in his memories, he couldn't remember if he'd spoken the words or not.

That was the thing about living alone in the wilderness for so long. A man's thoughts grew loud, and it was hard to know sometimes if words were actually spoken.

He exhaled a long breath, then scrubbed a hand over his face. He owed her an answer . . . and an apology.

His fingers brushed his beard, the scraggly hairs rough, even against his callused skin. What must she think of him? A wild-looking mountain man who claimed to be a doctor, yet couldn't even carry on a conversation or control his temper. She'd not asked about where he obtained medical training or anything about his past. In truth, he'd not given her much chance. And if she had raised the topic, he'd have been reticent to answer questions that would resurrect so many painful memories.

Still, holding back wasn't fair. The least he could do was set her mind at ease. Communicate with her in a civil manner.

It was the least he could do, but she would have no idea how much the effort would cost him.

The fire in her leg seemed to have spread throughout her body, and Ingrid struggled to find a position that eased the pain.

"Here. Can you drink some of this?" A gentle voice slid over her, and a solid, callused hand brushed her forehead.

She pried open her eyes to see Micah's face, all the anger now gone from his eyes and replaced with concern.

Parting her lips, she tried to lift herself to make drinking easier. His fingers slipped through her hair, cupping the back of her head to relieve the strain from her ribs. She relaxed into his hand, his strength.

The drink held the sharp bite of willow, but this time she didn't dread falling into the hazy slumber. What a blessed relief that would be. Anything to carry her away from the fire she'd stirred back to life in her body. Why had she so stubbornly attempted what he'd warned against?

"I plan to take you and the vaccines to Settler's Fort."

She stilled, forcing the words to penetrate her cloud of pain. Could he possibly mean what they sounded like? She pulled away from the cup and studied his face. "You will?" She tried not to let hope stir in her chest.

He nodded. "You're right. Those people need the vaccines, and we need to deliver them. Sorry I didn't tell you before. I had already decided to, just . . . didn't think to tell you." His mouth pinched in a sad kind of chagrin. "I didn't mean for you to hurt yourself."

Now she felt even more foolish for her bullheaded act. But she couldn't dwell on that. They had to make plans. "When can we leave?"

His brows pinched low. "You'll need a few days for the pain to come back down and the bones to begin healing again. If we pack snow on it several times a day and you *stay put*"—he gave her a very pointed look—"we can probably head out in three or four days at the earliest."

She nodded. "I'll do everything you say." Already, her pain felt lighter. Or maybe that was just the weight on her shoulders.

Micah eyed the back half of the wagon as his mind pictured the modifications he'd need to make for him to be able to haul it up and down mountains for weeks on end. He could build runners for the makeshift cart and pull her like a pony sled.

His gaze kept returning to that heavy iron axle. Even if he removed the metal-rimmed wheels, the entire contraption held too much unnecessary weight. What he really needed was something light that wouldn't jostle Ingrid over rocks and bumps. Maybe something like the drag sleds the Indians used to pull weight behind their horses. Just two poles crossed at one end. He could suspend a fur between them where Ingrid could lay. If he fastened it right, she could dangle from the poles and not be jarred by every bump.

He'd have to tie the ends to his shoulders with rope to lift her high enough and minimize wear on his body.

No matter what contrivance he built, trekking up and down mountains, pulling an injured woman, would be no stroll across a manicured lawn. Yet his discomfort would be a pittance compared to hers.

Over the next few days, Micah applied a steady treatment of snow to Ingrid's leg and offered willow tea every time she awoke. He was pretty sure she knew that he brought the brew to help her sleep, as well as to keep the pain at bay, but she faithfully drained each cup when he brought it.

More than once, he approached when he thought her asleep but found her eyes open, staring at the dried brush stacked to form the wall of her shelter. Red rimmed her eyes and colored her nose.

He never knew what to say in those times. What words could ease the loss of the person who was everything to you? No words had eased his pain.

Fighting the knot in his throat, he turned away each time. At least she grieved silently. He had no idea what he'd do if she wailed aloud or really did lose her senses, as he'd questioned right after the accident.

In truth, Ingrid Chastain was proving herself a remarkable

woman. With the loss of her father and maid—the last of her family—and the awful pain from her leg and rib, most people would have gone crazy. He certainly had all those years ago, and he'd not even dealt with the horrific injuries she endured along with her grief.

As he watched her now in the dancing light of the fire, the lines of her face resting in such angelic peace, he'd never guess at the pain that lay within. Nor the strength.

She stirred, her eyelids flickering open. Her gaze wandered the area, settling on him with a groggy sheen.

"You woke just in time for supper." He leaned forward to scoop a bit of watery stew into the cup. "Are you hungry?"

"Mmm . . ." Her murmur had a low, throaty tone that sent a shiver through his body like he'd not felt in years. He pushed the sensation aside, locking his jaw as he turned to hand her the soup.

She worked an elbow under her. "I'll sit up to eat."

As much as he wanted—and needed—to keep space between them, he couldn't let her struggle on her own. Setting the mug to the side, he helped lift her upright and stacked a couple furs behind her for padding.

When she sank back, she met his stare with a gentle curving of her lips as she took the stew. "Thank you. That smells delicious."

The knock on her head during the wagon tumble must have affected her sense of taste, because she'd given some far-too-flattering compliments about the food he cooked. He held his tongue, though.

As she ate, he sat nearby, arms wrapped around his knees. Her vision cleared and she seemed more alert than she had been since the morning she tried to stand.

"How are you feeling?"

"Better." She glanced at her leg. "It doesn't ache as badly."

"Good. What of your ribs?"

She arched her back, as though testing out the area. "Much improved, I think. I can draw a full breath now." Her gaze returned to his, a hopeful look in her eyes. "I think I'm ready."

His stomach knotted. "Ready for what?" As if he had to ask.

She raised her brows in an exasperated look. The kind he remembered all too well. "To leave. With the vaccines." Then her face turned eager again. "Can we start out tomorrow?"

So soon? He wasn't ready for the journey. Or to leave this peaceful haven. Somehow, leaving felt like a turning point, not just a simple trek there and back. As though everything would be different when he left this place.

Did he want things to change? Only if he knew for sure the changes would be better. Only if he could control the outcome.

He'd learned the hard way—losing control could be deadly.

# NINE

The way Micah marched around camp with quick efficiency the next morning made Ingrid feel so helpless. For at least an hour, he'd been taking things down and packing up, and the place looked almost as if they'd never been there, except for the ground cleared of snow and the black circle that had been their campfire.

Handsome followed along at Micah's heels for a while, but finally came to flop down beside her, weary from keeping up with the big man.

At last, Micah stopped to scan the area, probably checking for anything he'd missed.

"I'm so sorry I haven't been of help to you. I feel useless just sitting here."

He turned to face her. "I prefer to do the packing so I can know where everything is." He looked down at her leg, a fur covering the mound of melting snow packed around her. He'd taken this last opportunity to ice it before they headed out. "I need to tighten the splint before we move you."

She tried not to wince, just nodded, then moved the fur aside. As he knelt over her and attended to the strips of fabric

79

holding the wood against her leg, she searched for something to focus on other than his ministrations.

He didn't wear his fur cap this morning, and his black hair fell forward as he worked, brushing against his dark eyes. His coloring suggested Mediterranean descent. Maybe Italian or even Spanish. "Have you lived in America all your life?"

He glanced at her for a quick moment, then returned his focus to his work. "Yes."

"Where did you grow up?"

"Mostly Massachusetts and Connecticut. Then I moved to New York to study medicine."

Her attention narrowed on a very familiar word. "Where in Massachusetts?"

His jaw worked. "Lots of places."

"Like?" He obviously didn't want to say, but she couldn't help herself. Could they have lived in the same city?

"Like Worcester and Springfield. And Boston."

She exhaled. "Why didn't you say so? How long were you in Boston? What street did you live on?"

"Not sure. I was pretty young at the time." He pulled the knot tight and straightened. "Ready to move to the travois?"

He helped her shift onto the fur he'd stretched between two poles, although the feat was awkward. Handsome curled up in her lap the moment she settled in.

Micah covered her and the pup with two of the furs she'd been using, then folded another and placed it under her braced leg. His attention to detail was painstaking, and he never rushed in his care of her. In truth, the lengths he'd gone to help her were remarkable. If only she could thank him adequately.

At last he stepped back. "Comfortable?"

She nodded, her throat swelling as she forced herself to

look at him. "Thank you, Micah. For everything." Emotion clogged her voice, locking in everything else she should say.

He nodded and looked away, seeming self-conscious. "Let's head out, then."

A chirping sound at the edge of camp snagged his attention, and she looked that direction. Three tiny squirrels chattered, as though speaking to them. Or . . . perhaps those were chipmunks, with the black stripes down their backs.

"What are they doing?" She leaned forward to see them better.

Micah didn't answer, just took a step toward the animals, then crouched. "I wondered if you'd come." He spoke in low tones as he tossed something small on the ground in front of him. The chipmunks darted forward, chirping with every step.

He murmured something too low for her to understand as he scattered more bits on the ground—dried berries, maybe, or seeds of some kind. The animals gulped them down, creeping well within Micah's reach as they ate.

None seemed the least afraid of him, great strapping man that he was. He never attempted to touch them, just offered the gifts he'd obviously saved for the animals.

How often did these chipmunks come to visit him? How many other animal friends would he be leaving behind? As far away from people as he stayed, the creatures in this wilderness must become as dear as family.

And she was forcing him to leave.

Yet she had no other choice. This man was her only option to get the vaccines to the people at Settler's Fort.

He rose and turned back to her, although he didn't meet her gaze. He'd stripped all expression from his face—not sadness, not anger, not even determination.

He simply stepped to the front of the poles and positioned himself where they crossed. When he lifted the poles onto his shoulders, she rose up in the air. She couldn't help a squeal as she grabbed the rods, but it didn't stop her fur sling from rocking.

"Everything all right back there?"

"I . . . think so." She leaned forward, gripping the sticks. Truly, her life now hung completely in his control.

"I'll be as careful as I can, but call out if I bump you too much."

"Don't worry about me." She wouldn't complain for any reason, not when hers was the easy task.

When he started forward, the ends of the poles bounced on the ground. Even hanging suspended didn't keep the bumps from jarring her leg, and she gripped the rod with one hand to keep from crying out.

After a few moments, she settled into the feel of things. Except it was impossible to prepare for the frequent jarring when the ends hit an uneven spot.

An hour into the journey, Micah's labored breathing filled the air, increasing her level of guilt with each arduous intake. If she'd felt powerless while he packed, it was nothing compared to the utter helplessness that churned through her while he now struggled.

"Why don't you rest for a few minutes?" As much as they needed to cover distance, he had to keep from wearing himself out.

He stumbled to a halt, then the poles jostled as he worked his way out of them. The dizzying sway made her clutch the rails with both hands as he lowered her to the ground.

With his boot, he scraped the snow off a rock, then sank

onto the hard surface. She had to turn to see him clearly, and the sight of him sent a surge of concern through her. "Micah."

His cheeks had flamed red and sweat shone on his brow, curling the ends of his dark hair. He'd shucked his hat and coat a while ago, laying them atop the supplies strapped behind her, but he was practically dripping with perspiration. He raised a leather canteen to his lips and gulped, his Adam's apple bobbing once. Twice. He drank as though he'd not had a sip in days.

Finally, he lowered the flask and eyed her, his breath still coming in heaves. "I won't ask if you're comfortable." Was that a glimmer of humor in his face? After exerting himself for her comfort this past hour, how could he not summon anything but resentment?

"I'm well. Don't concern yourself with me." In truth, the throbbing in her leg had returned to the same level as when she'd foolishly tried to stand days before, but he was doing everything possible to make the trip easier. She wouldn't complain.

Besides, he was the one who needed help just now. She leaned forward. "What can I do for your relief? Maybe if you press snow against your face and neck it will cool you." He needed sustenance, too. "If you'll show me where the food is packed, I'll ready something for you."

He shook his head, resting his forearms on his knees. "No food. We'll stop at noon to eat. I'll keep 'til then." Leaning over the side of the stone, he scooped white snow into his drinking pouch. "I didn't mean to drink all the water. This was supposed to be for us both." Corking the top, he held it out to her. "If you'll keep this near you, the snow will melt into drinking water."

She followed his instructions, and within minutes, he lifted the poles to raise her up in the air again. Her splint jarred against a rod, sending a shooting pain through her leg. Clenching her jaw, she pulled the braced leg away from the pole and tucked a fur between the two.

But as they progressed, the steady bumping and sudden jolts ate away at her fortitude, and the pain began radiating through her body again. Especially through her skull.

Micah didn't stop for hours. And as much as she wanted to ask for a break, if she unclenched her jaw to speak, the moans wouldn't stay inside any longer. Her pain built up inside, pressing hard until she might explode. She'd stopped fighting the tears and let them stream down her face, as long as she could keep quiet.

They'd been traveling downhill for a while, a condition that tilted her rearward in a way that felt as if she'd tumble back on her head. One more reason to cling to the rails.

At last, Micah slowed to a weary halt.

The travois jolted and dropped, and she clenched her jaw tighter to hold in a squeal. Had he stumbled?

"Are you hurt?" She twisted to see him.

He'd dropped to his knees, his head bowed, even though the straps binding him to the poles held him upright.

"Oh, Micah." This was too much for him. How could she have forced him into this torture? Like the ancient Egyptians forced the Israelites into backbreaking slavery, she'd insisted this man haul her over countless mountains to accomplish her mission.

Her whim would save many lives, but would that be worth the cost of his own? As he knelt in the snow, his breath coming in hoarse gasps, his head lolling forward, she could believe he would work to his last breath to accomplish this journey to which he'd committed.

"Micah, come take a drink. Then stretch out on this fur and rest." She struggled to gather one of the pelts covering her and spread it out on the ground.

The contraption under her shifted again, jostling, then lowered to the snow. He struggled to his feet, then trudged around to her and sank onto the fur she laid out.

His handsome face flushed red, with lines of sweat streaking the sides. His damp locks curled in a mass of unusual angles where he'd probably attempted to swipe sweat and hair out of his face. He stretched out on his back, the manly scent of hard work drifting from him.

"Drink some water." She offered the pouch, its leather sides warm from where she'd held it against her shirtwaist.

He didn't open his eyes, just took the canteen, uncorked the top, and raised it to his lips. He lay within reach of her—so close she couldn't help but notice the strong contours of his face. His countenance wasn't angular and rough in the way of many men. Even with his beard, each part of the whole seemed like a piece of artwork, coming together to form an appearance so attractive, she'd need to protect her heart from becoming enamored with him.

He was her physician. A savior who appeared in her darkest hour and now performed his professional duty to treat her wounds . . . and carry her to a distant mountain settlement to save the lives of people he didn't know.

So, maybe he was a bit of a hero, too.

Micah's legs ached, yet he forced one step, then another, as he gathered firewood that evening. Surely his body would adapt to the extra load after a day or two, and the entire trip wouldn't be as hard as today.

He'd first thought to eat cold meat and leftover corncakes he'd brought with them, but a stew would be better. Warmer for Ingrid, who couldn't seem to shake her shivers as the evening chill settled over them, and more nourishing for them both.

As he reached for another rotting log, a bit of gray appeared underneath it. Mushrooms this late in the season? Probably the log had kept the spores protected. He carefully scooped the largest of them. This was definitely the variety he ate through the summer, and they'd been a good source of energy. An excellent addition to the stew pot.

One more log finished his load, and he headed back to where he'd left Ingrid in their camp at the edge of the woods. She'd not complained once today, but her pallor and bloodshot eyes proved the ride had been painful.

He should brew some willow tea with the evening meal, and extra for her to drink through the day tomorrow.

She cracked her eyelids when he approached, and he tried to ease his load down quietly so he didn't startle her with the clatter.

"What can I do to help?" Her words seemed to issue through clenched teeth, as though she were biting down on her pain.

"Just rest. I'll have the fire going soon, then I'll start supper." As he knelt beside the area he'd cleared for the blaze, the little dog rose from Ingrid's side, stretched each hind leg in turn, then ambled toward him.

As Micah laid out the tinder, the dog sniffed his hand. "You wanna help with the fire?" The pup licked him, then stared up into his face while wagging that curly tail.

Micah raised a brow at him. "I don't think you're old enough to play with fire."

The dog cocked his head, as though trying to make sense of Micah's words. He might be a perfectly useless little shadow, but he was kind of cute.

When he had a decent fire blazing, he pulled the pot from the supplies he'd strapped to the poles beside Ingrid.

"If you bring your pack here, I'll make the stew." Ingrid's eyes were open and she struggled to sit up. She still looked so weak, but lying there all the time was probably frustrating for her. She could cut ingredients into the pot and stir without injuring herself further. And he still needed to gather more firewood—enough for the night and a few pieces to carry with them in case he couldn't find dry wood tomorrow night.

By the time he finished the evening chores, Ingrid had the food ready. He sank onto a dry fur and took the mug she handed him. "Thanks. Sorry I don't have a second cup." Maybe he could carve one out of wood. But after they reached Settler's Fort, he'd no longer need it, so that seemed like a waste of energy.

And just now, he had no energy to spare.

# TEN

*M*icah woke to the sound of retching.

His shoulders ached, his own stomach churning as the miserable noises continued. "I'm sorry." He ached to take Ella's pain on himself. Relieve her of her awful symptoms.

Turning over in bed, he reached for her. But his fingers found only dirt. Cold, frozen ground.

Jerking his eyes open, he sat upright as the sound of heaving filled the air again. He strained to see in the dim light. He was outside. A figure bent over, emptying her stomach a short distance away. Not Ella. Awareness washed over him.

*Ingrid.* Was the pain from her broken leg so bad her stomach had to purge itself?

Pushing the covers aside, he struggled to his feet, ignoring the sharp ache in every part of his body. His own stomach churned, leftover remnants from his memories, but he forced that aside, too.

"What's wrong, Ingrid?" His voice was groggy from sleep, but he stepped toward her and dropped to his knees beside her bed. Loose tendrils had escaped her braid, and he reached to hold the locks out of the way of her heaving.

At last she stilled. Her breath came in ragged gasps, her back rising in rapid succession.

He had no handkerchief to hand her. "It may help to wipe your face with clean snow," he murmured. "I'll go fill the pot if you like."

She shook her head and reached for a clean patch of white to follow his suggestion, then sank back against her blankets. Her face glowed white in the dim light of the moon, her eyes dark pools.

A strand of hair covered one of her cheeks, and he brushed it away. Her skin was damp, clammy. Probably from the effort she'd just put forth, and maybe from the pain she endured, too. He rested the back of his fingers on her forehead. Not overly warm. At least there was no fever.

He could feel the strength of her gaze while he'd touched her, and finally he looked into the deep recesses of her eyes, shadowed by the weak moonlight. "I'll get some tea to help with your pain."

She shook her head, a bit of wildness in the act. Her hands moved to her midsection. "No. It's not the pain that made me sick."

"What then?" Could this be a common illness?

"I started feeling the discomfort not long after I ate."

His muddled thoughts came into focus with a clarity that made his own stomach churn. Could the meat in the stew have gone bad? He used the beaver he trapped the morning before. He'd taken every precaution, adding plenty of salt to the meat, keeping it packed in snow until he was ready to roast it.

The roiling in his gut surged, sending a pang so uncomfortable he jerked upright. This was more than worry churning his middle. He had to get to the woods posthaste. "I'll be back."

And as he sprinted through the trees, jumping a fallen log, the thought flitted through his mind. *Could it be the mushrooms?*

The night lasted forever.

Between his own trips to the woods, he sat beside Ingrid to help ease her misery. If only he had some ginger to settle her stomach, or black cohosh to remove the poisons he'd inadvertently fed her. When the vomiting came the second time, he rubbed gentle circles on her back while she heaved.

That gentle stroking had soothed Ella in those last awful days. So much of this horrible night felt like he'd fallen back five years. He'd not meant to feed Ingrid toxic mushrooms. Just like he'd not meant to bring smallpox home to his wife and daughter. And now Ingrid had succumbed in the same way his family had before. All he could do was sit by her side and offer water. Let her body cleanse itself. What kind of doctor was he? This was exactly why he'd given up the work all those years ago.

At least this episode didn't look to be deadly. For that, the relief sank through every one of his bones.

Another fact that brought him a sordid relief? This time, he partook, just a little, in the suffering. His own gut-churnings that sent him to the woods weren't as painful as Ingrid's, but at least she didn't have to bear the full weight of his misdeeds alone.

The effects of the mushrooms seemed to have subsided by the time dawn lightened the sky. After making sure they both downed another cupful of water, he crawled back to his bedroll and tucked inside. He'd need to get them moving again soon, but he wouldn't last a day of pulling without a few hours of sleep.

The sun peaked at the noon zenith by the time he helped Ingrid onto the travois. She sent him a smile that lit her weary face and thawed something inside him. Through all she'd endured—this last bit at his own hand—it was a wonder she could still muster a look that hopeful.

He slipped off his buffalo skin coat before strapping on the poles and raising Ingrid into the air.

"Do you think it will snow?" Her muffled words drifted over his shoulder.

Lifting his gaze to the low-hanging clouds, he searched for the sun. Only a spot of light brightened the clouds through the thick cover. The air seemed colder than it had in the night, too. "Probably."

And it turned out he was right. The icy flakes that drifted down several hours later were a cooling relief from the sweat rolling down his face. He pulled another hour or so while the snow thickened. The sky turned ominous as early evening neared.

He had to find a place where they could camp under the shelter of trees, but he'd been climbing the face of a mountain for a while now, and nothing larger than bushes and boulders poked above the snowy expanse.

A half hour later, he crested the slope and spotted a cluster of three trees ahead. That would have to do. The snow had risen almost to his knees, and still fell in a thick curtain. Tomorrow he'd need to strap on his snowshoes. The well-padded ground probably made Ingrid's ride smoother, so he couldn't be sorry for the extra depth—not much, anyway.

When he reached the downward side of the trees, he sank to his knees, lowering the travois to the snow. "This looks like the best spot to camp."

She didn't answer, and he worked his way out of the straps so he could turn and check on her. The buffalo hide was pulled up to cover her face completely, sending a jolt of fear through him. "Ingrid? What's wrong?" The fear rang in his voice as he scrambled back to her side.

The fur lowered to reveal her eyes. "Nothing. I'm just c-cold." Her teeth chattered, making the words stutter.

What little that showed of her face was pale, and her eyes seemed drained of life. He reached for the covering and pulled it down so he could see the rest of her features. Even in the dimming light, he could see the bluish tint of her lips. "Oh, Ingrid."

He pulled the fur back up to cover her nose, then reached for his own coat laying on the supplies above her head. After tucking it around her as much as possible, he placed both his hands where her arms should be and rubbed. He had to get a fire going, then he could work to encourage her circulation.

Even after he cleared snow from the area, the wet ground made building a fire achingly hard. They were high enough on the mountain that a steady wind cut through the area, dousing his flame every time he managed a spark with his flint and steel.

By the time he finally had a small blaze licking at the dry tinder he'd packed, darkness shrouded them like a thick fog. He cleared more snow for Ingrid's bed, then helped her move to the spot.

Her entire body trembled with cold, and he thought for a moment of pulling her close, trying to use his own body heat to warm her. It might come to that, but first he needed to find the right-sized stones to place in the fire to heat as bedwarmers, then he'd work to get her blood flowing through all her limbs.

While pushing aside the snow, he'd found a couple of fallen limbs that would make decent firewood once they dried out. He used his hatchet to cut the wood into smaller pieces, then placed them around the fire to dry. The logs he'd carried with them would last until these new pieces were ready to burn. Hopefully. By the time he had everything ready, Ingrid may well be frozen stiff.

At last, he settled himself beside her. Her face peeked out the side of the furs, buried in shadows. "Are you feeling warmth from the fire?" He settled his hand on the bump of fur that must be her shoulder and arm.

"A little."

"I'm going to work on getting your blood flowing better."

The fur shifted as she nodded. "G-Good."

He rubbed her arms through the furs for a few minutes, then took one of her gloved hands out from the cover to knead and stroke, forcing the blood to her fingertips. After tucking the fur tight again around her upper body, he moved down to her feet.

She still wore leather boots, and he removed the one from her good foot. The leather was thin, and she only wore a simple woolen stocking underneath. No wonder she was freezing. The wind blowing in from all sides as she hung suspended on the travois would make the chill worse, especially with the dropping temperature and snow. Thankfully, the falling flakes had ebbed to a few drifting down every now and then.

He wrapped his hands around her stockinged foot, feeling the intimacy of the touch more than he should. Her feet were slender and fine-boned, as was the rest of her. Underneath the wool, they were likely elegant—as much as any foot could be.

Forcing the image from his mind, he focused on working his fingers through the muscle to draw blood down to her extremities.

She sucked in a breath when his thumb worked up to her toes. He softened his touch. Surely she hadn't contracted frostbite. Not this soon. He'd need to check for that later. And she needed much better protection on her feet than those thin leather boots. They were clearly more helpful for fashion than protection against the elements.

Little by little, he worked his fingers over the appendage, pressing into her arch with his thumbs, working each toe by turn. After several minutes, she seemed to relax, her muscles softening.

"I never thought I would enjoy someone touching my foot." Her words held a relaxed sound. Not the stammering produced by chattering teeth. Finally.

As he worked, her words wove their way through his mind. She enjoyed this touch? Something about the thought warmed him—maybe more than it should. But at least he wasn't bringing her pain now.

After another minute or two, he cupped her foot in both hands and gave a final gentle squeeze, then pulled the fur over her again. He gathered two of the blankets he'd retrieved from the site of the wagon crash, then toed a rock from the fire. These blankets had been too flimsy to use in place of the thicker furs, but they'd do nicely for wrapping her feet.

He swathed the limb he'd rubbed in the thick layers of fabric, then tucked the hot stone beside her where the blanket would protect her skin.

"That feels . . . wonderful."

"Good." Because what he did next would likely make her forget all the pleasant sensations.

Turning to her left foot—the injured leg—he carefully unfastened the buttons and eased off the shoe. She didn't make a sound, but he could feel the tension in her.

"I'll be as gentle as I can, but we need to get the blood flowing through this leg." *I can't let you lose toes.* He clamped his jaw to hold in that last thought.

As careful as he was not to shift the position of her foot while he kneaded her muscles and worked her toes, he had no doubt he was causing pain. For that, he hated every second of his ministrations, even though this was for her good.

Finally, he wrapped her foot in the second blanket, then stood and kicked another stone from the fire to tuck beside this foot.

With that done, he straightened, his gaze roaming the length of her. She needed warm food now, and maybe some willow tea. He was running low on his supply, but he had enough for tonight and tomorrow morning. Hopefully, he'd find a creek with a willow growing alongside as they traveled tomorrow, so he could replenish their stock.

Something about Ingrid's shoulders caught his focus. She still had the fur covering all but her face as she turned toward the fire, and he couldn't place the reason for the prodding in his chest.

He knelt beside her, settling one hand on her shoulder and using the other to peel back the pelt so her face wasn't buried in shadows. What he saw constricted his chest. "Oh, Ingrid."

Tear tracks glistened on her cheeks, and fresh tears spilled from her beautiful eyes.

He stroked the hair from her face. "Did I hurt you that much?" He was a heavy-handed cad. He'd known he was causing discomfort but had no idea she was suffering this much.

She sniffed. "I'm not hurt."

Her attempt to soothe his concerns only showed how strong and truly good this woman was. He ran the backs of his fingers across her forehead and down her temple. Her skin was so soft—and warm now, finally. "I'm sorry, Ingrid. Truly. If I ever hurt you, I need you to tell me you're in pain."

She laughed, a choking laugh, and more tears leaked from the corners of her eyes. "I'm always in pain. Sometimes my leg hurts the most; other times it's my heart."

His chest ached the way hers must. He knew exactly how that felt—a heartache so real that simply breathing was sometimes too hard. Emotion clogged his throat. If only he could say something to help her grieve. To ease the awful hurt. But nothing helped.

He cleared his throat. "I wish I could say it gets better. That's what people told me: 'With time, the hurt goes away.' I don't think that's true. But I do know memories help."

She looked up at him, her eyes luminous in the moonlight. "You've lost someone?"

He nodded. He'd not meant to talk about Ella and Rachel. He never talked about them. But if anything could help her, he had to set his own preference aside. "My wife. And daughter."

She sucked in an audible breath. "Oh, Micah. I'm sorry."

This was why he didn't talk about them. He didn't want her sympathy. "Five years ago. That's why I stopped doctoring. The pain never gets easier, at least not for me, but I hold on to the memories. They make the pain bearable." Sometimes.

She reached from under the covers and took his hand. "I

have so many special times to remember. Papa was everything, my whole life. I would take lunch to him on the days he worked in his laboratory, mixing medicines. He taught me all about each ingredient, which blends worked well and which could be toxic."

"He was a chemist? I assumed a physician from the medical bag."

"Both. He saw patients on Monday, Tuesday, and Wednesday, then worked in his laboratory the other days. He and some friends studied and advocated for the use of vaccines for widespread diseases. Like smallpox." Her voice softened with the last words, her memories likely circling back to the reason she'd come to these mountains. The reason her father died on that cliff.

He squeezed her hand. "Hold on to the good memories."

Her eyes glistened, her mouth attempting to form a brave smile. "I will."

A glance at the fire showed he'd best get moving. "Rest now. I'll make something for us to eat, then we'll both get some sleep."

But sleep may be long in coming with this woman so near. Slowly but surely, he was coming to care about her more than he liked.

And far more than he should.

# ELEVEN

*T*he days seemed to meld together for Ingrid.

How Micah could endure such physical trial all day, then still care for her needs at every break, was unfathomable. Yet he did. Despite the fact that he was such a quiet, reclusive man, his attentions were gentle and achingly tender.

But that didn't stop the pain. Her leg throbbed constantly during the long days as she bounced over rocks and terrain only the mountain goats should attempt. By the end of the first hour each morning, her head pulsed so terribly that it felt as though her entire skull would burst—and what a blessed relief that would be. To be out of her misery at last.

She couldn't pray for that. Couldn't wish to be gone when she still had this life-saving task to accomplish.

What little sleep the willow tea brought was a muddled relief as she faded in and out of consciousness through days and nights. A few times she jolted awake at the sound of wolves howling, and once the cry of a mountain lion raised the fine hairs on her neck. Having Micah there made her feel safe. Whether the sensation was real or perceived, she didn't know for sure.

The days became almost impossible to distinguish. How long had they been traveling? Four days? Five? Maybe they were a third of the way through the journey. She could hope at least. And pray.

Midway through one morning, Micah eased to a stop sooner than she expected. "Looks like we've found someone."

A person? She sat up, craning her neck to see what he meant. A wooden structure—a rough home from the looks of it—sat through the trees, about thirty or forty steps ahead. "Who is it? Do you know them?"

"No." He shifted sideways, pulling her sled into a thicker grouping of trees. "Wait here. I'll be back when I know it's safe."

"Wait. Micah, no." She reached out for him, but he'd already moved away.

He paused and looked back at her. "I have my rifle. I'll return shortly." All sign of exhaustion had fled his features, leaving his shoulders squared in that virile mountain-man look he sometimes donned.

If any man could hold himself against a stranger in this wild country, Micah Bradley could. But she couldn't help saying, "I'll be praying for your safety." Because only God could truly protect him.

His expression shadowed, even as he nodded. Then he turned away and strode toward the house. A moment later, his voice sounded loud and clear. "Halloo, the cabin."

Micah paused in plain view of the well-built log home as he waited for a response, his Hawken rifle gripped in both hands. Every man in this country knew better than to approach a stranger's door without first calling out a warning, but if anyone was home, they were sure taking their sweet time to answer.

A scuffling sounded from within, just as the door cracked open. "Who be you?" The high, clear voice belonged to a child, no doubt about it.

He lowered his gun to make himself look less foreboding. "My name is Micah Bradley. Is your father around?" What was a child doing in this country? Most of the settlers in these parts were miners and trappers, although some did take Indian squaws as wives, so children weren't completely unheard of.

A head poked through the doorway, a shock of bright red hair pulling Micah's focus like a hungry dog to a chunk of meat. His chest tightened. Rachel's hair had been every bit as red.

"My pa's hurt. You wanna talk to Mama?" The child—a boy, he was pretty sure—couldn't be more than five or six. Who would let such a youngster greet a stranger at their threshold? The man must truly be bad off.

All Micah's muscles bunched. He wasn't a doctor any longer. Had turned fully from the job when he left Indiana, and he'd never been tempted to take it up again.

Until Ingrid.

In truth, he'd not been faced with a need, save his own occasional injuries. Now not only did Ingrid wait outside with a broken leg and ribs, he may need to treat the man who lived here, as well. Was God tormenting him?

"I'd like to talk to your mama." He eased forward, closing some of the distance between himself and the house.

The door widened to reveal a woman—a white woman,

of all things. A sight rarely seen in these parts. Wisps of hair stuck out from her brown coif, and her coat looked to have seen better days. Maybe those things were what caused her harried look, but likely it was the thin set of her mouth.

He took another step forward, bringing himself about ten strides from the cabin. "Hello, ma'am. I'm Micah Bradley, and I'm traveling with a woman who's injured. Would it be possible for us to come inside to get warm before we head on our way?" He wouldn't ask for food, but he'd not decline if she offered.

She didn't look inclined to offer. At least not from the way she pulled the door closer to herself, uncertainty clouding her stern features. "Where is she?"

He motioned toward the trees behind him. "Not far back. I wanted to make sure we'd be welcome before I brought her closer." A woman and boy didn't seem to be much danger, but he'd rather not give Ingrid's exact location and condition until he ascertained their safety. "Are there others in there with you?"

She straightened. "My husband is here." The boy's father who was injured. She was likely more concerned about her own family's safety than anything else.

He raised a hand, palm forward. "We mean no harm. I just thought to warm up for an hour or two. We've been traveling in the snow for days now."

That seemed to make up her mind. She opened the door wider. "Bring her in."

"Her leg is broken, so I'll need to carry her in." He closed the distance and poked his head inside. "I can lay her there beside your fire, if that's acceptable."

She nodded, holding the boy's shoulders to keep him beside her. He squirmed, trying to work his way out of her hold.

"Thank you. I'll be back in a moment."

Ingrid was sitting upright when he retraced his tracks to her. "Who are they?"

"A woman and boy. They say the man is there, but he's hurt." He gathered up the harness and strapped himself to the poles in the position that had become more familiar than sleeping these days.

He pulled Ingrid right up to the door, then eyed the flattened log he'd have to lift her over to enter the house. The floor inside was dirt, and she'd be most comfortable if she stayed in the travois, even inside the small building. After pulling the poles more than halfway inside, he balanced them on the transom as he moved beside her, then eased her the rest of the way in.

The effort brought him closer to Ingrid's face than he'd been in days, and her eyes widened at his nearness, drawing him into their depths. She really was a beautiful woman. Too delicate for this country.

He pried himself away from her gaze and straightened, looking around. The woman and boy stood against the back wall of the sparse room. She motioned toward the fire. "In front of the hearth is best. I'm Joanna Watson and this is my son, Samuel. We've hot water if you'd like tea. And there's stew in the pot if you're hungry. Bowls on the shelf." She pointed toward a ledge mounted beside the hearth.

A noise drifted from another room, like that of a person calling out. Maybe a groan. The woman jerked and released her grip on her son. "Samuel can show you where things are." Then she ducked behind a blanket hanging from the back wall, disappearing into what must be a bedchamber.

Micah pulled the travois forward until Ingrid was beside

the fire, then turned to face the lad. "Hello, Samuel. Is that your pa calling out?"

The boy's freckled face drooped. "Yeah, he hurt himself real bad. Mama told me not to come see him 'til he's better."

"He sounds like me." Ingrid spoke up from her position on the floor. "My leg is broken, but Dr. Bradley here is taking care of it. I'm getting a little better every day. Maybe he can help your pa, too."

Micah wanted to lurch forward and clamp his hand over her mouth. He hadn't decided for sure whether to mention his former occupation. He'd not doctored in so long, except for Ingrid. What if he forgot what was needed and caused further damage—or even death? He'd taken a pledge to do no harm when he spoke the Hippocratic Oath. A promise he'd already failed to keep once.

The boy's face lit. "That's 'zactly what we need. Let me tell Mama." He darted toward the blanket, then slowed when he neared it and poked his head inside.

Micah may not be ready to face the man in the back room, but he was more than ready to scoop the stew into a bowl for Ingrid. She needed nourishment, and although he couldn't say exactly what was in the lumpy soup, it was surely better for her than his simple meals of meat and corn mush.

His own stomach gurgled, but as he handed Ingrid's bowl to her, the hanging blanket flapped again and their hostess slipped back into the room.

"You're a doctor?" Her pale face held enough restrained hope to push the last of his hesitation aside.

"I haven't treated a patient in five years, save Miss Chastain's broken leg." He motioned toward Ingrid. "But I'll do what I can for your husband. I don't have many medicines or tools, though."

"Come then, please." She spun and motioned for him to follow her through the blanket-door.

He sent a last glance to Ingrid, who nodded at him. Would she be safe if he left her here? Surely she could hold her own with the boy. And she had the rifle beside her if danger appeared.

"Call out if you need anything." He swallowed, trying to push down the spurt of fear. Not for himself. Ingrid's well-being had come to mean more to him than a doctor should allow with his patient. How had he let this happen? But he didn't have time to chastise himself now.

Ingrid's eyes softened, as if she could read all the thoughts that had been swirling in him since they'd entered this place. "Go, Micah. Help the man." She motioned him forward.

Taking a deep breath, he pushed the blanket aside and stepped into the tiny room.

The dim space was lit by a single lantern on a table beside the bed. The woman stood on the far side of the mattress, leaning over a figure.

He moved around to them. The man lay with only a light-weight blanket covering him, his left arm resting atop the cover, a bandage wrapped around the forearm.

"His ax slipped and dug into the flesh as he was swinging. I've been using a salve, but it seems to be getting worse." Her voice trembled with the tears that had been falling already this day, if her puffy eyes could be believed.

She stepped back, and Micah took her place. The man didn't look conscious, but his labored breathing filled the quiet room. "What's his name?" He pressed a hand to the forehead. Burning. Likely from an infection.

"Robert."

He turned his attention to the bandaged arm and began unrolling the fabric. The skin above and below the gray wool bandage glared an angry red hue, so he prepared himself for what he would find when he peeled off the last of the cloth. Still, the sight of raw crimson flesh oozing with puss churned bile in his stomach. He worked to refrain from showing a reaction. "I'll need several clean cloths and a pot of warm water. And bring me that salve."

She moved to do his bidding, and his mind scrambled for anything else he could use to clear the infection. "Have you any peppers from a garden? Or perhaps a clove of garlic?"

She hesitated, her brow furrowing. "No. I'm sorry." Her words tapered into a mournful whisper, as though it was her fault she'd not thought to grow such things.

"Any whiskey or strong drink?"

She shook her head. "No, we only drink water and root teas."

"Just bring water and rags, then." But cleaning the pus from the wound likely wouldn't be enough to fight the infection surging in this man's body. Not when the poison was eating through his flesh.

Time seemed to span interminably as he worked, cleaning the gruesome wound, trying to cool the man's feverish skin, and getting him to sip a little water.

Robert's pallor continued to drain, his body seeming to sink in on itself. He wasn't getting enough water—that much was clear by a quick inspection of his skin. But with him unconscious, anything more than a dribble could easily choke him.

"We need to place wet cloths all over him. His arms, legs, face, middle—everywhere." Maybe his body could absorb the moisture through his skin while the cloths cooled him.

Mrs. Watson dove into the effort, pulling back her husband's clothing to apply the rags. She was younger than he'd first supposed, probably not much older than Ingrid. Yet her worries hung on her like a worn, tattered blanket.

And no wonder—her husband lay at death's door.

As the hours passed, Robert Watson slipped further away, no longer responding to even his wife's murmurings. The time had come to say something, but oh, he hated this part.

He cleared his throat. "Mrs. Watson."

Her face jerked up to look at him, her hands still cupping the cloths on her husband's cheeks. "Yes?" Fear made her voice ring high.

"I'm not sure he has much fight left. The infection's taken over his body. Now might be time for you and your son to say any last words."

Her expression hung suspended, as though his statement didn't penetrate. Then her mouth pressed into a hard line, trembling a little. Her eyes welled and she turned away, looking at her husband once more.

Time he left them alone.

He dragged his weary body out of the chamber, stepping through the blanket-door into the main room.

Ingrid sat where he left her, the dog in her lap and the red-haired boy at her side. The lad was talking to the pup as he held the black mop of hair away from the animal's eyes. All three looked up at his approach, searching his face.

The boy's expression was so innocent, pulling tighter at the knot in his gut. "Is my pa feeling better now?"

Not that question. How could he look this young, inno-cent child in the face—a face that reminded him so much of Rachel that he could barely breathe—and tell him his father would die? If only he could take that man's place. Leave this family whole and unblemished. Stronger for the trial they'd overcome.

And still *together*.

He lowered to a crouch so he was eye-level with the boy. "Your pa's very sick." His throat rasped with the words, and he cleared it. But what else could he say? What could possibly prepare the boy for the next few moments—and then the rest of his life without a father?

Micah knew exactly what a childhood alone felt like. And he would do anything to take it from this lad.

A hand found his, slipping soft fingers between his tired ones. Holding on. Soothing.

He raised his gaze to meet Ingrid's. Her fathomless eyes had the power to soak him in, to ease the pain from the past few hours.

"Samuel."

The boy jumped up at the sound of his mother's voice, leaving an empty place as he ran to her. Micah didn't turn to see the woman, didn't need to witness the sadness on her face.

Ingrid flicked her eyes up though, then lowered her focus back to him as sounds from the pair faded away. "Will he make it?"

Again the question. He let out a breath and sat back on his haunches. He was too tired for this. Why did the worst always seem to come when he was most exhausted? He tried to work his hand from hers, to find some semblance of control.

But she held tight.

"Micah."

He forced himself to meet her gaze again.

"You don't have to bear this alone." Her eyes begged him, pleaded . . . for what? Whatever she wanted from him, if he had it to offer, he'd gladly give it to her.

But the strength seemed to slide out of him. He dropped his head, letting it hang limp.

"Come sit. Eat. And rest." She took his arm, easing him down to sit on the floor.

He raised his head to respond, but she held a bowl out to him. "It's been cooling, but should be warm enough still." In her other hand she extended a tin cup. "Tea."

After two bowls of the stew, his body didn't feel as empty, and he stretched out beside her on a fur. He could sleep for days.

If only he could forget the awful loss happening in the next room.

# TWELVE

*I*f only she could get up and *do something* to help. Ingrid lay on the travois with the crackling of the fire on her left and Micah's deep breathing on her right. The noises she didn't hear were the ones that worried her most.

What was happening in that room where Joanna and Samuel had disappeared? From Micah's reaction, it didn't sound as if Mr. Watson would survive his injury. Her heart longed to be near to comfort his wife. No woman should have to endure loss like that alone.

And Samuel. Her heart ached for the boy. So young and innocent to lose his father. He'd never have his pa to teach him to fish or how to become a man. To help him navigate the trials of life. Was it worse to have a parent for a time and then lose them, knowing what was lost?

Her heart still ached for Papa with a pain that felt as though her chest were being wrenched in two. She'd felt the loss of her mother, too, especially as she grew into a woman. But Mama had died giving life to her, and she'd never known exactly what she was missing. That hollowness inside her that Papa was almost able to fill completely.

And now, the loss of him carved out that hole to a full crater. She turned toward the fire as a fresh wave of tears surged, burning their way down her cheeks. *Oh, heavenly Father. I feel so lost without him.*

The swish of the blanket-door sounded behind her, and she struggled to rein in her tears. *Lord, help me be strong for these people as they grieve. Show me how to help them, even if that means exposing my own wounds.*

She turned to them as Samuel trudged through the doorway, head drooping, while his mother led him with a hand on his shoulder. Joanna Watson's face held obvious signs of crying, even across the dim light in the room. Still, her shoulders were squared and her chin raised high.

Micah must have sensed their presence, for his breathing quieted and he raised up to a sitting position.

Joanna approached them. "It's over." Her words escaped on a breath, stilling Ingrid's pulse with their meaning.

"Oh, Joanna." She reached out for the woman, but of course she was too far away to touch. She craved to pull her into an embrace that would help take the sting out of the awful pain she must be experiencing.

Micah stood in a smooth motion, then stepped toward the woman and placed a hand on her elbow. "I'm so sorry, ma'am." The gentleness in his tone, the respect in his touch, had to provide at least a little comfort. His face took on that achingly gentle expression, the one he'd used when he told her about Papa's death. That look could only be given by a man who'd endured a world of loss and pain of his own.

Joanna nodded. "Will you help me . . . lay him to rest?"

"Of course." Micah paused. "With the snow, everything is frozen. I'll need to clear a spot and start a fire to thaw the ground. Or it might be better to cover him with stones."

"I'll help," Joanna said.

While they spoke, the boy had inched toward Handsome, who still lay snuggled in Ingrid's lap.

His mother turned to him just as Samuel knelt to stroke the dog's head. "Come, son. Let's put on our coats."

His crestfallen look made Ingrid's chest squeeze. She looked up at Joanna. "He can stay and keep me company."

Relief eased the woman's face. "That would be helpful. Thank you."

Sleeping with a roof over his head—a real roof, not a cave or brush shelter—was a luxury Micah hadn't experienced in months. He slept longer than he planned, maybe because there were no windows in the cabin for the sun's light to awaken him. Yet even when he awoke and glanced around to take stock of the morning, he felt as weary as if he'd been pulling Ingrid's travois all night.

Mrs. Watson worked at the table, cutting some kind of food. How had she fared through the night? She and the boy had retreated into the bedchamber after they finished the burial the day before. It was hard to tell from her outline how she was holding up this morning, but chances were good she'd had a rough go of it.

Pushing to his feet, he approached her. "Can I get water for you while I'm outside?"

Without turning to face him, she motioned to a pail by the

door. "There's a creek behind the barn, but it's frozen. If you can fill that with snow, I'll melt it."

He grabbed the pail and stepped outside. A hoarse bray filled the air as he passed the tiny barn tucked into the trees. Ah, yes. The donkey he'd discovered the day before. He opened the door and slipped inside, wincing as another high-pitched bray sounded in his ears.

"Hey there, boy. You hungry?" He could at least replenish the burro's water and toss him some hay while he was out here.

The donkey greeted his offering with hungry enthusiasm, nudging Micah's leg as he stepped into the little stall with the feed. After dropping his load, he stopped to rub the animal's thick brown coat, stroking the dark stripes that crossed its shoulders in the shape of a cross.

One of the trappers he'd joined with when he first came to this territory had kept a donkey. He'd told a story about how the lines were left from the shadow of the cross Jesus died on, a constant reminder of the burden He carried for everyone.

At the time, he'd been determined to hate every thought of a God who claimed to love His people, then let them suffer mercilessly. Now, he couldn't bring himself to begrudge this gentle burro.

For most of the day, Mrs. Watson seemed to be in a fog. He and Ingrid took turns occupying the boy's attention, but it was the little shadow dog who lifted the lad's spirits best. Samuel tussled with the pup on the floor of the cabin and took him for walks outside to visit the donkey, whose name was Jackson.

Each time the boy returned the dog to Ingrid, the little ball of fluff collapsed by her side in a heap. For her part, Ingrid looked to be feeling much better through this day of rest. He'd worried seeing this fresh loss would sink her back into the depths of her own grief. But she'd been a solid strength for both the woman and the boy, helping as she could, ever so gently.

By late afternoon, though, she began to look strained, and her frequent glances toward the door made him think her pensive look had nothing to do with her leg.

When he returned from a walk to the creek with the boy, Ingrid motioned him over. "Where's Samuel?"

After shucking his coat and gloves at the door, he stepped to her and crouched by her side. "He's building animals in the snow. I'll check on him in a moment." The shadow dog raised his head, and Micah reached to pet him. "Everything all right here?" He met her worried gaze.

"Joanna seems to be doing remarkably well. I think it's time we make a plan."

He raised his brows at her. "A plan?" He knew exactly what she meant, but he wasn't ready to commit to a course of action. Not when there were simply no good choices available.

She gave a sigh laced with tension, then motioned for him to sit beside her. "You know we can't leave them here alone. That means they have to go with us. Is there a sled or something the donkey can pull? I'd hate to think of either one of them having to walk."

His thoughts exactly. He settled into the spot where she pointed and wrapped his hands around his knees, working to organize his thoughts. "There is a little pony cart, but it's barely big enough for one person. I can put sled runners on it, but it won't be a smooth ride."

A single brow rose this time, and her mouth pinched as if she was holding back a smile. Probably, she didn't consider the travois a smooth ride, either, but she was polite enough to refrain from commenting. Instead, she said, "We have to speak with Joanna about it. Perhaps she'll have other ideas."

He let out a breath. "We can see what she says."

Less than an hour later, Mrs. Watson stepped from the bedchamber and approached the fire.

"Joanna, can we speak with you when you have a minute?" Ingrid wasn't letting grass grow under her feet. Surely she wouldn't rush this grieving widow into leaving her home.

Mrs. Watson turned, her face taking on a look of resolve. Had she heard them talking earlier? Would she be willing to abandon this place? Mayhap she'd be eager to return to a larger settlement.

"Yes?"

He could feel Ingrid's gaze on him, possibly wondering if she should do the asking. But this was his responsibility. "Mrs. Watson, have you thought about what you'll do next? Do you have family you can go to?"

The woman's expression dimmed, but then she seemed to find another bit of inner strength. "My family have all passed. My husband's mother lives in St. Louis, but I doubt she'd take kindly to us showing up on her doorstep. This is our home. We'll continue as before."

Except they weren't as before. A woman and child had little chance of surviving out here alone. He couldn't leave them, no matter what she said. But perhaps . . .

He turned to Ingrid. "You could stay here with them while I take the vaccines on to Settler's Fort. I'll return with help to travel the rest of the way when you're well enough." He didn't like the idea of leaving all three of them alone, but if they kept a gun at the ready and stayed close to the house, they might be safe enough. Maybe.

But she was already shaking her head before he finished speaking. "I'm going with you. We agreed. I know I've been a burden to you so far, but if the donkey pulls the pony cart, surely that would be easier. I'm sorry, Micah. Please." A hint of something flared in her eyes. Desperation? It looked almost like fear, yet he'd never seen fear on this strong woman.

Was she afraid to stay here alone? If that were the case, he couldn't leave her. *Wouldn't* leave her. If something happened to her, he could never live with himself.

He'd brought death on the two most important lives entrusted to him. He wouldn't let the same happen to Ingrid.

"I can't tell you how wonderful it feels to have clean clothing." Ingrid adjusted the wristband of her shirtwaist to make the ruffle lay straight. Having Joanna's help to freshen herself and her garments made her feel so much better, it was a wonder.

"I know what you mean." Joanna gave her a gentle look as she rolled another blanket into a tight bundle, but the expression didn't chase the sadness from her eyes. "I'm glad we had time to wash your things today."

Ingrid studied her new friend. Was that remorse in her voice? "I'm sorry we have to leave so quickly." They'd debated several times the day before, then finally agreed to take one day to pack, then leave out the next morning.

Joanna didn't look up, just reached for another blanket to roll. "I understand." Once she'd decided to come with them, she agreed to everything either of them had suggested. Did she regret her acquiescence now?

"How long have you lived here?" If Ingrid could draw this woman out, she could help bear some of the load, surely.

"Three years. We left St. Louis when Samuel turned one."

"What made you choose such a remote place for your home?" She imagined life would have been easier if they'd built near an established settlement.

"Robert came to the territory when gold was first discovered. He soon realized the chances of growing rich were slim, but he fell in love with the mountains. He didn't want us to be around the kind of men who came with gold lust, so we found this land and chose to build a life here." Her voice softened. "Robert was happy. Like he finally found peace. I thought this would be our home forever."

Ingrid reached for her hand. "I'm so, so sorry, Joanna. I know it's hard."

Joanna's face bore a sad smile. "I thought we'd found God's plan for us. Now . . . I don't know."

The familiar burn crept to Ingrid's eyes. "I understand. I'm struggling with that myself right now. My father and I came to this territory to deliver vaccines to Settler's Fort. We could have paid for them to be transported, but I knew in my heart we were to bring them ourselves."

She paused to inhale a long breath, searching for the memory of that certainty. "Now that the journey has cost Papa and the others their lives, I don't understand God's plan, either." Her voice cracked on the words, and she forced in another deep, painful breath, then released a steadying exhale.

"But I know in my very core"—she pressed a hand to her chest—"that God is leading me to His best plan for me. I have to trust that He is good." She squeezed her eyes shut, tears threatening to overwhelm. *You are good, Lord. Right? What could you possibly have for me that would be better than Papa? He was your blessing in my life.*

She couldn't dwell on that now, though. She had to stay strong for Joanna. Had to offer the only hope that could be the strength she'd need in the coming days. Opening her eyes, she focused on the woman through her blurry gaze.

"Thank you, Ingrid. I know you're right." Joanna's voice sounded stronger than her own had. "I don't want to leave our home. But I don't want to be here without Robert. It was . . . his dream." She sent Ingrid a pleading look, as though begging her to understand.

Ingrid squeezed her hand. "I'm glad you're coming with us. We'll discover the next step in God's plan for our lives together."

# THIRTEEN

*M*icah hammered the final wooden peg into the sled runner, then sat back on his heels to examine his work. He'd not done much craftsmanship in the past, so this had taken him longer than he expected, especially when he realized he'd need to carve nails to fasten the runners onto the little cart. This should hold, though—hopefully.

"Can I ride now?" Samuel jumped up from where he'd been stacking the leftover wooden pieces. He didn't wait for an answer, bracing a leg on the cart's side and clambering in.

Micah pushed to his feet. The boy moved so fast that keeping up with him could wear a man out before noon. "That's going to be Miss Chastain's seat when we leave tomorrow."

He inspected the cart a final time. He was more than happy to give up his job pulling Ingrid, but would the ride be too rough for her in this box? The space was just big enough for her and their supplies, which was all the little donkey would be able to pull anyway.

"Can I ride wif her?" The boy sat on the back panel and bounced.

"Maybe when we're going downhill." Micah grabbed

Samuel's arm as an extra high bounce propelled him backward. "Whoa there. Time to get down. What say we bring in more water for your mama?"

Samuel hopped to the ground and darted toward the barn door. "Race you to the pail."

Micah followed at a slower pace. That boy would keep them all busy, no doubt about it. But keeping Samuel occupied wouldn't be the hardest task on the rest of his journey. How was he possibly going to keep two women and a young boy safe through winter in this mountain wilderness?

*My Sweet Rachel,*

*Do you remember the hills we used to sled down after winter snows? When I finished seeing patients each day, you and I would hike to the hill behind our house, then you'd tuck yourself in the sled while I gave us a running start. Down the first hill and partway up the next, then I'd stand and push, running by the time we reached the top. I'd jump on, and off we went again. Three more sloping hills we took in that same way, you giggling so loud the sound echoed all around us.*

*Your face always turned red in the wind, and your nose would be as bright as a glowing coal. When you laughed, the gaps where you'd lost teeth would remind me just how fast you were growing. After darkness fell, you always begged for one more time over the hills. I could never resist your pleading, but one extra time turned into entreaties for just once more. I'm sorry I never gave in to the second round of begging.*

*If I could, I would ride those hills with you all night long, until you collapsed, too exhausted and sated with happiness to walk home. I would pull you on the sled until we reached our little house, then tuck you into a warm bed and brush the coppery hair from your flushed cheeks. I'd press a kiss to your forehead and thank God from the depths of my heart for one more day with my Ducky.*

*Papa*

❦

"Don't worry about me, Micah. Please."

He ignored Ingrid's protest the next morning as he shifted the pack supporting her broken leg. "Make sure this board doesn't press the splint into your skin." If that happened, it could misalign the break, which would cause horrific pain, not to mention reverse all the healing that had occurred thus far.

"Yes, Doctor."

He stilled at the word, his mind stuttering before he caught the teasing tone in her voice. He wheeled around to face her, to tell her not to use that title.

But then he caught the glimmer in her eyes. The way the corners of her lips pulled upward. Was she . . . baiting him?

The corners of his own mouth twitched. "Feeling better, are you?"

"Well enough you don't need to fuss over me." She gave him a grin that could have been called impish.

And just like that, the pressure that had weighed him down since they came to this place eased from his shoulders. Straightening, he dipped his head in exaggerated acquiescence. "As you please, Miss Chastain."

She nodded toward the donkey. "Just take care of my friend there. Jackson isn't accustomed to the work we'll be asking of him."

Micah stepped to the burro's side and rubbed his thick coat. "Think you can handle this, ol' boy?" The animal turned to nuzzle him, pressing into Micah's hand.

Samuel's high-pitched tones sounded as soon as the cabin door opened, and he and his mother stepped outside. Mrs. Watson held her shoulders squared in that way that had become familiar, yet as the pair neared, he could see the splotches of red that proved the final parting from her home had been difficult.

Ingrid extended her hand as they neared, and Mrs. Watson took it, the two of them sharing a look. Ingrid had such a way of connecting with people, reaching past their defenses to ease hurts and soften pain. He swallowed down a lump threatening to clog his throat. If she wasn't here to help, the trip with this grieving woman and feisty lad would be much more daunting.

"Can I lead Jackson, Mr. Bradley?" Samuel's voice cut through his thoughts as the boy appeared at his side. "He's my friend and he likes me to walk him."

Micah rested his hand on the boy's shoulder. "I suppose so. We can take turns as the day goes along. Just let me lace on my snowshoes." He motioned to the pair of frames in Mrs. Watson's hand. "It's not so deep you have to wear them now, but they'll make things easier."

She nodded, resignation marking her face.

"I don't got no snowshoes." Samuel wrinkled his freckled nose.

The look was so like Rachel that he wanted to pull the boy into his arms. Instead, he dropped his face to focus on his laces. "I think you'll be fine without them. You can ride on my back if you get tired."

"Really?" He'd not heard so much enthusiasm in a tone for five years now.

As they set off, the group found a quicker pace than he expected. Their speed would ease soon enough, but he let the donkey set the stride he liked. After an hour, they'd slowed considerably, and Samuel had handed over the rope and taken his mother's hand. From the looks of things, she was now doing her part to pull the boy along. At this rate, they wouldn't be moving much faster than when he pulled Ingrid in the travois.

By the time the sun crested the sky, he'd hoisted the lad onto his back and carried him piggyback style. The ground they'd been climbing leveled into a plateau, and he raised his hand to halt Mrs. Watson, who'd taken over leading the burro. "This is a good spot to eat a bite."

He lowered Samuel to the ground, then he stepped back to Ingrid. Her face had grown paler the longer they traveled, lines of pain etching around her eyes. She turned to open the pack of food, but he touched her arm to gain her attention. "Your leg is hurting?"

She looked at him, pain dulling her expression. "I drank the willow tea faster than I should have. Don't worry about me, though." Turning back to the pack, she asked, "Shall we have some of this good bread Joanna made?"

He let her shift the focus from herself, stepping back as she and Mrs. Watson prepared a hearty meal for them, even without a fire or a dry place to sit.

The food seemed to refresh Samuel before he was even halfway through with his portion. "I'm gonna build snow animals, Mama."

"Stay where I can see you." Mrs. Watson sat propped on one corner of the cart, her shoulders sagging in a weary arc.

Ingrid turned to him. "Micah, did you know Joanna's been to Settler's Fort before?"

He looked to the woman. "Did you ride or walk?"

"We had horses back then and traveled in early summer, so the going was considerably easier." She raised her brows. "I remember the journey taking at least a week each direction."

"That sounds right. Since we're on foot and moving slow, I expect it to take us close to two weeks to reach the Mullan Road, then a few days or so after that." He couldn't remember exactly the distance to Settler's Fort from where they joined that trail, but it shouldn't be too far. The going would be easier once they reached that more established road.

"What happened to your horses?" Ingrid gave the woman a curious look.

Mrs. Watson's face turned down. "Golden took sick one spring. The following winter, Nugget broke his leg on the ice. Robert hated to end his life, but we couldn't let him suffer."

The memory of that poor mule from Ingrid's wagon flashed through his mind. There was nothing easy or good about taking a life—even when it was the only merciful option.

"Samuel?" Mrs. Watson sat up straight, turning to scan the area around them.

Micah turned to where he'd last seen the boy playing near a boulder. No sign of that copper-colored hair. His muscles tightened as he strode toward the spot as fast as his snowshoes allowed, his gaze sweeping all around it.

"Samuel!" Mrs. Watson's frantic call filled the air.

Tracks littered the area, especially around a mound of packed snow that might have been a likeness of any four-legged creature. He checked behind the boulder, then scanned the area surrounding the tromped-down section. *There.* A trail leading around the side of the mountain. How had the boy disappeared so quickly?

"Samuel." Mrs. Watson tromped close behind him, lifting her legs high to maneuver her own snowshoes.

They rounded the curve in the rock, and a figure appeared in the snow twenty strides ahead. The boy was crouched beside a stone, staring intently at something.

Micah slowed to a walk, and Mrs. Watson did, too, but didn't ease her determination a bit. She easily outpaced him, her frames spraying snow with each step.

"Samuel." Her tone had turned from desperate to frustrated, but her call finally turned the lad's focus to them.

"Shhh. You'll scare him away." His loud whisper reached them easily, even with a gloved finger to his lips.

As Micah strained to see what had captured the lad's attention, a white form darted through the snow, blending almost completely.

Samuel lunged after the hare, chasing it with as much determination as his mother now possessed.

"No, sir." The bark in her voice rang hard, stilling him while the animal dashed out of sight.

"Yes, ma'am?" Samuel's dejection was evident in every line of his posture, reminding Micah too much of another expressive form he still saw in his dreams. Another freckled nose that wrinkled when she was frustrated and a mouth that spread in wide abandon when she celebrated. No matter what she did, Rachel threw every part of herself into every act. A trait that often frustrated Ella, who worked so hard to teach their daughter proper manners.

Secretly, he'd been thankful Ella hadn't successfully tamed Rachel's eager personality, although he'd not wanted his wife to be unhappy, either. He'd worked hard to please them both, but in the end, he'd failed at everything.

Mrs. Watson strode toward him, Samuel's hand clutched tightly in her own. Micah fell into step behind them, the weariness of the day settling over him. In truth, it wasn't just today's efforts that weighed him down.

He had to do a better job of protecting the people in his care.

Before the gray light of dusk hit, they reached a valley with a cluster of trees and a frozen creek. A good place to camp for the night.

Micah's little band looked exhausted. Even Jackson, the donkey, stood with his head hanging low while he waited for someone to unfasten his harness. This would be no small task to ready camp.

"What should be done first? Shall I unfasten Jackson?" Mrs. Watson stepped toward the animal.

"Yes, good." He removed his snowshoes, then began kicking aside the snow, clearing a place for their fire and bedrolls.

"Samuel, gather all the sticks and logs you can find from under the trees, then put them in a stack where Mr. Bradley shows you. You might find some covered with snow." His mother pointed to a lump in the white powder that looked suspiciously like a fallen branch.

Mrs. Watson kept herself and the boy busy over the next half hour, organizing their things, gathering all the loose wood in the area, and even feeding Jackson his corn ration. Which left Micah with far fewer chores than he was accustomed to.

After he built the fire, she took over the spot to prepare the meal. Ingrid occupied Samuel with her pup, leaving Micah with little else to do except cut down more wood in case they ran low through the night. Green wood wasn't ideal, but if the fire was already roaring, he could intersperse a few pieces with the dry wood to help the flame last longer.

The stew Mrs. Watson prepared warmed him all the way to his core as he sat on the outskirts of the little group. The day seemed to have caught up with them all, but none more than Samuel. He leaned against his mother while he ate, sloshing broth from his spoon as he raised unsteady bites to his mouth. With added dishes from the Watsons' supply, they finally had enough tinware to go around.

When Micah finished his meal, he pushed to his feet to rinse his bowl in the snow.

"Please let me clean up." Mrs. Watson stood as well, reaching for his dish and spoon.

He shook his head. "I'll take care of it." Turning to Ingrid, he glanced in her bowl to see if she was finished. She looked as though she'd fall asleep any minute, her head lying back against the cart as she raised a slow bite to her lips.

"Please, Mr. Bradley. Samuel and I need to take a moment in the woods, and I'd like to clean the dishes while I'm out there."

He turned back to her. She'd prepared the meal and did more than her share of the camp chores; she should focus on her lad now. But her expression brooked no opposition, and maybe she had a reason for wanting to clean up after the meal. Most of the dishes were hers, after all. He held out the bowl and spoon. "Thank you."

She nodded, and within less than a minute, she ushered her tired son toward the copse of trees.

Silence eased around them as he turned back to Ingrid. Her weary face was raised to him. "Sit, Micah. Talk with me." She motioned to the ground beside her.

Her words made something inside him spring to life. He may not be needed as much for work around the camp, but the idea of being *wanted* stirred him more than it should.

# FOURTEEN

*M*icah dropped to his knees beside Ingrid. "Are you warm enough?" Several layers of furs covered her, but night had cooled the air considerably.

"Much better after that stew." Her voice sounded as tired as she looked.

"Shall I brew willow tea for you?" Perhaps if the tea dulled the edge of her pain, she could sleep.

"In a minute."

She must have something to tell him, then. He held his tongue, letting his gaze wander to the leaping flames of the fire. She would speak when she was ready.

It didn't take long for her gentle voice to break the quiet. "Do you have a home, Micah? I realized today I don't even know that about you."

He glanced toward the darkness. "These mountains are my home. I set up camp in one spot and stay there until it feels like time to move on."

"The mountains are beautiful, aren't they? I never imagined this wilderness would feel so majestic. Even with everything that's happened, I feel so much more alive here."

He turned back to her, and the soft smile that touched her lips, even through the exhaustion marking her face, made his heart lift. She was so beautiful, yet it was her inner strength that drew him like he'd never expected to be drawn to a woman again.

He forced himself to look away.

"Do you miss having one place to call your own? Or for that matter, do you miss having a place to store things? It must be hard having no more than you can carry with you."

Was she simply making conversation, or was there a serious question she wanted to ask? He wasn't sure he was ready for a deeper discussion, so he took the lighter path and slid her a look. "I've found I can carry more than one would expect."

She gave a soft chuckle. "It turns out you can even haul an injured woman when forced to."

Her tone sounded so demeaning, it made him want to turn and face her to make his point clear. But he forced himself to stare into the flames. "I'm thankful I can help, that I found you on that mountainside—alive. If I'd been a day later . . ." He couldn't finish the thought. It brought back too many memories of times he wasn't able to help.

Her hand touched his arm, and he could feel the heat all the way through his coat. "I'm thankful you found me, too. More thankful than I can say."

He finally met her gaze, but shadows made her thoughts impossible to read. So he nodded, then looked away, back to the flame—a welcome distraction.

She pulled her hand from his arm, leaving a barren place, and only the crackle of the fire sounded.

Usually, he loved the quiet. The peace of silence, where nothing was expected of him. But a part of him couldn't stand to let go of the connection that now stirred between them. So he searched his mind for something to keep her talking. "How do you know the doctor in Settler's Fort?"

"He and my father worked together as chemists after graduating from their university."

"When did your father begin doctoring?"

"After I was born. My mother died giving birth to me, and I think he hated feeling helpless as she slipped away. He went into doctoring a few months later." She was quiet for a moment. "His first love was studying medicines that would provide new cures, but he loved working with patients, too."

"So you never knew your mother?" The thought struck him harder than it should have. Even though she'd lived among Boston's elite, her world hadn't been free of hardship.

"My father raised me, with the help of a nanny, then tutors. But he was always there. The center of my world."

He swallowed down the burn in his throat. Now her world had shifted off-kilter, though she didn't seem afraid or unsure of what to do next. How had she developed such a strength?

"I lost a parent when I was born, too. My father. Except he left by choice, not by death." The words slipped out before he even knew they were coming. But maybe they would take her mind off the loss of her father.

"Oh, Micah."

Those two words, soft in the stillness of the night, settled over him like a thick blanket.

"If only he'd known what he was missing out on." Her voice, so gentle, soothed like a healing salve.

A knot clogged his throat, and he had to clear it to speak what he'd always wanted to say. "It didn't bother me so much that he wasn't around, but that he left my mother to fend for us alone. She worked as a laundress most of my youth, taking in work from wealthy homes, slaving over hot fires and boiling pots, ironing and mending by lamplight late into the night." He paused, swallowing down that knot again.

When he shot a glance at Ingrid, she was looking at him with an odd expression. "Did your mother ever work in the homes on Cambridge Street?"

He looked away. Should he tell her? A part of him wondered if she really was that little girl in his favorite memory. "Yes."

"Did you ever go with her to the houses? Do you remember how old you were?"

"Sometimes. We lived in Boston until I was about nine, I think." He couldn't help turning back to her. "Why do you ask?"

"I wonder if we met. I have a tiny memory of a boy who came with his mother for some kind of business with the housekeeper. I was so lonely that day, waiting for Papa to come home for the midday meal as he'd promised. That boy played stones with me, and Papa even came and played with us for a while. I remember being so happy. It was almost like a real family, with a brother to play with and be my best friend."

He swallowed again, and his voice barely croaked through the knot in his throat. "That was one of my favorite memories, too."

Her gasp sounded over the crackling fire. "That was you."

He nodded. "It must have been. I remember it just the way you described." And he couldn't help sinking back into that day, the pure pleasure of feeling like he was a part of something special. He could even remember the rich ring of her father's laughter.

He couldn't have said how much time passed before Ingrid

spoke again, pulling him from the memories. "Tell me more about your mother. And how did you become a doctor?"

"Mum worked so hard. I apprenticed with a doctor when I was barely old enough, mostly because he was the only man I could find to take me on. I didn't want her to feel like she had to take care of me for even one more day. When I set out my own shingle, I planned to begin providing for her. Finally.

"But she'd passed away the year before. The woman who sent me a wire to tell me said she thought Mum's heart went bad. But I think it was pure exhaustion."

He'd never told anyone that. Not even Ella. Why he was saying it now, he couldn't have said. Maybe the lateness of the hour and his exhaustion clouded his good sense.

Gathering what little strength he had left, he turned back to Ingrid. "I'd better make that tea now so you can sleep."

Ingrid eyed the brooding sky as the sled finally settled over a smoother section. The jostling today didn't ache as much as the past three days on the trail, but the thought that the coming rain or snow this afternoon might end their travel early filled her with more lightness than it should.

Every day it took to get these vaccines to the people of Settler's Fort mattered, but her entire body ached with the pain radiating from her leg and rib—not to mention the pounding in her skull.

She glanced at Micah, who led their procession, with Samuel riding on his back. The boy's tousled hair bounced against Micah's wide shoulders as he slept. Not a bad way to ride.

What did Micah think of the coming storm? Camping in a

downpour wouldn't be pleasant, but maybe they could build a quick shelter and use the furs for protection.

A quarter hour later, Micah stopped them with a raise of his hand. "The sky looks to snow any minute, but there's a cave about half an hour ahead. A good place to get out of the weather."

Her chest surged. That would be so much better than a makeshift shelter.

That half hour seemed to double as snowflakes began to fall. They'd crested a ridge and begun a downhill descent, which kept them moving at a faster pace than before. Micah led them at an angle, his stride sure as he began to weave around boulders, finding a trail that would have been impossible to discover under so many layers of snow.

At last, he stepped sideways, leading them into a crevice in the mountain. The opening became a cave, and Jackson's hooves clicked on the stone floor as they passed through the entrance.

"Look, Mama. An outlaw cave. Do you think there's hidden treasure?" Samuel's voice rang loud in the small enclosure.

"I don't know, son. We'll look after we make camp." Joanna's voice dragged with weariness. She'd handled more than her share of cooking and camp chores—not to mention climbing mountains for three days now.

"The cave doesn't reach much deeper than we can see. Go ahead and settle in. I'm going to gather wood." Micah turned back toward the entrance and stepped out into the falling snow.

Joanna set to work with her usual efficiency, assigning Samuel simple tasks. When she asked him to pour corn for the donkey, the boy plopped down on the stone floor. "I'm tired, Mama. I don't wanna feed Jackson."

Here was a chance she could help. Ingrid leaned forward. "You know what? Your little donkey is so smart, I bet we can teach him a trick or two."

"A trick? Like magic?" He sat up straight, then struggled to his feet.

While she entertained Samuel with the donkey, Micah brought in three loads of wood, forming a large pile near the fire Joanna was kindling to life.

After dropping the last of the sticks, he brushed the snow from his coat and turned to scan their camp. His attention hovered on the boy, who now sat with Handsome in his lap. Something in Micah's eyes looked almost haunted, but then his gaze shifted again, landing on her. Or rather, her leg. His focus roamed the length of her propped limb before coming back to meet her eyes. "Would you like to stand for a minute?"

Hope surged in her chest. Could he be sincere? "Yes, please." She pulled the furs aside, ignoring the blast of icy air that hit her lower half.

He stepped beside the cart as he still studied her. "I need to adjust the splint first so your foot can rest on the ground. We'll need to move you out of there so you can sit flat on the floor."

"What can I do to help?" Joanna appeared at Micah's side, wiping bark from her hands. Twin lines formed between her brows, a sure sign of worry.

"Let's raise her out, just like before. You support her legs." He stepped around the cart so he was on the side of her good leg, then bent low, his face coming near hers. "Wrap your arm around my neck." His breath heated her face, his eyes not quite meeting hers.

She did as he asked, while he fit one hand around her waist

and the other under her good leg. He was merely her doctor, assisting her to a more comfortable position, yet the gentleness with which he touched her made her feel cherished.

Until her broken leg shifted, and a knife plunged through the bone. "Oh." The sound slipped out before she could clamp her jaw shut, and she clung to Micah.

"I've got you," he murmured in her ear, his breath fanning her hair. Then his voice shifted. "Let's ease her down."

The stone floor was hard and cold, but she did her best to ignore the sensations as Micah knelt beside her broken leg. He fiddled with the cloth wrappings for a minute, then wrapped his hand around her ankle as the wood pieces fell away from either side of her limb. The release of pressure sent another pang through the injured area.

She fought the sting pricking her eyes, then pressed them closed as tears threatened harder. After inhaling a deep breath, she paused, then exhaled, focusing on releasing a steady stream of air.

When she forced her eyes open, Micah was studying her, worry creasing his brow. "Does that hurt a great deal?"

She shook her head. "Not a great deal." Not as much as those first few days after the crash.

Slowly, he released her ankle. "Sit exactly like this for just a minute while I cut the wood shorter. Don't move at all, understand?"

She nodded, afraid to unclamp her jaw lest the tears spring up again.

He stepped away, taking the two boards with him, then the sound of a hatchet on wood echoed through the cave.

"What're you doin', Mr. Bradley?" Samuel's little boy voice blended with each blow.

"Cutting these shorter." The hatchet blows ceased, then Micah stepped back to her side and knelt again.

"What're you gonna do with those?" Samuel crouched beside Micah like a shadow.

"I'm going to tie them next to Miss Chastain's leg so the bone heals straight." His tone stayed calm and relaxed, as though he was perfectly accustomed to explaining his every action to a child.

"Samuel, come help me lay out the blankets." Joanna's voice interrupted the boy's next question.

"Aw, Mama. I'm helpin' Mr. Bradley now."

"I can handle this for a bit. Best help your ma." Micah placed the wood and wrapped the first cloth around her leg.

"Yes, ma'am." Samuel released a long-suffering sigh as he pushed to his feet and ambled toward his mother.

Ingrid braced a hand on either side of the wood pieces to help hold them in place while Micah tied. "You're good with him."

One corner of his mouth tipped. "It's hard to have so much energy sometimes." He spoke as though he'd experienced such.

"Was that the way you were as a child?" She kept the question soft, gentle so he didn't feel like she was prying.

His mouth lost any sign of a smile, and he was quiet for several heartbeats. "My daughter was like that."

She froze, searching his face for what emotion might show there. He didn't take his focus from his work as he fastened the second tie. "She sounds like a special girl."

The corners of his mouth flicked. "She was."

"What was her name?" Maybe she shouldn't press for more details, but he might like the chance to talk about her.

"Rachel. She had red hair and freckles just like Samuel. She used to scrunch her nose like he does, too."

Her heart panged as an image formed of a little girl with copper curls and Micah's dark eyes, snuggled in his lap while he read her a book. "She sounds adorable. How old was she?"

"Seven." The light left his eyes, and he pulled the cloth snug, then straightened.

The tight line of his jaw proved she'd pushed too far. She should have focused on happy times, not asked a question that would remind him of her death. "I'm sorry, Micah."

"Ready to try standing?" He rose, then stepped around behind her. "I'll lift you. Don't try to use the broken leg, just let it rest."

She did her best to obey, working her good leg underneath her as he lifted under her arms. The injury ached, and her damaged ribs let themselves be known, too. But she forced herself to move past the pain as she rose to a full standing position.

The cavern swirled around her as she reached a height she'd not experienced in well over a week. She grappled for something to hold on to, especially as Micah's grip on her loosened.

Before she could inhale a breath, she felt herself falling.

# FIFTEEN

$\mathcal{I}$ngrid grasped for Micah's arm.

"I've got you." His hand shifted to her waist, wrapping around her as he came to stand at her side. "Keep your weight on your good leg."

She gripped his shoulder, reaching up much farther than she'd expected. "You're tall." This was the first time she'd had the chance to stand beside him. Her gaze roamed up to his face, landing on his jaw. His beard looked shorter than before, barely covering the strong lines of his face. When had he trimmed it? How could she not have noticed before this moment?

"I like this shorter." She reached to brush his chin.

He shifted, turning to look at her with those dark, penetrating eyes.

Her breath stalled. What had she been thinking to say such a thing? And to touch him?

She dropped her hand to his shoulder, moving her gaze to that same spot. "I'm sorry. I think the altitude must be muddling my mind."

He chuckled—actually chuckled—and if she wasn't mistaken,

it felt as though his hand at her waist gave a gentle squeeze. "How does your leg feel?"

The words shoved the ache to the forefront in her mind. "Hurts a little. Not bad." Not so bad that she would tell him anyway.

"Hmm." His tone gave no hint as to whether he saw through her light words.

"Look, Miss Ingrid. Handsome wants to play with me." Samuel's high voice broke through the shroud that had seemed to separate them from the others.

She turned to the boy, who was playing a game of tug with the pup using one of the furs. "Yes, he is. See if he'll pull on a stick instead of the pelt. We don't want to damage one of Mr. Bradley's animal skins."

"Yes, ma'am." Samuel grabbed a piece of bark and waved it in front of the dog's nose. "Here, boy. Bite this."

Of course Handsome ignored the wood, tugging harder on the white pelt locked between his teeth.

"It's not a problem." Micah's voice rumbled low in her ear.

She braved a glance at his face. That corner of his mouth twitched as he met her look. Gracious, he was attractive. More so than any doctor had a right to be.

Dropping her eyes, she scrambled for something to say. "I think I should sit now." That wasn't quite what she'd been looking for, but maybe some distance between them would be good.

"All right, then. Let's lower you to this pallet Samuel did such a fine job laying out." He eased her down the same way he'd lifted her, his strong arms doing all the work. She hated relying so completely on him, but he seemed more than capable of bearing whatever she couldn't.

When he had her settled, Micah moved to the cart and began sorting through the supplies they'd need. Joanna, of course, kept busy with meal preparations and ten other things. Indeed, the woman could accomplish more in half an hour than most people could in half a day.

"What can I help with, Joanna?"

Her new friend looked up. "Are you close enough you could stir this while it simmers on the coals?"

"Of course." She scooted forward a few inches to make sure of it.

While she performed the simple task, her gaze drifted toward Micah, as it did far too often these days. He'd completely emptied the supplies from the cart and appeared to be reorganizing everything.

"How long do you think we'll stay here?"

He slid a glance to her from the corner of his eye. "Restless already?"

Heat surged to her face. "I guess I meant how long do you think the snow will last."

He accompanied that sideways glance with a raised brow. Did he know that wasn't really what she'd meant? Part of her wanted desperately to hear him say they'd not stay a moment past the end of the snow. They had no time to waste.

"It's hard to say about the snow. Hopefully it will have stopped by the time we wake in the morning. Then I need to do some hunting to keep our food stores high. We'll leave as soon as that's done."

She eased out a breath. He knew what she'd meant. And his plan was good. She'd have to be content with the short wait.

Silence fell over them, except for Samuel's steady chatter as he played with the dog. Handsome had done more to keep the boy occupied than she ever would have imagined. What a blessing for them all. She still kept an eye on them, but Samuel showed a remarkable gentleness with the dog that seemed at odds with his spirited approach in every other part of his life.

"Mr. Bradley, can we sleep in a cave every night?" Samuel lay back on his blankets, propping his hands behind his head.

Micah pulled the tie closed on the pack in his hands, then pushed it aside. "That'd be nice, but I haven't found that many along our path."

"How'd you find this one?"

"I stayed here for a time last winter." He leaned forward, resting his hands on his knees. "There was a lot of snow, and I had to stay in here for days at a time, so I taught myself some things to make the time pass. You wanna know what they were?"

"What?" Samuel sat upright, leaning forward in the exact position Micah held.

Micah opened his mouth, but the bleat that came out made her jump. It sounded like a cross between a calf and a sheep.

"What was that, Mr. Bradley?" Samuel sat up excitedly on his knees.

"That's the exact sound the mountain goats make. Then there's this—" A high-pitched keening filled the cave, turning hoarse as the call ended. "The sound of a bull elk."

"I can make that, too." The boy cupped his hands around his mouth and screamed.

Even Micah winced at the ear-piercing sound. "That's close, but there's a funny way you hold your tongue so it doesn't sound as much like two cats fighting."

For the next quarter-hour, man and boy sat beside the fire, Micah showing the steps to make sounds for a bull elk, a mountain goat, a wild boar, and even a honking goose.

Samuel studied each movement, absorbed each word, and accomplished each animal noise. At least somewhat.

After one attempt at a boar pitched higher than he intended, he flashed his mother a toothy grin. "Did you hear that, Mama? I sound like a baby pig."

"The perfect baby pig." Joanna attempted a smile for her son, but the weary turn of her eyes belied the look. "How about some stew and corn bread for you piggies?"

Tonight Ingrid needed to bear more of the load Joanna tried to take upon herself. She may be trying to forget her sadness, but working herself to exhaustion would be far worse for them all.

Micah stepped out into the steadily falling snow the next morning. This wasn't a good time to hunt, but he couldn't stay closed up in that dark hole for another minute. Ingrid's presence had become too strong in the place.

He never should have wrapped his arms around her when he helped her stand the night before. Getting so close . . . well, he'd not been able to clear her from his mind since. Even when she slept, he was tempted to just sit and watch her.

Maybe a good, icy shave would clear his head. And no, he wasn't doing it because Ingrid liked his beard shorter. He was doing this to purge her from his head, not mire his thoughts deeper around the woman.

After clearing the bristle from his face—and nicking himself several times in the process—he took a few extra minutes to hike along the frozen creek at the base of the mountain. If the willow trees were still there, he could replenish the supply of bark for Ingrid's teas. Her leg appeared to be healing straight, which was a wonder with all the jostling he'd put her through.

She made light of the pain, but anyone could see the lines of strain around her eyes and mouth and the way she eased through any movement, as though even turning her head too quickly would send a bolt of agony through her. And after a mere hour on the trail, her face usually lost its color.

If only he could take the pain from her. Bear the weight of her suffering—both the physical agony and the anguish of losing her father. It didn't seem right that she should be forced to endure both crushing blows at the same time.

Nothing about this life was fair.

By the time he climbed back up to the cave, the falling snow had lessened to a few final flurries. As soon as he had a bite to eat, he'd head back out to see what game might be venturing from their shelters.

As he stepped into the cave, his eyes took a moment to grow accustomed to the dim interior. When he could finally see more than utter darkness, he was able to make out the form of Mrs. Watson kneeling by the fire—preparing food, most likely—and the boy sitting with Ingrid. The pair were occupied with the dog, and Samuel's steady chatter filled any possibility of silence.

Honestly, the only time the boy wasn't making noise, he was sleeping. The constant talking was still hard to get used to. So different from the quiet he'd been surrounded with for the past five years.

But he couldn't be angry with the lad. Not with the way he brought back so many memories of Rachel.

He set the bark in a safe place on his bedroll.

"Micah, you're back." Ingrid glanced up at him with a strained smile, then her eyes grew wider.

"You're just in time to eat." Mrs. Watson held a plate out to him.

"What happened to your face, Mr. Bradley?" Samuel, too, was staring at him.

"Samuel." The boy's mother sent him a furtive glare. "That was unkind. Apologize to Mr. Bradley, then come sit beside me to eat." She darted a glance at him, then focused on the food again.

Micah brushed a hand against his cheek, his fingers finding one of the places where the blood had dried. "No harm done. I simply wasn't careful with my knife."

He forced himself not to look at Ingrid, instead focusing on the beans and corncake on his plate.

"Sit, Micah. It's not healthy to eat while standing."

He raised his gaze to Ingrid. "Where'd you hear that?"

"Dr. Faulkner, a friend of my father's, says it often. He and my father are partners in their medical practice. Or . . . they were." Her voice dipped, fading a little at the end. "He was always telling Papa to take dedicated times for eating. Says it's unhealthy for the digestion to eat while standing."

Micah eased down on his fur pallet. After a request like that, one that spurred such sad memories, how could he not comply? "I'm going out hunting for a bit. We'll pack up as soon as I prepare the meat from whatever I find."

"I'll have the rest of our things ready." Mrs. Watson still hadn't sat to eat while the rest of them partook, but appeared to be cleaning the utensils she'd used while cooking. Should he tell her to rest for a minute or leave her be?

"Joanna, please sit. Eat with us while the food's hot."

Ingrid's gentle tone made the words in his head sound so much better than he ever could.

The woman paused in the midst of wiping out a bowl, looking up at Ingrid with a startled expression, as though the idea hadn't occurred to her. "I suppose I can." She reached for the plate she'd set aside, then adjusted her position on the stone floor and raised a corncake to her mouth.

Had she always been so industrious, or was this determination to stay busy an effort to keep her mind from straying to her own loss?

Soon, he'd thawed from his morning hike—thanks in part to the hearty meal—and reached for his Hawken. The sun now peeked through the clouds, warming the air a little.

"Can I go with you, Mr. Bradley?" Samuel pushed his plate aside. "I'm good at hunting."

"Best stay and help your ma this time." He slipped his shot bag over his shoulder.

"But I've done all my chores this mornin'. Ma said so."

"Samuel." Mrs. Watson's tone held a warning. "Let Mr. Bradley go alone."

The boy looked so crestfallen, tucking into himself as though guarding against a blow. Did he think Micah didn't want him around?

He strode toward the lad and squatted in front of him, reaching a finger to tip his chin up. "The kind of hunting I'll be doing isn't safe for you. But I'll need your help when I get back. For now, do what your Ma says. If you get bored, practice those animal sounds we worked on. Remember to tuck your tongue in the back of your mouth for the bull elk."

The boy sniffed, his countenance lighting as Micah talked about the animal calls. That was the kind of thing he would have loved to learn when he was that age. Much more thrilling than how much soap to put in a pot of wash water, or how to properly starch a collar.

"I will, Mr. Bradley." Samuel wiped his nose on his palm. "Yes, sir."

"Good." He clapped the boy on the shoulder, then stood and headed for the cave's entrance.

Half an hour later, he was regretting his suggestion to Samuel. Just when he had the rifle aimed at a red fox, the unmistakable cry of a five-year-old attempting a bull elk's call echoed across the valley. The sound ricocheted off the icy cliffs around them as the fox darted for cover. The animal probably assumed the mountains were falling down, as ear-splitting as the noise was.

He lowered his gun with a frustrated sigh. Should he hike back until he was close enough to yell for the lad to quiet down? Or move on until he and his quarry were out of earshot from the camp?

Best try for the first, because he could be hiking an hour on these snowshoes before he was far enough away that Samuel's animal sounds didn't scare the game.

Another shrill scream filled the air, this one more high-pitched—like a mountain lion's call, yet clearly still the boy's attempt at an elk's cry. His skill hadn't progressed to the point he was in danger of attracting a female elk.

As he slogged in that direction, following the winding path of the valley along the edge of the tree line, a flash of white movement ahead grabbed his focus.

A snowshoe hare hopped from behind a rock, stopping in the path before jumping again. Micah raised the rifle to his shoulder, aimed, and fired in a quick motion. The crack of the gun reverberated from the mountains around him, echoing for several heartbeats after he pulled the trigger. He strode forward to see to the hare, but a hissing sound caught his attention, making the fine hairs on his neck stand on end.

He scanned the trail. The sound couldn't be a snake during the winter months. Nothing seemed out of place in the snow around him, so he looked higher up the surrounding cliffs.

*There.* Up on the mountain before him, high above the cave, a white cloud billowed, shifting downward. Growing wider, bigger, faster.

An avalanche.

# SIXTEEN

*H*e had to get to the cave. Get them out. Keep them from being buried alive. Micah's heart surged as he charged forward.

The snowshoes hindered his progress. He pulled his knife and sliced through the ties. Plunging through the snow took more effort, but he could move faster. He raced through the cluster of trees separating him from the mountain. How fast was the avalanche moving?

A flowing cloud still sped downward, ever widening. Already covering half the distance to the cave.

He'd never make it. He gulped in a breath of air and cupped his hands around his mouth. "Ingrid!"

*Please let them hear me inside the cave.*

The rush of snow drowned out his voice. "Samuel!" What was the other woman's given name? His thoughts muddled as he worked to pull them free. "Joanna!"

The billowing cloud had almost reached the opening. They'd never be able to get out, especially with Ingrid crippled.

*God, help them.*

He could only watch as the torrent of white curled over the

151

dark circle that was the entrance to the cave, engulfing everything in its path. Plunging onward, ravenous to consume more.

His chest ached, his throat tightening. Did the snow fill the cave completely? He couldn't lose them all. Not again. Why did God keep destroying everyone he cared about?

The wave of snow descended to the base of the mountain, surging forward with the very real possibility the swell may cover him where he stood. Maybe the Almighty planned to take him out with the others.

*Come and get me.* The pain could finally be over.

But the white clouds slowed, easing to a stop not twenty strides before him.

His heart thudded in his chest. He was alive. But why? *Why leave me to grieve again?*

As he looked back up the mountain to where the cave opening had yawned just minutes before, a wave of helplessness sank through him. How would he ever break through to them?

He had to try.

Turning back, he retraced his steps to his snowshoes. With so many layers of icy powder covering the trail, he'd need these to walk atop the fluff. It took some doing to retie the cut laces, which left time for his mind to churn.

Was the snow secure enough to walk on? Or would it shift out from underneath him, starting another avalanche, like the aftershock from an earthquake? He'd gladly let the massive white blanket smother him into oblivion, but Ingrid and the others were counting on him. He had to get them out.

Finally he pulled the knots tight, securing the frames to his feet. He also needed something to shovel snow when he found the cave. A sapling was the best thing he could find, and he used his knife to cut through the green wood. Perhaps he should leave his rifle by the trees so he didn't have to worry about keeping it dry. Still, it went against his instincts to be without a gun in these mountains. He'd keep the weapon with him.

Finally, he turned toward the wall of white.

The mountain towered above him, and he mentally marked the spot where the cave should be. Hopefully.

Climbing upward seemed to take an hour. Two hours, as he inched his way over the sliding snow. Twice, the loose powder slid from under his feet, plunging him face-first into the icy mix.

At last he reached the place where he'd judged the cave to be. There was no indentation in the bed of churned snow. No sign that he'd gauged correctly. He might dig for hours, only to hit solid rock.

"Ingrid!" He pounded the snow with his stick.

Nothing answered, save a faint echo. He'd best not make another loud noise. Had it been his rifle shot that loosened the avalanche?

*Please. No.*

He dug in with the stick, pushing aside the loose powder. His actions had buried Ingrid and the others alive.

He would *not* let another woman he loved—

No, he couldn't say that. However he felt about Ingrid, he wouldn't let her die. Nor the other woman and boy. These people would *not* suffer the consequences of his actions.

For what felt like hours he dug, tunneling through the white mass. He'd had to remove his snowshoes early in the process, and he'd now pushed aside enough snow to sink to his thigh when he stepped into the hole. Digging took longer now, for he had to loosen the packed ice with his stick, then scoop out the powder.

He would dig as long as it took to find them. Or until the mountain took him, too. If only he knew for sure he was in the right place.

When he'd gone deep enough that he stood in snow to his waist, his stick hit something hard. He stabbed at the ground. *Let it not be rock.*

As he chipped away at the packed snow, a dark surface appeared beneath the white. He'd reached the stone of the cliff.

He sank back against the snow wall of his hole, disappointment stealing the strength from his limbs. The wrong spot.

Inhaling a long breath, he scanned the snow blanketing the cliffside around him. Had he dug too high or too low? Maybe the right height, but too far to the left or right?

He turned to stare down the mountain at the trees below, summoning the memory of exactly how the view had appeared from the cave entrance. He needed to be to the left a little.

Grabbing his stick, he hoisted himself out of the hole, then pushed to his feet. Without his snowshoes on, he sank to his buckskins in the loose snow, the icy wet seeping through to steal his breath. He slogged forward, stopping a couple of times to check the outlook on the trees below.

Finally, he found the spot that looked right. Although . . . maybe he should be a few steps higher.

At last, he started digging again. Shoveling the snow aside, scooping it out of the hole that gradually sank deeper and deeper. The snow had been waist-high in the other area, so that was a good estimate for how far he'd have to dig here.

Unless . . . If the snow had fallen into the cave, he might

be digging for hours. Maybe the others would be clawing out from the inside.

Sweat dripped down his back as he worked. The sun glared off the white crystals. His mouth grew dry, but he stuffed in a handful of snow when it became unbearable.

He dug through to waist-height but didn't reach stone. Maybe that was a good sign, or perhaps the avalanche had simply deposited more snow here.

Pausing to wipe the perspiration from his brow, he poked at the bottom of his hole. "Ingrid? Joanna? Samuel?" Just the thought of them freezing down there refueled his energy, and he stabbed at the snow again, shoveling loose powder out of the way.

He forced the stick harder with each jab. The sapling might break any moment, but he had to make faster progress. How long would the air inside last with the fire blazing and all three of them breathing? Not to mention the donkey and dog. He'd not even thought of the animals in this ordeal.

With a jerk, one of his thrusts broke through. He tumbled forward, landing on his elbows in the snow.

"Micah!" The voice inside barely drifted through the tiny opening. But the sound of it flooded him with joy. And fear.

And a fierce jolt of energy.

He jerked the pole out. "Ingrid. Are you hurt?" What a silly question when she had a broken leg. "The others. Are you all safe?"

"We're safe." Joanna's voice sounded louder than Ingrid's had. She must be standing near the opening. A bit of skin showed through the hole, then an eye.

"I'll have you out soon." He shifted to dig again.

"We'll help from this side."

"No." He practically yelled the word, images of the snow where he stood caving in on them. Burying them again. "Pack our things. As soon as I make a hole large enough to get you out, we're leaving this place."

Ingrid hated this feeling of helplessness.

She listened to the sounds of Micah hacking at the snow. Of Joanna bundling their things back into the pack. Her quiet murmurs to Samuel.

Through it all, there was no way she could help, sitting here with her back pressed against the cave wall, her bulky leg extended in front of her. The wood planks bracing her broken bone were so heavy, the only way she could move was by scooting backward, dragging the limb behind her.

A scuffle sounded from the snow wall, and she turned to see Micah's face, the whole of him. With the light behind him, his features were cast in shadows, but still she could sense his fear.

"Ingrid." His voice strained with emotion.

She found a smile for him. "We're well, Micah. And so thankful you found us."

"I'll have you out soon." Heavy breaths slowed his words.

He was such a good man, Dr. Micah Bradley. Yet he didn't seem to know his own strengths. This man who would spend himself to keep those in his charge safe. Do whatever necessary to make them comfortable.

A ball of black fluff crept toward her, breaking through her thoughts. "Handsome." She reached for the little dog and snuggled him to her chest. "You're the perfect man, too, aren't you, fella?"

Now that Micah had widened the first tiny hole, the going went faster than before, and soon, he cleared an opening wide enough for him to step inside.

He was by her side in a moment, his eyes searching hers. "Are you hurt?" He looked as though he wanted to take her in his arms, to prove to himself that she was safe from the avalanche.

In truth, she wanted him to do just that, but she couldn't ask him to. Still, the fact that they were alive, that he'd found them . . . they had to celebrate this miracle.

She reached for his hand and squeezed it. "We're well. All of us. I can't believe you were able to dig us out. God answered our prayers."

She couldn't see the nuances of his expression with the light shining behind him, but she could feel the way he clung to her hand. The desperation in his grip showed just how much he'd feared losing them.

"We're well, Micah. God used you to save us."

He nodded. "I'm glad." It might be her imagination, but it sounded as if his voice hitched on the words.

He exhaled an audible breath, then released her hand and stood. "Let's get everything out of here."

He and Joanna worked together to push the sled and supplies through, with Samuel bouncing around them, jabbering about how brave he'd been when the snow closed them in.

A moment later, Micah stepped back into the cave and stopped in front of her, his hands propped at his waist. "Your carriage is ready, m'lady."

Joanna stepped in behind him, Samuel at her heels.

The thought of the forthcoming pain made all the muscles up through her shoulders tense. She also hated to add so much work for the others.

She extended the pup toward the boy. "Can you carry Handsome until I'm settled?"

"Yes, ma'am." He ran forward, then slowed as he took the dog in his arms. No matter how much energy bounced through the lad, he somehow always managed to move carefully when he held Handsome. It was a wonder, really.

Micah stepped around to her side and crouched. "We'll do this the same way as before. I'll lift you, and Joanna—I mean, Mrs. Watson—can stabilize the injured leg."

Ingrid looked to her friend, who let out a sigh. "I suppose you should call me Joanna. We've no need for such formal address when we're climbing mountains and surviving avalanches together." She looked at Micah with a sad smile.

Something about the intimacy in the look planted a new thought in Ingrid's mind.

Surely it was too soon after her husband's death for Joanna to have feelings for another man. Yet she and Micah were experiencing so many of the same challenges on this journey. Such shared moments were bound to build a connection between them. When Joanna's grieving passed, it would be only natural for her to realize the exceptional man Micah was. The two could be an ideal match. Both of them skilled, hardworking, and devoted. What a blessing for this woman who was becoming a dear friend.

The thought seared all the way to her chest, making it impossible to draw breath. Her gaze found Micah's face as he reached forward to lift her. He tucked her so close, his strength wrapping around her, making her eyes sting. She ducked her face, willing the tears away.

Joanna carried her feet, working in perfect tandem with Micah. A team. Tears stung harder, the sense of loss almost devastating. She should never have let herself develop affection for Micah. No matter how easy it was to admire him.

As they settled her in the cart, Joanna wrapping the furs around her, she kept her face down, eyes averted. She could feel the weight of Joanna's stare, but maybe her friend would think the pain caused the tears in her eyes.

*Be thou my strength, Lord.* God was truly all she had left. And Handsome. She took the dog from Samuel's arms, forcing a smile of thanks for the boy. Then she buried her face in her pup's soft fur and closed out everything else.

# SEVENTEEN

*T*hat evening, Micah stopped them early. He still needed to hunt, as they were almost out of meat.

Mrs. Watson did a remarkable job of stretching their limited supplies. Probably she'd had a great deal of experience doing so. Now that the danger was over, using her given name seemed wrong. And he suspected she preferred hearing her husband's surname. Something to keep his memory alive.

In the faint light of dusk, he found a herd of deer and brought down a young buck. A *coup*, as the Indians would call it.

"What a blessing." Ingrid bestowed a weary smile on him as he came to sit by the fire after preparing the meat. "Will that be enough to feed us until we reach Settler's Fort?"

"Possibly. I hope at least until we reach the Mullan Road. I may need to hunt again at that point." He glanced around the campsite, empty except for the two of them. "Where are the others?"

"Joanna took Samuel for a short walk." Something in her tone shifted, as though the topic perturbed her.

"Seems like we did enough walking to get here."

Her eyes tinged with something that looked like sorrow. "I'm sorry I haven't been able to share in the load. I've only made things harder for you."

Was she berating herself? His heart quickened. "You don't make things harder. In fact, this journey would be worse without you." And he hoped she didn't ask why. He wasn't ready to divulge the way he felt about her. Best change the conversation. "Would you like to stand again, or would you prefer I rub your feet? We need to keep your blood flowing correctly."

A corner of her bottom lip slipped between her teeth. "I'd like to stand, if it's not too much trouble."

A thrill slipped through him, a feeling he shouldn't allow. He was her doctor, assisting her with proper blood flow. He shouldn't crave the nearness that accompanied this action.

She pushed her blankets aside and straightened her legs, then he bent behind her and lifted. "Remember, put all your weight on your good leg. Just let the other rest."

As soon as she was upright, he shifted around to her front so she could hold on to his shoulder. She did so, bringing her face close enough so he could feel her breath on his neck. She was the perfect height for him. The perfect height to brush a kiss against her forehead.

He fought the urge to move closer. Fought the desire coursing through him. He couldn't be attracted to her. He still loved Ella. Still craved the family they'd had.

The reminder did exactly what he hoped it would—cleared his mind and senses like a bucket of water sluicing away the dirt.

He must have pulled back—probably his unconscious attempt to put distance between them—but the movement made

Ingrid teeter. She gripped harder on his shoulder, throwing her weight into the hold.

"I have you." He moved in again, placing a stabilizing hand on each side of her waist.

"I'm sorry. I'm so unsteady."

He made the mistake of looking down at her, catching the glow of moonlight pooling in her eyes. He couldn't see much of her face in the darkness, but those eyes were luminous. Drawing him in. Resurrecting every bit of desire he'd just tamped down.

His focus dropped to her lips, another part of her lit by the moon's glow. Full and calling to him. Did he dare? He flicked his gaze back to her eyes. He shouldn't, but the look there drew him like he'd never been summoned before.

As he lowered his mouth, she reached up to meet him.

Sweet perfection. Her lips were soft, full, unschooled—and achingly sweet. Just as the woman herself.

She made a noise. A gasp.

He paused, pulling back to look in her eyes. Did she want him to stop? Above all else, he wouldn't push her. He shouldn't have gone as far as he had.

But she rose up again, pulling him down for another kiss. This time her lips met his as though she knew exactly what she wanted.

And she wanted him.

The thought filled him with a heady joy, but caution restrained the parts of him that he'd thought died long ago. His hands longed to cradle her face, to cherish her. But he couldn't release her waist or she might fall.

Summoning all his strength, he caressed her lips with a final kiss, then pulled away, resting his forehead on hers. Her eyes had widened even more, touched with a wonder that magnified her innocence. He knew that wonder. The same feeling beat in his chest. He might be a bit more jaded, yet how could he not thrill with the thought that this woman saw something in him? Something worthy.

"Micah." Her hand brushed his jaw, cupping his cheek. He leaned into the touch. "You are the best man I've ever known." Her words sent a burn through him, clogging his throat with more emotion than he'd thought he could feel.

He forced the mass down. "I wish I was." His words came out raspy, as though dragged through a dry, rocky creek bed.

A familiar little-boy voice sounded in the distance.

Ingrid jerked her hand from his face, straightening as she gripped his shoulder again.

He didn't want to put her in a compromising situation, but he couldn't regret the connection between them. "I'd best sit you down again."

She nodded, averting her eyes. The darkness shadowed her features, but it looked as though her cheeks had turned cherry red. Maybe that was the cold.

"Mr. Bradley, we found some grass for Jackson. He loves it, too. We took him there and he started eating and digging at the snow."

"Is that right?" He eased Ingrid down to a sitting position. "I'm sure he liked that." As he tucked the furs and blankets over her legs, she sent him a shy smile.

The last thing he wanted was for her to be reticent around him. He didn't regret that kiss. Didn't regret letting her know she'd become more special to him than he'd ever expected. He had to let her know his feelings about what just happened between them.

"Lie down now, Samuel." Joanna's gentle murmurings sounded across the fire.

He spared a glance to make sure they weren't watching, then pressed a kiss to Ingrid's hair. "Do you have everything you need?"

She met his gaze, finally. "Everything." That wonder brushed her eyes again, and he had to fight the urge to press a final kiss to her lips.

He settled for stroking his thumb across the back of her hand. "Sweet dreams."

But as he laid down on his own pallet, his mind replayed their moonlight rendezvous. For the first time, doubt crept into his thoughts.

Had he started something he wouldn't be able to finish?

It was a wonder Ingrid slept at all. Yet she did, slipping into a dream where they arrived safely at Settler's Fort. Upon reaching Dr. Stanley's office, she found her father, sitting in an armchair. He rose and greeted her with one of those hugs he'd given when she was a girl, running to meet him as he arrived home at the end of the day. The kind of hug that wrapped around her, holding her close, as though he'd been missing her every moment they were apart.

When the hug ended, she stepped back and reached behind her for Micah's hand. "Papa, I want you to meet someone special."

Micah took her hand, but that's where the dream had ended. She'd not seen either face while she introduced the man who was winning her heart to the father who'd held it her whole life.

She'd not seen the exchange of respect she desperately hoped for. Would Papa like Micah? Would he approve?

She'd like to think so. Her father had held her so close, even after she more than reached the marrying age. Looking back, it seemed like he'd begun to allow her to help more in his laboratory as she'd reached the age to enter society. Had he been keeping her from the possibility of marrying and moving away? She'd been so thankful for the chance to spend more time with him. Even now, she wouldn't exchange those days with him for society functions or any other reason.

*Especially* now.

Micah acted normally as they ate and packed camp for another day on the trail. Only when he bent to lift her into the sled did he do anything that made her think he even remembered their kiss from the night before.

As he scooped her up, he cradled her close. Closer than in times past—she was almost positive. He set her gently in the sleigh, then covered her with the furs, like always. But this time when he finished, his gaze found hers and his face softened. He leaned over her and pressed his lips to her forehead, sending warmth all the way through her.

Then he straightened. "Let's head out. Samuel, will you lead Jackson first?"

"Yes, sir, Mr. Bradley." The boy jumped to his feet and charged toward the donkey.

A heaviness poked through Ingrid's awareness, and she looked over at Joanna. Her friend was looking at her with a kind of knowing half-smile curving her mouth. Heat flamed up Ingrid's cheeks. How much had she seen? What did she suspect? She'd need to find a way to explain when they were alone.

But what would she explain? That her heart was slowly melting for this man? She wasn't sure she could claim nothing was between them without giving away the lie.

Still, she needed to talk with Joanna. To make sure she understood nothing untoward had happened between her and Micah . . . if she didn't count that kiss.

"Come on, Jackson." Samuel's voice broke through her thoughts. The animal eyed the boy with a wide eye and a swiveling ear, but started forward without a fuss when he pulled.

They settled into their usual pace, with Samuel talking steadily. Their path followed a valley between two mountain ranges, winding along a frozen creek.

The day already promised to be colder than the few sunny hours they'd enjoyed the afternoon before. Ingrid pulled the fur tighter around her shoulders and snuggled in. If she were up and carrying her own weight like the others, she wouldn't suffer nearly as much from the cold.

If only.

A couple hours after they'd begun, Joanna gasped and pointed at something in the distance. "What is that?"

Ingrid strained, but Jackson's big ears blocked her view of the spot.

"I can't see. Put me down, I can't see." Samuel bounced from his position on Micah's back, kicking him as he wiggled to get down.

Micah obliged, and the boy's feet were already running when he touched the ground.

"What is it?" She leaned sideways to get a better view.

"Something that sparkles. I can't really tell with the trees in the way."

"A waterfall. But I'm betting it's frozen." Micah took the donkey's rope from Joanna, probably so she would be free to chase after her son if she felt the need to.

"Don't go near the water, Samuel," she called ahead, and her words actually slowed the boy's pace to a walk.

As they neared, Ingrid had to blink a few times against the brilliant sparkle of the ice crystals. The water seemed to originate from a rock partway up the mountainside, except it had frozen solid. The flow appeared to stair-step down in three little waterfalls, each about the height of Samuel. All three falls were frozen in partially clear, shimmery ice crystals.

Micah halted the donkey at the water's edge where she could look her fill. "It's beautiful. More than beautiful." To think that not only did God have the ability, but also the creativity to conjure this masterpiece. More lovely than anything man could make. "Our God is a wonder, isn't He?"

"He is." Joanna's voice sounded as awestruck as she felt.

"I wanna touch it, Mama." Samuel wiggled under his mother's hold.

Joanna took a firmer grip on him. "We'll just walk to the edge and reach out. We're not going to step on the ice. Understood?"

Ingrid bit back her smile at the sudden change in her friend's tone. Nothing could be hallowed for long with a little boy around.

After they'd spent a few minutes marveling over the natural ice sculpture, Ingrid noticed Micah studying the mountain from which the waterfall started. His brows knit in a troubled look.

"What's wrong?"

He was standing near enough that she didn't have to raise her voice, but he didn't turn to look at her.

"I'd hoped we could hike up the cliff face to go around the water, but we won't be able to do that with the sled."

She followed his gaze to the icy rock. The mountainside wasn't straight up, but the stone slanted enough that the cart stood a good chance of falling over. She wasn't game for another wagon crash just yet.

He looked down at the frozen creek. "Is there any chance we could go over the ice?" The stream could be crossed in three or four long strides, and it didn't look very deep, even if the ice broke through. "Do you think it's strong enough to hold?"

Micah studied the stretch she was looking at. "I can't tell without walking on it to test it. That may be our best option."

He stepped forward, shuffling down the steep bank. The edges of the icy stream were covered in snow, and he stepped gingerly onto the first section.

An image formed in her mind of his foot crashing through the crust, sinking into the icy water. The exposure would surely give him frostbite. Or maybe a broken leg. Which would be worse?

"Micah, wait." She sat up straight, itching to reach out and pull him back. "Don't try it. Let's find another way to test the ice."

He sent her a quick glance. A smile? Surely not. "It's holding. I'll be careful." He eased another step forward, sending her heart into her throat.

"Please take care." What would they do if something happened to him? Micah was their protector, their guide, their strength. They'd have no idea how to go on without his help.

Her conscience panged. God was her protector, her guide, and her strength. He'd sent Micah to help, but He could as easily accomplish the task another way.

Still, the thought of Micah being hurt made her chest ache as deeply as her broken leg. *Lord, keep him safe. Please.*

# EIGHTEEN

*S*tep by achingly slow step, Ingrid watched Micah travel across the creek. The ice held.

The moment he reached the other side, she drew in a long breath, then released it, forcing out her pent-up nerves with the spent air.

His white teeth gleamed in the kind of smile that came from deep down. A smile she'd not yet seen on him. "The ice is good."

He stepped back across, taking a different path this time, and not nearly so carefully. She didn't breathe until he reached land again.

After trotting up the bank, he moved to the spot where the harness attached to the cart. "Here's what we'll do. Mrs. Watson, you and Samuel take the donkey up the hill and around the spring. He's surefooted, so he won't give you trouble. I'll pull the sled over the ice. I'd rather not chance the weight of the burro."

Her stomach knotted. She'd rather not chance Micah again, either. But she couldn't deny his plan made sense.

After tucking up Jackson's harness so it wouldn't drag,

Joanna took her son's hand on one side and the donkey's lead in the other. "Let's go climb a mountain, boys." Her bravado swept away a layer of worry from Ingrid's shoulders. Joanna was a brave woman, and no matter how much struggle she faced, she didn't shy away from making the best of it. Samuel was blessed to have such an example.

"Ready for our turn?" Micah's voice pulled her back to the present. He met her look with raised brows, a hint of adventure gleaming in his eyes.

"I suppose if we have to." She gripped the sides of the cart as he pulled her toward the frozen creek. When she tilted over the ledge and down the slope of the bank, she had to clamp her teeth to keep from crying out.

The sled tried to rush down the little hill, but Micah held it back, digging in deep with each step. Finally, they reached the edge of the frozen creek, and he gripped the cart's shafts to haul it forward.

She hated sitting here, at the complete mercy of those willing to help, looking up at the world around her and watching others manage her responsibilities. She'd be happy never to be in this position again.

Micah stepped onto the ice, leaning into his efforts. The cart crept forward, and he had to strain to move the runners on the snow-covered edges of the frozen stream. When his boots reached the part not covered in snow, his foot slipped, and he gripped the shafts harder to stay upright.

"Please be careful." She couldn't help the words. Her own hands gripped the sides of the cart until her fingers ached, as though that would help Micah.

His only reply was a grunt as he eased her forward, but then his foot slipped again. He paused, appearing to study the ice.

Releasing the shafts, he stepped forward to the snow lining the far edge of the stream, then turned and grabbed the poles again. With a tug, he hauled the sled forward.

He'd almost pulled it to the snowy patch when the sound of a shot rang out and the back of the sled dipped.

She screamed, grabbing for the front. Water splashed, and the rear runners dipped lower.

Micah strained to pull the shafts, leaning his entire body backward as he fought against the weight sinking through the broken ice.

Should she climb out? That would put her in even worse trouble, crawling on the ice and snow. Was the water deep enough to come over the side of the cart? Surely not. Micah would get her out of this fix.

*No.* God would get her out of this fix.

*Sorry, Father. Keep me safe. Please.* Her spirit eased with the prayer.

Leaning all his weight back, Micah dragged the sled forward. The back end came up with each inch of progress.

Then another crack sounded, and the back end dipped with a splash.

Micah growled, bending his knees as he worked to repeat the progress.

Twice more, Micah inched the sled forward, raising the runners up almost out of the water. Then the ice would give way, crashing into the flowing stream, dipping the rear of the sled into the water with it.

At last, the front of the runners reached solid ground. Micah's face was scarlet as he hauled her the last few steps off the ice. He still had to get the sled up the sloped embankment, but maybe the donkey could help with that.

He released the poles, turning to brace his hands on the cart as though to hold himself up. His head dropped forward, ragged breaths filling the air. "Are you hurt?" He raised his head to look at her, exhausted concern filling his dark eyes. Sweat dampened the edges of his black hair.

"I'm not hurt. Are you?" In truth, she was breathing almost as hard as he was, although she had little cause for it.

"No." His shoulders heaved with his deep inhales.

"Mr. Bradley, Miss Chastain. Did you fall in an' get all wet?" Samuel came running, heels kicking high to clear the snow.

"Not a bit." She worked out a smile for the boy. "God gave Micah extra strength to pull the sled out."

Samuel turned wide eyes on the man. "Did you feel God give you ex'ra strength?"

Micah straightened. "How about you and your mama bring Jackson here so we can use his extra strength to pull the sled up the hill?"

"Yessir." The boy spun and sprinted back the way he came.

He'd been an overconfident fool.

Micah forced himself to turn back toward Ingrid and face her. The moment he'd let his guard down, he put her in danger. "I'm sorry. I shouldn't have let that happen."

Her brows lifted, widening her eyes. "Did you break the ice on purpose?"

A flare of anger burned through him. "Of course not. I should have checked the ice better."

She reached out her hand and rested it on his arm. "You did everything right, Micah. Sometimes accidents happen, but

I'm not hurt. I'm sorry you had to work so hard to pull me out, but we're not injured. God protected us."

He fought harder to force the anger down, but it leaked out. "The ice cracked, Ingrid. If that was God's protection, I'd hate to see how bad things get when He turns His back."

She straightened, her look turning curious, though maybe a bit guarded. "We're safe, Micah. God brought us through without injury."

He turned away from her questioning eyes. "I learned long ago trusting God to help never makes things better. It only makes me weaker. When I let my guard down, people I care about get hurt."

A sadness crept into her eyes, making his chest squeeze. He'd not meant to cause pain.

"I'm sorry you feel that way, Micah. I actually feel the opposite. Relying on God fills me with an inner strength much greater than I could possess on my own."

"Here's Jackson, Mr. Bradley." Samuel's voice broke through their conversation, and not a minute too soon.

He turned to reach for the donkey's rope, but as he fastened the harness to the shafts, her words radiated in his mind. *Relying on God fills me with an inner strength much greater than I could possess on my own.*

She did possess inner strength; he'd recognized it from the first time they spoke after her accident. Even as she mourned her father and the others, she'd not grown hysterical. She'd endured her pain without complaint. And she willingly endured great sacrifice for the hope of saving lives from smallpox. He'd assumed she was simply a remarkable person—in truth, she *was* remarkable. But could part of her ability be God's strength, too?

Even now, she didn't seem ruffled. Not upset or struggling to rein in her emotions. He wished he could say the same for himself. Which of them seemed weakest just now? But he pushed that thought aside.

If she wanted to think God was protecting her, fine. Still, he wouldn't be letting his guard down again.

⌖

Ingrid couldn't sweep that determined look on Micah's face from her mind, even though the next two days were mostly without mishap. His past struggles had been awful, no doubt. And they clearly still haunted him. Somehow she had to help him see that turning control over to God would give him peace. In truth, it was the only way she was dealing with Papa's death and the utter desolation of her plans. Their plans.

They stopped for the midday meal near the crest of a mountain, but the frigid wind made the break less pleasurable than it might have been otherwise. Still, the view was remarkable, with the snowy descent all around them and blanketed peaks stretching in every direction. This land was so rugged, so much bigger than her sheltered world in Boston. Even though she was bound in this tiny sled, one glimpse over the vast landscape made her feel free, brave enough to step outside the confines of what she'd always known.

Could she leave Boston for good? Make a life in Settler's Fort or whatever mountain town the Lord called her to? What would she do there? *Guide me, Father.*

The wind swept icy fingers across her unprotected skin, and she pulled the fur tighter around her shoulders. The gust appeared to almost bowl over Samuel. She motioned him toward her. "Come sit on this side of the cart where you'll be shielded."

The boy tucked tighter into his coat and dragged himself to where she pointed. "I'm cold."

"I know, honey. Let me lay this fur down so you don't get wet." This icy wind was enough to exhaust them all, especially a five-year-old boy. "Maybe if you promise to be very still, you can sit on my lap when we start again." She slid a glance at Micah as she spoke, who'd been standing with his hands propped at his waist, eyeing the low-hanging clouds.

He turned to her, a frown drawing his brows low. "I'm not sure Jackson can pull the extra weight."

She glanced at the donkey, who was eating the corn Joanna had just poured out for him. The woman still stood with the animal, stroking the coarse hair of his mane.

"What about if I carry the food pack?" Joanna's quiet suggestion seemed to catch Micah off guard. She didn't often question something Micah said, but she must be concerned about her son.

He turned to eye the cart, and it looked like his gaze hovered on Samuel. "We can try it down the mountain. If the pull seems too hard when we reach level ground, I'll carry the boy."

Of course he would. Micah would take the brunt of the work every time to ease the load for those around him. It was one of the things she loved about him, but might it also be part of his drive to make the situation better himself, without relying on God? She'd not thought of his actions in that light before, but his declaration by that frozen stream made her see him differently now. Not that her opinion of him changed, but it was like she could see glimpses under the mask of self-reliance he wore.

When they prepared to start out again, Micah took the two

larger packs from the wagon and strapped them on his back, making room for Samuel beside her.

"You can put one of those back here, Micah. There's enough space." Honestly, the man didn't have to put himself through so much.

He shook his head. "This is how I travel when I'm on my own. It's not a problem."

He was telling the truth, most likely, but that didn't stop her from wishing he would carry a lighter load.

As they set off down the mountain, dodging rocks and cutting left then right in switchbacks, Samuel squirmed. He wiggled. He writhed in the tiny compartment she'd made for him. Twice, he accidentally kicked her injured leg, sending lightning bolts of pain down to her foot and up through her back. Not even gritting her teeth could keep in her cry.

But the way Samuel snuggled in, his sweet little boy hand tucked inside hers, made all the discomfort worth it.

And, of course, he talked.

She only had to answer questions every so often, because the boy occupied the silence with practiced ease. It was as if part of him had to be moving at all times. Since his feet were confined in the cart, his mouth refused to be contained.

Even so, she wouldn't have traded those moments tucked in with the fidgeting boy for a hundred calm ones. What was it about children that soothed a person's soul, that little voice reminding you of the simple pleasures in life?

When they reached the bottom of the mountain, Samuel grew quiet for the first time. She breathed in the silence, closing her eyes to enjoy the feel of the wind at this lower altitude. None of the former iciness raised gooseflesh on her skin, only the caress of this new breeze.

A gust flapped at the hood of her coat. Perhaps this wasn't a breeze, maybe more of a gale. But with its warmth soothing the parts of her that hadn't thawed in weeks, she'd take the heavier wind without complaint.

"Looks like a chinook is coming in."

She opened her eyes at the sound of Micah's voice. They'd come to a stop, and he stood in that same posture as before—hands propped at his waist, eyes lifted to the heavy sky.

"What's a chinook?" Joanna followed his focus.

"It's a warm wind that sweeps through. Raises the temperature so it feels like summer's coming."

"Oh, we had that two years ago. It came right after a snowstorm and melted everything within an hour."

He nodded. "I've seen it melt a foot of snow in the space of a morning."

"How long will the chinook last?" Ingrid shifted to protect Samuel from a particularly strong gust. A glance at the boy explained why he'd not joined in the conversation with eager questions. His face softened in sleep, his long red lashes resting against wind-chapped cheeks. She couldn't help but smile at the sweet scene.

When she looked up, Micah was also watching the boy. She met his gaze, drank in his soft smile. Who couldn't love this boy who talked for hours on end and approached life with such fervor? Micah had said his daughter had been much the same. No wonder he still missed her so much. *Bring healing to his heart, Lord.*

Micah straightened and turned back to the direction he'd been looking. Almost as though he resisted the tug of her prayer. "You never know how long the chinook will last. Sometimes hours. Sometimes days."

"It feels wonderful." Joanna stood in the wind, skirts billowing, hair flying, as though the gusts swept away all her inhibitions. All her sorrows. The heavy weight of her losses. With the warm gale buffeting her, she seemed to be reveling in the freedom.

Within minutes, Micah motioned them forward. As they slipped into their familiar procession, with his broad shoulders leading the way, she couldn't help but notice the way he stiffened against the wind. If only he could find the same freedom in casting off his fears and worries that Joanna had discovered.

# NINETEEN

The chinook blew all through the night, keeping temperatures balmy enough that they didn't need a campfire. Which was good, because the gusts would have blown out the flame the second it formed.

"Can I take Handsome for a walk, Miss Chastain?" The nicer weather seemed to infuse an extra dose of energy in Samuel the next morning.

"He would like that, if you stay close. And if your mama says you may." She tacked on that last sentence with a glance at Joanna. As usual, the woman had been working steadily since dawn's first blush. She might want the boy to stay and help.

"Stay where I can see you." Joanna wiped her sleeve across her brow. "When Mr. Bradley gets back with Jackson, we'll be ready to leave."

"Yes, ma'am. Come on, puppy." And he was off, a limitless bundle of energy.

"If you'll bring me a pot of water, Joanna, I'll clean the morning dishes." How frustrating that she had to have help to accomplish a simple chore like that.

But Joanna didn't complain, just brought over the pot that

had been sitting at the edge of camp. "I filled this earlier." She offered a gentle smile, the look softening the lines that had begun to creep in around the edges of her face. "How are you feeling this morning?"

"Well. I'm enjoying this warm wind. I just wish I could help more. The burden of everything falls on you." She studied her friend's face for signs of agreement.

Joanna shook her head. "Not everything. In fact, it almost seems easier being on the trail than back home. You and Mr. Bradley help so much to occupy Samuel."

Just the sound of Micah's name conjured the image of him, trekking forward on snowshoes, Samuel clinging to his back and chattering away. She couldn't help a smile. "He is good with the boy, isn't he?"

"I'm surprised Samuel's constant talking doesn't make him grumpy, but he just adds a word every now and then and carries on as though he's used to such."

Now was her chance to talk to Joanna about what the other woman might have seen between her and Micah the other day. But how to bring it up?

Joanna seemed to read something in her face, and a sparkle touched her eyes. She reached out to touch Ingrid's shoulder. "You two seem like a good match. The perfect complement to each other."

Heat flamed to her face. "We're not—I mean, I wanted to talk to you about that. To let you know that there's nothing untoward happening between us. He's merely helping me take the vaccines to Settler's Fort. And he cared for my wounds from our wagon accident." She was rambling, but none of her words seem to hold any substance. She wouldn't believe her if she were in Joanna's shoes.

Joanna rubbed Ingrid's arm, maybe trying to silence her. "He seems like a good man. I've come to treasure your friend-ship, even though it seems we rarely have a spare moment to visit. You deserve to be happy, and I see the smile that lights your face every time he comes near. Don't let him go." She straightened, and that twinkle crept back into her eyes. "And I'm happy to act as chaperone."

A lump clogged Ingrid's throat, making it hard to answer. Joanna may have taken her budding feelings further than In-grid would like her to think, but having her friend's support soothed her insides like a cup of tea on a cold day.

She reached for Joanna's hand. "Thank—"

A scream ripped through the air, stilling her mid-sentence.

They both spun toward the source. The voice had sounded like Samuel. Was he hurt? Caught by a wild animal?

Joanna scrambled to her feet and sprinted in that direction, raising her skirts high, her feet sloshing through the melting snow. In the distance, the boy began crying, lifting up great wails as though something was very wrong. Handsome barked around him, his frantic yip pulling the knot in Ingrid's chest even tighter.

Micah's footfalls sounded through the trees where he'd gone to water the donkey. He appeared from the shadows, sprinting with long strides toward the spot where Joanna now knelt. A large rock sat beside her, several more nearby.

The boy's cries didn't cease, only grew louder, more an-guished. Something was very wrong.

Ingrid scooted backward, dragging her splinted leg until she reached the cart. She had to go help them. By levering her good leg under her, she eased up, gripping the cart's sides to pull herself upright. It had been more than three weeks since the injury; surely she could walk a little if she could find something to lean against. She could just drag the bad leg behind her.

But as she stood, bent over and bracing herself on the cart, there was nothing around that would provide the support. Nothing tall and strong enough.

She could hear Micah's deep tenor amidst the boy's wails but couldn't make out his words. Thankfully, the dog had ceased barking. Micah would be able to fix what was wrong with Samuel. He had to. If Joanna lost her son, too, after everything else . . . The idea was too horrible to give thought to.

*Lord, please save the boy. Give Micah wisdom. Give Joanna peace.* Her spirit breathed the prayer, stilling her fear with the same peace she'd petitioned for Joanna to receive.

Micah stood and—with Joanna on Samuel's other side—helped the boy ease to his feet. As they turned to walk back to her, it looked like Micah was supporting the lad's left arm. Or maybe just the wrist. Handsome plodded through the snow behind him, as though sorry he'd not protected the boy like he should.

As soon as they reached the camp, Ingrid couldn't contain herself any longer. "What's wrong? What can I do?"

Samuel raised his tear-streaked face to her. "My arm."

"Come sit here so I can wrap it." Micah's entire focus was on the boy—or, more specifically, the arm. Was it broken? Would he have moved the lad if it was?

When Samuel was seated, Micah motioned for Joanna to come closer. "Hold his wrist still, just like this." He was so engrossed in the boy and the injury, a professional intensely focused on his work.

After he was satisfied with the positioning, he stood and

turned toward the packs, then stalled when he saw Ingrid. "You shouldn't be up. Sit back down." He strode toward her. "I'll help you."

She pushed away his outstretched hand. "I'm fine and I want to help. What do you need?"

He froze, looking torn. He glanced toward the mother and boy, then spun back to the pack. "I don't think the wrist is broken, but there are lacerations, and it's likely sprained. I'll wrap it and make a sling to let the arm rest."

Poor Samuel. "You can use some of my skirt for the sling." She grabbed the hem of her blue muslin.

"I found a bandage. It will be enough." He stood and moved back to the boy.

What else might be needed? "I have some willow tea left. Will it help with his pain?"

Micah paused. "Probably." He moved toward her and she held out the canteen of bitter tea. After taking it he squeezed her hand. "He'll be all right. Just in a bit of pain for a while."

She nodded. How had he known she needed to hear that? Her chest throbbed for the heartache Joanna must be feeling. For the searing pain Samuel was struggling to cope with. For Micah's anguish as he had to face another hurting child. Someone who depended on him to make things better.

*Be with them, Lord. Fill each with your loving strength.* She may not be able to do anything else, but she could do the most helpful thing—cover them with prayer.

Each of the boy's cries plunged another knife into Micah's chest.

He'd wrapped the forearm firmly and strapped it to his chest to restrict movement, and now Samuel sat in his mother's arms. Deep, shuddering sobs still slipped out every few seconds.

"Try to drink a little more, honey. This will stop your arm from hurting." Joanna raised the cup of willow tea to her son's mouth.

The boy took a sip, then turned away with another sob.

"I know that stuff doesn't taste so good, but I'll bet you're brave enough to drink it anyway, aren't you?" Ingrid stroked the boy's hair. She'd been more worried about the injury than Micah had expected.

Micah had been so engrossed in wrapping the arm and securing it properly—especially in case there was a fracture to the bone—he'd almost missed the distress on her face. Seeing her standing there, clutching the cart to hold her upright, his heart had surged to his throat. If she'd fallen, her leg could easily have broken again.

The anguish on her face finally took hold of him. He couldn't even remember what he'd said, but the connection that passed between them as he took her hand seemed to be what she needed. Now she'd regained that strength that always surrounded her. A calm in the storm.

A power he wished he possessed.

"*Relying on God fills me with an inner strength greater than I could possess on my own.*" Her words from before rushed back at him. How did she get that strength? Surely she didn't sit down one day and hand over her will to God, like baked goods sold to a neighbor. "*Here, God. I'll trade you this in exchange for inner strength. Would you mind signing this receipt, please? I wouldn't want you to back out of the bargain.*"

Something inside him tightened at the thought. He may not be very close to the Almighty these days, but not even he was so blasphemous as to think such things. *Sorry, Lord.*

He looked around the campsite. He needed something to do. They should stay here another few hours at least, to give the boy time to calm down. He should take the chance for a little more hunting. Enough to carry them through to Settler's Fort, plus a little extra in case they experienced delay.

Another delay, that is.

His gaze slipped to Ingrid. She was handling this pause in their journey well so far, her attention focused on helping the boy feel better. Her head bent close to his, and he had to focus on her mouth to tell what she was saying. Or rather . . . singing?

Was she crooning a lullaby?

His heart ached with the sensations flowing through him. This woman . . . how had she become so special? She poured out her beautiful heart for others in so many ways. If only he were worthy of the affection she freely showered on him, too.

But he wasn't.

Pushing up to his feet, he reached for the rifle. "I'm going to check the donkey, then do some hunting. Call out if you need me. We'll leave after the noon meal, if everyone is up to it."

His boot caught on the small satchel that carried his personal things. Maybe this was a good time to do some writing, too. Reaching inside, he snagged his journal, then strode toward the woods.

Perhaps the time alone would help him settle his thoughts. But then again, five years of solitude hadn't accomplished that feat.

It would take a miracle for it to happen now.

*My Sweet Rachel,*

*Do you remember the song I used to sing to you at night? I can't remember when our habit began, but every evening I wasn't out doctoring someone, I would tuck you into bed. I'd lean close to your ear and sing,*

*"You are precious, you are precious,*
*You're the one, you're the one.*
*Jesus made you special, Jesus made you special,*
*For His love, for His love,*
*And my love, too!"*

*Then I'd tickle you while you giggled so hard, you'd snort and gasp like a little piggy. When you grew older, you learned how to tickle me back, and our little song turned into a full tickle-fight.*

*Often, we only stopped when Mama came to tell us to settle down. She always said I was making you too excited before bedtime, but I couldn't resist hearing you laugh so hard.*

*There's nothing I wouldn't give to hear you laugh again, my sweet Rachel. I miss you more than I can say.*

*Papa*

When they finally stopped for the night, Joanna looked more exhausted than Ingrid had ever seen her. Samuel had ridden in the cart some of the afternoon, but there were many moments when his tears and cries of "Mommy, please" were too pitiful to ignore. In those moments, Joanna would take her son and carry him, soothing away his sobs as only a mother could.

The effort took a toll on Joanna, though, as was evident by the deep lines under her eyes and her pale face.

After setting up camp, Micah handled meal preparations so Joanna could tend to her son. Now that the heavy wind had left, he'd been able to build a fire—a good thing, since the air dropped to icy temperatures.

"Stew's ready." Micah filled a cup and handed it to Joanna.

She took the mug as she wrestled her son into an easier position. "Come, Samuel. Let's eat a few bites. This will help you feel better."

"No. It hurts." He'd been whining those same words for hours, a heartbreaking refrain.

"I know, son. But you have to eat." Joanna's tone picked up a twinge of frustration. Nay, desperation.

"How about if I sit with him for a minute?" Micah stood and handed Joanna her own mug of stew as he stepped toward them and Joanna scooted back so he could take her spot.

He settled in, taking the boy on his lap, cradling him as though the two had sat together many times before. "Did I ever tell you about the time my little girl broke her arm?"

The boy's eyes rounded as he looked up at the man. He shook his head and sniffed, then wiped his nose on a sleeve.

Micah lifted a bite of stew to Samuel's mouth. "Have a bite here and I'll tell you." The boy opened obligingly. "She was about a year younger than you, and her name was Rachel."

The past tense word *was* made pain clog in Ingrid's chest. How hard must it be for him to talk of his child who no longer lived.

But he continued the story. "She loved to climb trees and

rocks, just like those boulders you were climbing today. One day a boy came running to tell me Rachel had fallen and I needed to come quickly." He spooned another bite into Samuel's mouth, even as the lad's eyes were fixed on him.

"I ran faster than I've ever run in my life. When I got there, I saw she'd broken her arm in the same place yours is hurt." He touched the boy's bandaged wrist. "I carried her home and wrapped the arm up just the way I did with yours, but she still cried. And her tears made me so sad inside that I wished it was my arm that was broken instead of hers." Micah's words quavered a bit as he gripped his own arm in the same spot.

Ingrid knew well the pain of a broken limb and could only imagine the grief of watching his child with that ache, not being able to remove the agony.

He inhaled audibly. "I knew what she needed most was something to take her mind off the hurting. Something unusual. Do you know what I did?"

"What?" Samuel was so engrossed in the story, he didn't seem to notice as Micah fed him another bite.

"First, I gave her a licorice stick, because that always helps. But then, I remembered a game I played when I was a boy called 'Guess What I'm Thinking.' It goes like this.

"I say, 'I'm thinking of something that makes noise.' Now you can ask me five questions to find out what it is, but I can only answer with a yes or no. After five questions, you have to guess. Understand?"

Samuel sniffed and nodded.

"Good. You could ask me something like 'Is it alive?' or 'Does it move?' Anything that will help you guess what I'm thinking of that makes a noise."

"Well then, is it alive? An' does it move?"

Micah chuckled and fed the boy another bite. "Yes and yes."

"Is it an animal?"

"Yes, it is."

"What kind?"

He raised his brows. "Best to ask me something that I can answer yes or no."

"Oh, um . . . does it have four legs?"

"It does. One more question."

"But, Mr. Bradley, you didn't answer yes or no."

Another deep chuckle rumbled from Micah's chest. "You're right. Yes, the animal I'm thinking of has four legs."

"Hmm . . . for my last question . . . does it make a noise like a neigh?"

Ingrid had trouble biting back her laughter at the pair. Samuel was catching on quickly.

Micah scrunched his face as though thinking hard. "I suppose . . . yes."

Samuel's expression changed to weary triumph. "I think it's a horse."

"And I think you're right." Micah spooned another bite of stew into the boy's mouth. "Now it's your turn to think of something and I'll ask the questions."

They made it through two more rounds before Samuel's eyes grew droopy. He'd eaten the full cup of stew and drank most of the willow tea she'd poured for him.

For a few minutes, man and boy lapsed into silence. Then Samuel's little voice broke the quiet. "Mr. Bradley?"

"Yes?" Micah looked down at the boy, the firelight reflecting off the tenderness in his features.

"My arm still hurts." His voice was low and soft. No trace of the whining from before.

"I know. But you're being very brave. I'm proud of you."
His voice roughened with the last words, then his Adam's
apple bobbed.

Silence settled over them again as Samuel's eyelids drifted
shut. Micah stared into the fire, his face a mask. Was he remembering the time he'd played that game with his daughter?
Remembering the challenge of holding her, unable to take
away the pain?

She wanted, more than anything, to move closer. To soothe
away his hurts. To hold him until she could ease his heartache.
But she stayed where she was.

*Be his strength, Lord. His peace.*

# TWENTY

They pushed on the next morning, the boy riding in the cart with Ingrid again. Jackson didn't seem bothered by the extra weight, and Micah kept to the valleys, skirting around mountains as much as he could. He'd much rather carry the packs and let Samuel ride in relative comfort if they could make the situation work.

"The rest of you aren't allowed any injuries," Ingrid proclaimed as they started out. "There's no room left in the hospital cart."

A smile tickled the edges of his mouth. "That suits me fine."

Samuel grew restless early in the journey, and although he didn't cry from the pain, he certainly lacked his usual cheery disposition.

Micah kept them moving, but it was hard not to focus on the conversation between his two patients.

"Would you like to play 'Guess What I'm Thinking' like you did with Mr. Bradley last night?" Ingrid infused her voice with a merry tone.

"No."

"Are you sure? You can think of something first."

"My arm hurts. I want my papa."

Micah cringed at the words. Of course this trauma would meld with the greater suffering of losing his father. How would Ingrid answer him? Surely she'd have something more profound to say than anything Micah could summon.

He glanced back to see her wrap the boy in a tight hug. "I know, honey. I lost my papa not long ago, too. And it still hurts."

Micah looked away to stop the emotion clogging his throat. The raw ache in Ingrid's voice resurrected that same pain inside him.

"But you know what? I'll see my papa again one day in heaven, just like I'll bet you'll see your papa there. That makes me feel better."

"When will I see him?"

"Only God knows that, but as long as you trust God, He promises we'll go to heaven someday and see all those people we love who are waiting there for us."

Samuel was quiet then, and Micah didn't turn to see what they were doing. He wasn't sure he wanted to hear more.

But she spoke again. "How about if I tell you a story?"

The boy answered too softly for Micah to hear. His response must have been agreement, because Ingrid started in.

"Once upon a time, there was a man named Gideon. He lived a long time ago, in a land where the people didn't have much to eat. There was a king who lived in the next country who was very mean to the people. Every time they grew grapes or wheat for food, the king would send soldiers to come and take their crops so they barely had enough left to eat.

"Just like all his family and friends, Gideon was afraid of the soldiers. He'd rather be hungry than face their swords and knives.

"One day, when Gideon was hiding away a little food so the soldiers wouldn't take it, an angel appeared to him. Don't you think that would be exciting, to be working at your chores, then an angel appears in front of you, just like that?" She snapped her fingers.

"Did the angel have wings?"

"I don't know."

"I think it did." Samuel spoke with the certainty of youth.

Ingrid's voice held a hint of chuckle. "Maybe so."

Over the next half hour, she kept the boy spellbound with the tale of how Gideon gathered an army of people to fight the evil king, then sent most of them home before the battle, at God's direction. That sounded like the God he knew. A deity whose actions never seemed to make sense.

As she unfolded the tale, what he'd assumed was a story direct from the Bible turned as mystical as a fable. When Gideon and his army of three hundred surrounded the enemy army, they blew trumpets and waved torches.

"God made the bad soldiers confused from all the noise, and they started fighting each other. When the battle was over, Gideon and his countrymen were free to keep the food they grew and to worship God any time they wanted. And Gideon learned God could use anything to accomplish what He promised to do." She settled into silence.

"Miss Chastain, was that story really true?"

"It was, and it's one of my favorite stories from the Bible. Whenever I'm afraid or hurting, I remember how God made Gideon brave. I pray and ask God to give me courage, too."

Her words tugged in Micah's chest. Did she really believe God granted her request? How did she know for sure? Over these past days, he'd come to grips with the fact that her inner strength came from her faith. But could it actually come from God himself, not just the strength of her beliefs? In response to her prayers?

If only he could see that play out with his own eyes. Maybe the idea would be easier to believe in.

The next few days weren't easy for any of them, but Ingrid did her best to entertain Samuel so the weight of his care didn't smother Joanna. Thankfully, the boy's arm seemed to be healing well.

But even with her help, Joanna seemed to grow more weary and drained with each passing hour. Perhaps the hill they'd been climbing all afternoon had been too much, because she looked like she may not make it to the top. Micah didn't seem to notice how pale she'd grown, nor the way she staggered with each step.

"Maybe we should stop for a minute," Ingrid called up to him.

He slowed, then straightened and turned to her, his breaths clouding the air. "All right. Anything wrong?"

She slid a glance to her friend, who still stood hunched over, huddling in her coat. The weather was cold, but she'd expect Joanna to be warm from her trek up the mountain. In fact, a sheen of sweat glimmered from her brow.

"Joanna, are you well?"

"I'm just tired." Her voice quavered, as though from shivers.

Ingrid glanced back at Micah to see if he noticed the unusual symptoms. He studied the woman, concern knitting his brows. Joanna was clearly unwell.

"Come here, Joanna," Ingrid said. "Let me feel if you're feverish."

The woman actually complied, which meant she must really feel ill. As Joanna leaned against the cart so Ingrid could feel her forehead, her labored breathing filled the space between them. Her skin burned at first touch, and her cheeks flushed with bright red circles. "Joanna, you're not well at all. You should be in bed."

Ingrid looked up at Micah, who'd stepped closer to them. "Is there a place we can camp?"

He nodded. "We'll have to hike down the mountain, then we can make camp in the woods."

Turning back to Joanna, she studied her. "Can you walk that far?"

The woman straightened. "Of course." Yet she still hugged her coat tight around herself as she turned downhill.

Joanna seemed to have renewed energy for the first few minutes after they started again, but it faded quickly. By the time they neared the cluster of evergreens spanning the base of the mountain, she'd returned to her huddled posture, stumbling forward as though each step was a challenge.

What could be wrong with her friend? Her joking words from before clanged loudly in her ears. *The rest of you aren't allowed any injuries. There's no room left in the hospital cart.* This trip had been beset by one trial after another, slowing them each step of the way.

*Why, Lord? You called us to bring these vaccines to help the people at Settler's Fort. Why haven't you prepared the way for us? Why are you allowing these awful things to slow us down?*

And poor Joanna. She'd endured so much already. What

could be the Lord's purpose in adding one more affliction to her load?

Although still an hour or two before they normally stopped for the day, they made camp as soon as they reached the trees.

After helping her son from the cart, Joanna found her bed pallet and sank onto it while Micah unharnessed Jackson. Ingrid hated being confined to the cart until Micah was generous enough to come hoist her out. Joanna always helped lift her splinted leg, but this time they'd need to accomplish the task without her.

As soon as he removed the straps from the donkey and entrusted the lead line to Samuel so the animal could graze, Micah stepped to her side. "You ready?"

She nodded. "If we had a pair of long poles, I could do this part myself."

He bent down and slipped his hands under to lift her. "I don't mind helping."

As much as she wanted to be independent, feeling his strength so close was a small dose of heaven. His touch always formed a connection between them. She was hard-pressed to resist his nearness, nor did she want it to stop.

"Do you want to stand for a moment?" He lifted her from the cart and cradled her, waiting for her response.

"Yes, please." She shouldn't distract him from building a fire and tending Joanna, but the chance to stand was too alluring. "Just for a minute." She gripped his shoulders as he lowered her feet to the ground.

While she worked to find her balance, she could feel the thudding of his heartbeat as the sound intermingled with her own. He kept his hand tight around her waist, holding her to him. She didn't push away. Didn't try to put space between them so she could stand on her own. These few moments were the best part of her day.

But then the memory of why they'd stopped early brought a stab of remorse. She leaned back to look into Micah's face. "What do you think is wrong with Joanna?" She kept her voice to a whisper so the other woman couldn't overhear.

His gaze slipped over her shoulder, and she turned her focus in the same direction. Her friend had curled up on one of her blankets, pulling the others over her as she huddled underneath.

"I'll have to examine her to see what's causing the fever." Micah's deep voice rumbled deliciously in her ear, sending a wash of chill bumps through her.

She let her eyes drift shut for a quick moment, relishing his hold one last time. The bristles of his jaw brushed her temple as his lips touched her skin, achingly sweet.

"I need to set you down so I can see to things." He whispered the words, his warm breath caressing her skin.

"All right." She responded in a matching whisper.

But he didn't move to lower her, nor did she shift away from him. They stood suspended, his mouth brushing her temple, her clutching him as though her life may slip away if she let him go.

At last, he inhaled a long breath, then released it as he pulled back. "Can you hold on to the cart side until I get your bedroll unpacked?"

She waved him away. "I'll get it. See to Joanna first."

He seemed hesitant to release her, his hand slipping along her back as he let go. At the angle she leaned, she couldn't see the expression on his face. But in her imaginings, the look was tenderness, not concern. A desire to be near her, not angst for her safety.

Finally, he turned and moved toward their friend. She worked to unload the things they'd need from the cart, which was an awkward business the way she stood, but not impossible.

At least this, she could do.

Micah pressed two fingers against the artery passing through Mrs. Watson's neck, counting the beats in his mind. He had no stopwatch to measure them against, but it was easy to tell the pulse was faster than it should be.

Her face had drained to a dim pallor, except for spots of color on each cheek brought on by the fever. She lay with her eyes closed, her breathing deep, but not as if she was sleeping. There wasn't a raspy edge that would come from congestion in her nose or lungs.

"Can you open your mouth?"

She obeyed, still not lifting her eyelids, as though that took more energy than she possessed.

He peered down her throat, adjusting her jaw so the light would aid his view. Her tonsils didn't appear inflamed. "Does your throat ache?"

She shook her head.

With a final glance around her mouth, he started to move his focus to her eyes, but a red spot on the side of her tongue caught his notice. Maybe it was a trick of the shadows, but that surely looked like a set of raised bumps. An exact replica of so many he'd seen before.

A weight slammed into his chest, knocking him backward. He sat on his heels, studying the woman with an eye for the symptoms that had become so familiar to him five years before.

"Does any part of you hurt?"

She raised a hand to press her temple. "My head."

Urgency quickened his senses. "Anywhere else?"

She was quiet for a minute as her eyes squeezed. "It's hard to tell. I feel like . . . everything hurts."

He forced himself not to show a visible reaction. Head and body aches often accompanied fever. "May I see your hands, Mrs. Watson?"

She extended both arms toward him, and he unwrapped the cloth strips she'd been using for gloves. Her fingers were icy, which was not uncommon with a fever. Or perhaps merely from the frigid temperature around them.

No rash marred her white skin. A good sign. But it usually began in the mouth, so the sickness probably hadn't progressed that far.

If this was even smallpox. He had to keep from leaping to that conclusion.

He rewrapped her hands and tucked them under her blankets. "Can you open your mouth again, please?"

She obliged, and he peered inside. This angle allowed more light to flood the cavity, and he studied the red spot on the side of her tongue.

"Press your tongue to the top of your mouth." As she obeyed, another red spot came into view. This one left him no doubt. That was the beginning of a pox if he'd ever seen it.

He sank back on his heels again, tapping her jaw. "You can relax now."

Weariness sank over him, stealing his strength. This couldn't be happening. Not again.

# TWENTY-ONE

*I*ngrid stayed close to Joanna that evening, offering sips of water or willow tea and handling the chores she could from her seat. Micah did everything else, usually with Samuel in tow. The man was clearly troubled by Joanna's illness, but he wouldn't share his thoughts about what she suffered from.

The boy was clearly troubled by the change in his mother, too, but Micah kept him busy enough that he didn't have time to brood.

When it was time for Samuel to bed down for the night, he moved to his mother's pallet where he normally slept.

"Why don't you sleep over here with me, lad?" Micah motioned toward his own stack of furs. "We'll let your mama rest tonight so she can heal."

Samuel glanced where Micah pointed, then sent a worried look to his mother.

Joanna opened her eyes, giving him a slight reassuring smile. "That's a good idea, son. Mr. Bradley will help you get a fine night's rest. I'll feel better in the morning."

Ingrid should probably offer the boy a spot on her pallet, but she needed to be free to care for Joanna. And the two males seemed to have formed a bond through these days of hardship. Micah's influence could have a strong positive effect on the lad now that he'd lost his father.

Micah sat beside Samuel as he snuggled under the blankets for sleep, and Ingrid couldn't help but steal glances at the man from where she sat with Joanna. After only a few minutes, Samuel's face slipped into the relaxed expression of sleep, and Micah rose from his blankets.

Instead of moving toward the woods, he came around and sat beside her. "Are you awake, Mrs. Watson? I need to ask you both a question."

"Mmm . . ." Joanna's eyelids flickered open. "What is it?" Her voice sounded so groggy.

Ingrid flicked her gaze back to Micah. Was he finally going to tell them what he suspected was the cause of Joanna's illness?

He looked at her with eyes so bleak, her chest tightened. She started to reach out for his hand, but something stopped her. "What is it, Micah?"

His jaw flexed. "Have either of you—or the boy—been vaccinated for smallpox?"

Ingrid sucked in a hard breath. *No.* "Is that what you think this is?" She studied his face, seeking the truth.

The desolation in his face showed his answer, but also revealed so much more. How hard this must be for him, to relive the death of his wife and daughter. The brutal end that sent him wandering like Moses into the wilderness.

She did take his hand then, slipping her fingers around his palm. "I was vaccinated as a girl." She turned to Joanna. "What of you and Samuel?"

Her face was so white it shone in the moonlight. "No. Neither of us."

Ingrid's heart dropped into her stomach, or at least it felt that way. She tightened her grip on Micah's hand, knowing the words likely strengthened his certainty about what she suffered. Intensified the fear that must be engulfing him. *Be with him, Lord. Use this situation to bring him healing. And protect my friends in your mercy.*

She turned back to Micah, her mind spinning as to what should be done next. "It won't help her to be vaccinated now, will it?"

He shook his head, his mouth a thin line.

"What of Samuel? Should he be inoculated if he's been exposed to the virus?"

Lines formed across his brow. "Yes, I think it's safe. The vaccine is made from cowpox, which is different from smallpox. If he hasn't already contracted the disease, taking the injection may save his life."

She looked across the campfire to the boy's sleeping form. "In the morning when he wakes?"

"Yes." The dread in Micah's tone was hard to miss, even with that single word.

She brought her focus back to him. "What should we do to help Joanna? What stage is she in?" She'd heard enough from her father about smallpox to know what to expect each step of the way.

"I've only seen the rash in her mouth. Tomorrow we'll need to check her body for more pox marks. For now, she needs to eat and drink as much as she's able. Likely she won't be hungry, but she needs all she can force down."

He studied the woman, and Ingrid turned to look at her, too. Joanna's eyes were open, and she met Micah's gaze. "I'll recover from this. Just take care of my boy. Don't let him get

205

sick, too." Her voice broke with those last words, and her jaw worked.

Ingrid touched her shoulder. "We'll do everything we can. You and Samuel are in the best care possible. Both with Dr. Bradley"—she squeezed his hand again—"and God caring for you."

Micah didn't sleep much that night, his mind replaying too many vivid memories. Ella, with the pox marring her pale skin. And Rachel, her vibrant personality drained from her those last few days. Lifeless. His heart wrenching. So helpless to heal them.

Nothing he did stopped the misery. Nothing kept them from slipping away—and taking the best part of him with them.

The memories would swallow him whole if he didn't force them away. He worked to focus on Mrs. Watson, picturing the rash in her mouth. It was possible the marks and fever could be from something else. Maybe a reaction to something she'd eaten. Perhaps even varicella, which some people called chicken pox.

He shouldn't assume smallpox just because of his nightmares with the disease and because of a known outbreak in the area. Had Mrs. Watson been exposed to other sick people? He'd have to ask about recent travels or visitors they'd hosted.

With the first light of dawn spreading across the eastern sky, he rose and saw to the morning chores: gathering water and more firewood, feeding the burro. When he returned, Ingrid had prepared coffee and corn gruel. Samuel sat on his pallet, his sleepy eyes and rumpled hair making it clear he was still working out of the night's sleep.

As Ingrid handed him a bowl of gruel, Micah motioned toward the sleeping woman. "How was the night?" He knew the answer, as he'd heard her restlessness through the long hours.

Ingrid showed dark circles around her eyes this morning, too. "Her fever seems a little better now."

"We need to check for pox or rash as soon as she wakes." He studied her. "Do you want to handle it, or should I?"

As the doctor, he probably should. But Mrs. Watson would likely be more comfortable with Ingrid accomplishing the task.

"Is Mama better?" Samuel's little-boy voice broke through his focus.

Micah turned to him and slipped an arm around his shoulders. "She needs her sleep right now, and she'll likely be sick for several days. But there are things we can do to make her feel better. Do you want to help me with that later today?"

An eager light flickered in his eyes. "I want to help."

"Good boy." He squeezed the lad's shoulder. They needed to build a brush shelter in case more snow came, and that would be the perfect thing to keep him busy.

But first, the boy had to be vaccinated.

He eyed the box peeking above the side of the cart. He'd not opened it since the first time he retrieved it from the site of the crashed wagon. Stepping toward it, he raised the lid, revealing the neat rows of vials inside. Each one had been so carefully wrapped that still none had broken. He couldn't have wrapped them better himself.

He glanced over to Ingrid, who was watching him with

intense scrutiny. He swallowed. "They're all safe. Whoever packed them did an excellent job."

A wash of sadness flowed across her features. "Papa. He was meticulous in everything he did."

His tongue clogged his throat, and he turned back to the box. He never had the right words, but he could already admire the man. Taking up one of the vials, he found the section where the bifurcated needles were stored and pulled one free. It'd been so long since he'd done this. Could he inoculate the boy without causing undue pain?

He'd do his best. Unless . . .

With the tools in hand, he turned back to Ingrid. She was scooting away from Mrs. Watson, toward the lad. She must plan to help. Or maybe she'd read his thoughts before he'd had time to think them.

When she reached Samuel, she gave the boy a sideways hug. "How are you this morning, love?"

"Fine." He rubbed his eye with a fist.

She kept her arm around his shoulders. "Mr. Bradley is going to give you some medicine that will help you stay well. So you don't get sick like your mama."

Perhaps she hadn't read his mind.

The boy looked up at her with questioning eyes. "Is my mama going to die?"

The words plunged a knife through Micah's chest, leaving him breathless from the pain. He couldn't watch this child lose his mother. He couldn't.

"Oh, honey. God's helping Mr. Bradley take care of your mama. We're praying she will get better very soon." She pulled Samuel close. "In the meantime, Mr. Bradley needs to give you medicine in your arm."

Her gaze lifted to Micah, calling him forward. He forced himself to walk to them. To kneel beside the boy. To clear the knot clogging his throat so he could speak. "Have you . . ." His voice pitched high, and he cleared his throat again, working to lower his tone. "Ingrid, have you given the vaccination before?"

She met his look, her eyes asking all the questions he didn't want to answer. "I've assisted. My father always used the inoculation point."

His chest squeezed tighter. He had to be the one to perform the painful task. *God, if you care about this boy at all, let my hands remember what to do. Don't let me make this worse for him.*

While he opened the vial, Ingrid unfastened the boy's coat and uncovered his arm, talking to him the entire time. "You're going to feel a few little pinches in your arm, but what I want you to do is squeeze my hand every time you feel a poke. Do you understand? Your job is to let me know what you feel."

She'd clearly done this before, and the boy looked at her with as much trust in his big brown eyes as Micah felt inside him. With Ingrid assisting, this wouldn't be so bad.

When he made the first puncture, Samuel jerked away from him. "Ow!"

Micah held the boy's arm steady while he squirmed. "Ow. Mr. Bradley, that hurts."

With the second puncture, Samuel let out a howl, which turned quickly into sobs.

Ingrid soothed him as tears ran down his freckled cheeks. "Don't forget to squeeze my hand when you feel a stick in your arm. You're doing fine, Samuel. Squeeze my hand." Through the torrent of howls, her voice kept a steady singsong melody.

Never ruffled. As though she was strolling through a meadow of flowers.

After the fifth successful inoculation, he pulled back. "There now. All done." He slid his fingers down the boy's arm, feeling for bumps and soothing the skin.

Samuel hiccupped another sob, his cries winding down. "No more?"

"No more." Ingrid pulled him close again. "Mr. Bradley did a wonderful job, and you're all done."

"You're my brave boy, aren't you, son?"

The boy whirled to see his mother sitting up on her sleeping pallet. Her hair fell around her face, and her eyes were rimmed in deep shadows.

Samuel jumped up and ran to her. "Mama."

Micah reached to grab him, but the boy was too fast. He surged to his knees so he could rise and follow the lad, to head him off before he could be infected by the vicious disease.

Ingrid grabbed Micah's arm, stopping him mid-rise. He jerked to free himself. He had to stop Samuel from reaching his mother. If he contracted smallpox because Micah allowed them to be together, he'd never forgive himself.

"Micah."

Something about Ingrid's tone stilled him. He paused, there on his knees, and turned to her.

Those clear brown eyes softened. "They can have just a moment, can't they? Both of them need it." When she pleaded like that, he couldn't bring himself to deny her. Still . . .

He forced himself to look away, turning back to mother and son. Samuel curled into his mother's lap, tucked inside the security of her arms. Her chin rested on his head, tears running down her cheeks. The look in her eyes no longer seemed as drawn, replaced by a look of peace. Almost . . . joy. Was it better to be together and happy, though ill? Or to be separate and miserable until each one's fate was determined?

The true answer might lie in the outcome of the illness.

He forced himself to stay put, kneeling beside the pallet Samuel had just fled. He should put away the vaccine materials, but he couldn't seem to pull away from the tender scene across the fire. His jaw ached from clenching it.

A hand slipped around his, gentle fingers brushing his skin. Ingrid, always supportive. Always there when he needed her.

He turned his gaze to hers, willing his eyes to show his thanks. She was becoming far too important to him. Yet he couldn't seem to stop craving her attention.

After a long moment, he forced himself to turn. To focus on the instruments lying on the blanket. "I'll put these away."

And then he'd take a walk amongst the trees. Some time alone might be the only thing to rein in his wayward desires.

# TWENTY-TWO

When Micah returned, the camp seemed mostly back to normal. Despite the fact their lives may never be the same. Mrs. Watson ate a bit of gruel, and Samuel played with the pup.

He motioned to the pair. "Shall we take that little shadow for a walk to gather limbs? It's time we start on the shelter for your mama."

The boy's gaze held a little bit of reservation, but he nodded and stood. "Come on, Handsome. Let's go to work."

As Samuel started toward the trees, Micah caught Ingrid's eye, then motioned toward Mrs. Watson. "This is probably a good time to look things over."

She nodded, clearly understanding his meaning. "We'll do a thorough inspection." She seemed to know a fair amount about the disease, which made him more comfortable allowing her to handle the task of looking for pox marks. Hopefully her knowledge was learned through medical tomes, not firsthand experience with the gruesomeness of a severe case. That sight would be seared in a person's mind forever.

It took longer than he expected to gather enough limbs

and poles, but finally they dragged the wood back to camp. In truth, the boy was a welcome distraction.

As they neared, Ingrid looked up at him from where she worked by the fire. The lines of her face were strained, but not overly so. Did that mean she'd found something?

"Stack those branches here." He motioned to an empty patch of ground beside the poles he'd carried.

The boy dropped to his knees as he dumped his load.

"Samuel, would you check Jackson for me? You can take him the water in this pot." Ingrid motioned toward their cooking pot. Was she sending the lad away to show Micah something worrisome on Mrs. Watson?

"Yes, ma'am." Samuel huffed a resigned sigh and pushed to his feet.

As soon as he slogged away, she motioned Micah over, turning to raise the blanket from Mrs. Watson. His gut clenched as he moved in. The sick woman looked at him with exhausted eyes, deep shadows giving her a haunted look. He brushed his hand across her forehead to check the intensity of her fever. Maybe a little less than the day before. A tiny bit less.

"We found five spots on her midsection." Ingrid pushed aside the hem of her shirtwaist to reveal the bright red dots, which looked almost like shiny blisters.

Mrs. Watson touched one of the spots and rubbed.

He grabbed her wrist, an instinctive action. "Try not to scratch them. If the blisters break open, the poison will spread faster."

He studied the marks. They didn't have the dent in the center that was characteristic of smallpox, but they may not have reached that stage.

Moving back toward the woman's face, he searched her skin

for a red mark or blister they'd missed. It was highly unusual for the pox to break out on the trunk before starting on the face and hands. He took each of her hands, removed the cloth strips, then studied her skin. Nothing yet.

Next, he peered into her mouth again to see how those blisters had progressed. They had the same shiny, puss-filled shape of those on her abdomen. Without the indented centers.

He straightened. Which did she have: smallpox or chicken pox? None of her symptoms fit neatly within the normal activity of either illness.

A motion from Ingrid pulled his attention, and he blinked to clear his thoughts. "You can cover her back up."

"Are you certain it's smallpox, Doctor?" Mrs. Watson huddled into the blankets as Ingrid tucked them tightly around her.

How much should he say? In his experience, people wanted to know precisely what was wrong with them, but medical diagnosis rarely fell into a defined package—a fact that always frustrated him.

In this case, the possible outcomes for either of his suspicions were so drastically different that she needed to know the full extent of both possibilities.

He made his face take on that old expression he'd used at so many bedsides. The one that presented a frank, though caring, manner. "I'm not sure."

As he laid out his thoughts, Mrs. Watson's pallor regained a small bit of color. When he finished, Ingrid gripped his arm. "Oh, Micah. Chicken pox is so much better than smallpox. I'll pray that's what she has."

Their relieved expressions only tightened the urgency in his chest. "You need to know that it's just as possible at this point she's suffering from smallpox. We have to watch carefully. If the pox spread to her hands and face and develops an indentation in the center, it's most certainly the more dangerous illness." He focused his attention on Mrs. Watson. "Either way, you need to drink as much as you can."

"Have some water now." Ingrid slipped her hand behind the woman's neck to help her drink.

Micah pushed to his feet and stepped back to give them room. But as he watched the pair, he couldn't seem to soften the knot in his gut. If she suffered from smallpox, he couldn't stand to watch another patient die in his care.

It would be the end of him.

Ingrid watched Micah through the day as he and Samuel constructed a brush shelter to cover Joanna. The boy's chatter had returned in full force, which made her think his arm must be feeling better. Through his host of questions and comments and imaginings, Micah seemed more distracted than usual.

And definitely more somber.

In truth, he reminded her too much of the Micah she'd first met all those weeks ago—silent and more likely to slip away from camp than sit and talk with her. Of course, he didn't leave them for hours at a time today. But his shuttered gaze swung as often toward the woods as it did to check on her or Ingrid.

For her part, Joanna seemed to itch all over. They found spots on her back and a few more on her abdomen, and she writhed against the burning itch much of the afternoon.

Keeping Samuel away from his mother was no small task,

and by the time they finished the evening meal, he'd begun to cry as he reached for his mother.

Ingrid curled the boy on her good leg, tucking him tight against her. "I know, honey." She stroked his back as they snuggled under the weight of a blanket. "Your mama's getting better, but we don't want you to get sick."

"Hold me, Mama." No matter what she said, the boy still reached out for Joanna with a pitiful whimper.

"I have you, Samuel." She pressed his face to her shoulder, rocking. The fear racking his little body made her chest ache. He'd lost his father barely more than two weeks ago. And now he must fear losing his mother in the same way.

Losing his entire world.

"Mama." The desolation in his tone made her eyes burn.

"I know, sweetie. I know."

Micah pushed to his feet and turned toward the woods. "I'll be back."

Her heart ached, for the boy, yes, but just as much for the man. Had he held his own daughter close as she cried for her mother? His own tears mixing with hers?

*Lord, show Micah your grace. Wrap your love around him to heal the raw places as his suffering springs back to life. And please, Lord, restore Joanna to health.*

Because if this woman died, she had a feeling neither Micah or Samuel would ever be the same again.

Two days later, Ingrid studied Micah's face as he examined the blisters that had cropped up all over Joanna's body. Twin lines furrowed his brow, and more worry creases radiated out from his eyes. He fingered the scab on the back of one of her hands.

"What do you think?" Joanna scrutinized his every movement, strain tightening her expression.

He raised his focus to her face. "The blisters are starting to scab. That's a little quicker than I've seen with smallpox, but only by a day or so. How do you feel?"

"Just so tired and cold. And I have to fight not to scratch. The itching is the worst part." She wrapped her arms tight around herself, as though to keep her hands from scratching the bumps.

Ingrid stroked her friend's shoulder. "You've showed remarkable restraint. Better than I would have if I itched all over."

Joanna appeared to pull into herself, her focus still on Micah. "What should I be doing?"

"The same as you have been. Rest. Drink as much water as you can. Stay away from Samuel to keep from infecting him."

Her gaze shifted to her son, sleeping on Micah's pallet. Micah had taken him on a long trek through the snow to gather firewood, and the boy succumbed to sleep not long after returning. The way Joanna looked at him now made Ingrid's chest ache. Such longing, almost desperation. Her eyes rimmed red, and she looked as though she may lose control any moment.

"We don't want Samuel to get sick." Ingrid gave her shoulder a strengthening squeeze. "And you've moved through the stages of the illness so quickly, it will likely be only another day or two before you're better."

"When the scabs fall off." Micah's voice held a firm edge. "When all the scabs are gone, you'll no longer be contagious."

Joanna appeared to be working to contain her emotions, assembling her features into a look of resolve. She gave a firm nod.

"We'll keep praying God brings the illness to an end quickly." Ingrid's words seemed to tug a softer look from the other woman.

"Thank you." Red tinged her eyes again, and a weary look settled over her.

Micah turned to Ingrid. "We found something for you."

She raised her brows at him. "Really?"

He stood and moved to the stack of firewood, then extracted two long sticks from behind the logs. Each was about the thickness of her wrist and mostly straight, except for a curve at one end.

Did he mean them to be . . . ? Her heart surged at the thought.

He moved to an open patch of ground and held one in each hand. "It took a while, but we finally found two poles with curved ends where the branches forked out. I think these should work for walking sticks." A smile tickled the edges of his mouth. "Would you like to try them? If they're right, I'll need to wrap the curve to make them more comfortable. Let's check them first."

She was already scooting toward him before he finished the question. With her skirts and the brace slowing her down, she didn't make it far before he scooped her up in his strong grip. She squealed at the sudden feeling of being airborne and grabbed tight around his neck.

"I've got you." His words murmured near her ear.

She couldn't help snuggling in. *Finally*. He was offering her the freedom to move around on her own. Although if he'd carry her like this all the time, she'd prefer it even over walking sticks.

He glanced down at her and caught the smile on her face. "What's so funny?"

Trying to bite back the grin did no good. "I'm just happy to be up."

When they reached the spot where he'd dropped the poles, he eased her feet down to the ground. She kept one hand on his shoulder, and he held her waist as he leaned down for one of the poles.

"It will take a while to learn how to walk with these, but make sure you don't put weight on your injured leg. Not for another week at least." He helped her fit the pole under one arm, then reached for the other.

When she had both sticks tucked under her arms, he eyed the positioning of the curved ends, still not releasing her completely. "I can shorten them a little if that helps."

"They're perfect." With these to lean on, she'd be able to walk. To move at her own whim. It was hard to imagine a more glorious thought.

"Try to take a step." He shifted away, yet still kept his hand on her back.

She moved the right pole forward, then hopped on her good leg, then positioned the left pole and worked to drag her injured left leg to rejoin the rest of her. The step was awkward, but she accomplished it.

This time she moved both sticks forward, then swung her body forward in a hop. Faster and not quite as clumsy, but a lot of work for a single step. The wood pressed into her underarms, and a twinge of pain shot through her left thigh. Next time she'd need to be gentler.

But still . . . she was walking.

She turned to grin at Micah. "I love them. Thank you, thank you."

His face softened in a smile that lit his features. He was a truly handsome man, with those piercing eyes and the dark beard stubbling his jaw. Enough to make any woman's knees buckle.

Especially when he looked at her like that. Her pulse sprinted through her, pushing her nearer to him. Would he kiss her again? Every part of her longed for that kiss with an ache she'd never felt before.

He wanted it, too. His eyes showed clearly as his gaze dropped to her lips, than raised to her eyes again.

Then his focus flicked right, and he stilled. Hovered. Backed away.

Her chest squeezed the breath from her lungs. Why hadn't he kissed her? She followed his gaze.

Joanna.

She lay in plain sight, her eyes dropped to the fire. But there was no way she could miss them.

Heat surged up her neck, flooding her face. Oh, heavens. Had she really been about to kiss this man in front of an audience? She backed away, but didn't get one of the walking sticks moved in time.

She teetered, working to move her leg or a pole behind her to keep from falling. But the stick tangled in her skirts.

Micah lunged for her, his strong hand closing around her arms with a solid grip. He wrapped an arm around her back, pulling her upright, pulling her to his chest.

Her heart raced as she leaned against him. With his speeding pulse also in her ear, the sparks racing through her felt as though they might explode any minute. She focused on breathing slow, steady breaths.

"I think . . . you should have someone with you when you use those poles." His words held a gravity that would have been appropriate had he just saved her from falling off a cliff.

She pulled back, forcing some strength back in her joints. "I'm well, truly. And I can use these. As long as"—she looked around for the stick she'd lost—"I have them both."

He didn't release her as he reached down to grab it, then helped her position the bent piece under her arm. "Why don't you walk back to the blankets?"

Yes, that would be a good start.

But as she limped in slow progress toward her seat by the fire, Micah never left her side. Clearly, she'd have to prove her abilities before he trusted her to walk alone.

# TWENTY-THREE

*M*icah, you have to leave."

Micah scrubbed a hand through his hair to avoid Ingrid's pleading look. He'd returned from checking his traps that next morning to find Ingrid and Samuel taking the dog for a walk. They'd managed at least thirty strides away from the campfire, and she looked worn out already.

He shouldn't have brought her the walking sticks. Why had he thought she'd use them sparingly?

"All those people, Micah. If they're not already suffering from smallpox, they need these vaccines. We're settled here, and you can move much faster by yourself than if we slow you down."

Could he leave them? The town should be less than a week ahead, but just the thought of walking away made his stomach churn. Every part of him revolted against the idea.

He shook his head. "I'm not leaving you alone. When you're all well enough, we'll move on together."

She leaned on the crutches tucked under her arms and placed a hand on his forearm, forcing him to meet her eyes. Those brown pools were pure liquid. "God is here, protecting us. I believe in the depths of my heart"—she placed her other hand on her chest—"that He wants you to take the vaccines the rest of the way. We'll be here in His hands, covered by His protection. When you come back, we'll be safely waiting. And you'll have saved people's lives."

She spoke with such fervor, she made him almost think she was right. He raked a hand through his hair again, pinching the ends and tugging. The flash of pain from the action helped clear his mind, and he pulled back, staring at the boy, who was running in circles with the dog.

"If I go, I can take Samuel with me." What was he thinking with words like that? How could he walk away and leave two injured women alone in the wilderness?

She loosened her grip and ran her fingers down the length of his forearm to settle in his hand. "Leave Samuel here. He's a help to us, and you can move much quicker without him." She squeezed his hand, bringing his focus back to her. "Go. Accomplish this work God called us to do, then come back to us."

Her eyes said so much, filling in all the words she hadn't spoken. He wanted to come back to her with every part of his being. To stay with her for the rest of his sorry life. But he couldn't subject her to that. He couldn't hold her back. She was so much more than he'd ever be, no matter how much he tried. She was Boston's elite, with money and every resource she needed at her disposal.

Except family.

But surely she could overcome that hindrance in time. She could marry into a family that would provide anything she lacked. With her noble heart, she could do great things. Things he didn't have the courage to even imagine.

"Micah, God called me to this place. To you. I'm not leaving until I fulfill all His plans for me. Every part."

The way she said it, the earnestness in her voice, the certainty in her eyes, he knew without hearing the words that she meant *he* was part of that plan.

But that seemed too wonderful for God to include him in the plans for this woman's life. God had never given him anything so fantastic—at least not something He didn't jerk away within a few years. How could he believe the Almighty would bless him so much now?

But none of that had bearing on whether he would take the vaccines or not. He had to focus on this decision.

"I know you need time to think about this, but don't wait too long." Her words softened, turned almost hesitant, all the certainty slipping out of them. "The people need those vaccines."

He made the mistake of looking back at her, seeing the vulnerability on her face. Despite her deep strength, she made him want to protect her, to fight her battles.

She squeezed his hand again, and it felt as though she drew him forward, closing the distance between them. He raised his hand to brush the hair back from her face. Her skin was so irresistibly soft, like balm to his fingers, rough and numb from the cold. She leaned into his touch, and he cradled her cheek.

Her lips, red and chapped, called to him, and when her eyelids drifted shut, there was no turning back. He touched his mouth to hers, letting her soothe the raw places inside him, taking his time as her tender lips responded.

She was strength and gentleness, her belief in him so pure it made him want to weep with all he'd lost. All she could be to him. If only he could be as much to her. But he had nothing to give. At least not what she needed in a man.

Still, he drank her in like water, his fingers threading through her hair, hands cupping her jaw. Cherishing her.

Sounds from Samuel broke through his awareness, and he knew he had to end the kiss. No matter how much every part of him relished it. With one last touch of his lips on hers, he drew back enough to study her.

Her eyelids drifted upward, and a smile turned her full lips. Pleasure laced her expression. "God was so good to me when He brought you into my life."

The same pleasure washed through him like a mountain river during spring thaw, and he couldn't help but return her smile. "You make it hard for a man to leave."

Her look turned soft and knowing. "We'll be in God's hands. And I'll be here waiting when you come back."

Some of the joy squeezed from his chest. Could he really leave her? Leave them all here alone?

He had to. He knew in his soul this was what he must do. Lowering his forehead to rest on hers, he inhaled her sweetness one last time. "This might be one of the toughest things I've ever been asked to do."

When Ingrid awoke the next morning, Joanna was sitting up on her bed pallet. She still appeared pale, but not nearly as close to death as she had the past few days. "You look like you feel better."

Joanna smiled, and the shadows beneath her eyes weren't quite as deep. "I do feel better. I think my fever may be gone."

"Thank the Lord." She inhaled a deep breath of the frigid morning air, pulling her coat tight as she glanced around. "Where are the boys?"

"Mr. Bradley took Samuel and Handsome to feed the donkey."

Just the sound of Micah's name made a warm puddle in her chest. She reached for her walking sticks and maneuvered to her hands, then knees so she could rise. "I'm going to the privy." What a relief to finally be able to take herself away instead of using the bedpan that one of the others had to empty.

"Tell the boys to come back for the morning meal." A corner of her mouth tipped. "At least, tell Samuel to come. I suppose Mr. Bradley can eat when he chooses."

Ingrid worked the poles under her arms, feeling the ache from using them so much the day before. The left stick had rubbed a raw spot through her coat, even though Micah had wrapped the wood in cloth. Maybe that one was a little shorter than the other. That would explain why the hip on that side ached more than the other. She forced a smile into her voice. "If I see them, I'll bring Samuel back with me."

"*If* you see them?"

The suggestive tone of Joanna's words made her turn back for a look at her friend. Joanna's brows were raised, her face giving that expression that said she knew everything Ingrid wasn't willing to admit.

She fought a sheepish look and turned away. "I'm going to the privy." And if she happened to walk a little farther for the sheer pleasure of being able to, she'd pass along Joanna's message.

Micah and Samuel had ventured beyond what she expected, and the raw spot under her left arm burned like she'd poured boiling water on it by the time she found them a few strides up the base of the mountain. Micah sat on a boulder, a lone silhouette against the backdrop of the rising sun. The boy and dog played on the ground below, and she paused a moment to watch them—and to catch her breath from the hike. Handsome was becoming so much more playful under Samuel's care, just like a young puppy again. They were good for each other.

And Micah . . . from the set of his shoulders, it looked as though he carried the weight of the world. Or maybe just the load of a hard decision. He felt such a burden for their care, and, in truth, they wouldn't have made it this far without his strength and help. But God had settled them in this nook of safety, and the urging in her spirit was strong for Micah to take the vaccines the rest of the way.

Would he feel God's prompting and obey? If he chose not to, she wasn't sure what she would do. *Lead him, Lord.*

Micah must have heard her, or maybe just sensed her presence, because he turned. His face registered surprise, then a hint of friendly reprimand. "This was too far for you to come."

He started to rise, but she motioned him to stay. "I'll come sit."

He stilled, but didn't leave his crouched position as she shuffled forward. That was Micah—ever the guardian.

When she reached the rock, it was just tall enough that she couldn't pull herself up without a great deal of scrambling, which would likely hurt her mending leg.

He jumped to the ground and scooped her up, just as he'd done so many times to place her in the cart. After easing her into a spot where her leg could rest, he pulled himself back up beside her.

"Miss Chastain, look what Handsome can do." Samuel waved a small stick at the dog.

She leaned forward to watch the pair. "Show me."

The boy threw the piece about five strides away, and the dog charged after it. He dove onto the twig, then started gnawing like he'd found a scrap of jerky.

Samuel slapped his leg. "Bring it here, boy. Bring it to me."

Handsome ignored him, biting into the toy with relish.

"I think they're good for each other." Micah chuckled.

"That's exactly what I was thinking."

Easy silence settled between them as the youngster tried the trick again, with a similar result. They continued playing, but something about Micah's demeanor seemed to change. She couldn't say what exactly, but a tension needled through the silence. Where had his thoughts turned?

After a moment, he straightened. "I suppose I'll head out whenever you and Mrs. Watson feel comfortable with me leaving. But if I'm not back in ten days, I want all of you to pack up and start toward town without me. I'll draw out a map that should get you to the main road into Settler's Fort."

She turned toward him, taking measure of his expression. He'd shaved his jaw clean again the night before, and its lines stood strong and hard. Worry creases edged his eyes, even before he turned to look at her. His eyes took her in, searching.

She pushed aside the fear that struggled to the surface of her emotions and reached for the certainty of knowing they were in God's plan. Then she took Micah's hand. "We will if we need to, but God will protect you. And us."

He nodded, even as the Adam's apple at his throat bobbed. "Just let me know when you're ready for me to leave."

She forced herself to say what she had to. "I think as soon as possible."

He raised his brows. "Today?"

She caught her breath. Was she ready? Not in the least. But she could trust the Lord's guidance.

Squeezing his hand tighter, she nodded. "Today."

Neither of them moved. He seemed to be clutching her as tightly as she held on to him. They had no control over what would happen from here on out. If Micah made it safely to Settler's Fort with the vaccines. If he arrived in time to save the town from the epidemic. If they were still alive and well when he returned to them.

Only God knew the answers.

An urging touched her spirit. A desperate need. "Micah?"

"Yes?"

"Can we pray?"

His chest rose and fell as he blew out a long breath. "Yes."

Micah pushed as late as he could that night, making almost double the progress they would have traveled with all four of them and the donkey. He'd left the animal and most of his things with the women so he could move more quickly, taking only the vaccines strapped to his back and a few necessities.

Including his pistol.

He felt defenseless without his rifle, but the thought of leaving the women without a solid means of protection made him want to cast up his breakfast. He at least had his knife and more strength than them, not to mention two good legs, although his body ached from the strain of the day's hike.

*Lord, let this be enough for my defense.* The prayer came before he even thought about it. Ingrid must be rubbing off on him.

He couldn't help but smile at the thought as he stretched out on his bed pallet and pulled his furs over him. She believed so firmly that God would care for her. For them all. How did she trust so securely? He would have called it naïveté before she came to the mountain country. Despite the loss of her mother, her life seemed like it had been close to ideal.

Yet with her father's death and the pain and immobility from her broken leg, how could her faith remain so steadfast? What had she said to Samuel when she'd told him the story of Gideon? Something about when she was afraid or hurting, she remembered that God made Gideon brave. Then she prayed and asked God to give her strength, too. *God was the giver of her strength.* Not just the foundation of her faith. But God actually poured strength into her when she asked Him.

*I want that, too, God. I need your strength to become a better man.* Not just through the trials of these next few days, but to overcome the man he'd let himself become these past years. In truth, he'd never been the man he wanted to be. Not even when he'd been Landsburg's doctor and husband to Ella, father to Rachel.

Could God make him into the steadfast man he'd wanted to be, but never seemed to attain? "I don't know if it's that easy, God. But if you can do it, show me what you need from me. Show me what I need to do." The words rang loud in the clear night, as though they drifted far out into the sky. All the way to heaven?

He had the sense that God heard him. But . . . should he do something else? Say something else?

A long, slow breath leaked from his chest. "You're going to have to show me, Lord. I don't read minds very well."

He closed his eyes, letting his weary body take over.

# TWENTY-FOUR

*T*he next morning dawned with low, heavy clouds—the sure sign snow would be joining Micah soon.

What about the women? His spirit churned as he went through the motions of packing camp. Part of him wanted to turn around and head back. But what could he do, more than he'd already done? Maybe build a second shelter. He should have done that before he left.

If they needed to, Ingrid and Joanna could always stretch a fur off one side of the shelter. They would stay warmer if the three of them huddled together in one place. Except . . . that would place Samuel too near his mother's contagion.

He wanted to shout at the frustration filling his chest. This was so hard being away, not being there to help them. No way to control their situation.

He stood and heaved his pack onto his back. "God, you're going to have to take care of them because I can't do it." He raised his gaze heavenward. "Please."

Only the wind whipping across the mountainside answered him, but the chaos in his mind eased a little. *Thank you.*

Breathing in a deep draught of icy air, he started out.

For the first few hours, only the wind blew against him. But midway through the morning, the snow began, drifting down in large flakes. Each cluster of ice crystals pricked his face as he marched on, continuing without a break.

Finally, he stopped for a drink from his canteen. He'd crested the mountain a few minutes before, and the fresh white blanket covering the landscape made everything feel different. The scene he'd expected from this view didn't sit the way it had in his mind. The Mullan Road should be within view at the base of the next mountain, but all he could see was a cluster of scrubby trees.

Of course, it had been a year since he'd seen this route.

After taking one more swig of the icy water, he capped the canteen and returned it to his pack. Lord willing, he was getting closer.

Ingrid stared out at the falling snow, a white curtain in the darkness around their little shelter. Samuel squirmed in her lap, pulling her focus away from the growing mounds.

"I wanna do something, Miss Chastain. I'm bored." The boy's whining ricocheted off her already raw nerves, and she pressed her eyes shut to keep her frustrations tamped down.

"How about if we . . ." She scrambled for something to occupy the lad, but nothing came to mind. At least, nothing she hadn't already exhausted in the hours they'd been hiding away from the snow.

"Why don't you lie down, son, and I'll tell you a story." Joanna patted the blanket in front of her.

Ingrid stiffened, her arms wrapping around the boy as she

looked at her friend. They were trying to keep him away from her contagion.

Joanna returned her gaze with weary determination. "I'm feeling much better, and we laundered my clothing and blankets earlier. I don't think he'll be in danger."

The longing in her eyes was hard to stand firm against. How could she separate mother and child? And Joanna did seem better. She'd risen for a while earlier in the day, saying she was desperate for a washing. They'd heated pots of water over the fire, and Ingrid scrubbed fabric while Joanna cleaned herself. The activity seemed to exhaust her, but hopefully the effort had cleared away her contagion.

Samuel squirmed into place beside his mother, tucking under the blankets with the childlike innocence of pure pleasure.

"Now, what story would you like to hear?" Joanna pressed her cheek against her son's hair.

The sight of them snuggled together, secure in each other's love, raised a burn to her eyes. She could still remember sitting like that with Papa when she was Samuel's age. Like this boy, she'd lost a parent early, and her father had become her world.

Now, her world . . . She inhaled a deep breath. Her world hadn't crumbled, but it did look very different than before. *Hold me, Father.* She wrapped her arms tightly around herself. Perhaps a walk would help soothe the ache in her heart. A little time alone with her heavenly Father always settled her.

She scooped Handsome from his place beside her leg and laid him next to Samuel. "I'm going to check on Jackson one last time. Keep this boy warm for me." The poor dog wasn't pleased by all the new snow. After reaching for her walking sticks, she pulled herself up to stand.

Joanna paused her story to watch. "You're doing quite well with those."

"I'm happy to practice." She limped forward, ignoring the bite of the left pole in the raw spot under her arm. She'd trimmed the end of that stick to make it more even with the other, but the wound wouldn't go away.

As she shuffled through the snow, the white all around illuminated the darkness. Her mind flew across the mountains to Micah, hopefully tucked in a shelter of his own, snuggled in his furs before a roaring fire.

*Lord, keep him safe and warm.* She couldn't be there to help him, but she could pray for him. A pressure settled in her chest, weighing down her spirit. Something didn't feel right about Micah. *What's wrong, Father?*

A sense of urgency for him—for his safety and health—surged inside her. If she didn't have this clumsy splint, she would have dropped to her knees, right there in the snow. Instead, she whispered, "Lord, hide him in the shadow of your wing. Form a hedge of protection, no matter what he faces."

Words cleared from her mind, so she let her spirit lift the prayers she wanted to say. As she remained there, snow falling on her upraised face, the deepest parts of her connected with the Father, easing the turmoil inside.

Micah was in the Lord's hands—the very best place for him.

Micah awoke to shivers racking his body. Every part of him ached, as though he'd fought with a bear and hardly escaped alive. The fire was low, but still had a flame, so it must be early in the night. Summoning all his willpower to face the cold, he sat up and reached for the stack of logs he'd gathered, then piled as much on the blaze as he dared. He sank back down, pulling his furs over his head so he could burrow inside. He hadn't been this cold in years.

A new thought slipped in to his benumbed mind. Was he feverish? He worked his coat sleeve back to reveal a patch of bare wrist, then raised it to his forehead first, then his cheek.

*Yes.* He didn't have a doctor's bag with him to make sure, but it felt like steam might be rising from his face.

A knot of dread formed in his gut. Had he contracted Mrs. Watson's illness? He'd been vaccinated for smallpox, but there was always a small chance the vaccine wouldn't be fully effective. Maybe this was a unique strain of the disease that reacted differently to the inoculation. Perhaps that was why he'd had so much trouble confirming whether Mrs. Watson suffered from smallpox or chicken pox.

His mind ached as his thoughts chased every possibility, and he pressed his eyes shut to block out the horrors. He needed to determine his other symptoms so he could make a diagnosis. Running his tongue across his teeth and gums, he felt for sores. His mouth was so dry, he had trouble distinguishing one sensation from another. There, on the side of his tongue, was that a raw spot?

He had to pull off a glove to feel with his fingers, and his hands were so icy, it took a moment for sensation to return to his finger. That did feel like a lesion. Maybe.

But did it really matter? There was nothing he could do to cure himself. He had no medicines, nothing to reduce the fever or ease the pain. And nothing in the world could cure smallpox once a person was infected. The disease had to run its course, bringing either devastation or weak relief.

He let his groan roll out. Was this his final punishment? If God was going to take him the same way He'd taken Ella and Rachel, why had the Almighty made him suffer all these years?

Squeezing his eyes shut, he tried his best to block out the convulsive shivers, the powerful ache in his bones, and, most of all, the torture of his thoughts.

Ingrid jerked awake, her heartbeat racing with urgency. What had awakened her?

The fire's flame had died low, which meant it was probably sometime around midnight. Joanna and Samuel lay curled together, both more settled than she'd seen them since Joanna took sick.

So what was it that made her palms sweat and her pulse thunder in her neck? Had she contracted Joanna's illness? No. It was more her inner spirit that weighed heavier than any physical ailment.

*What is it, Lord?*

An image of Micah slipped into her mind, huddled on his bedroll before a campfire. *What's happening, Lord?* No clear answers came. Just the same urgent dread in her chest.

She pressed her eyes shut, lifting Micah to the Lord in thought and spirit, praying protection and healing for him.

*Healing?* The thought slugged her in the midsection. Was he sick? Was that why she felt this fierce reaction in her body? Or maybe he'd been injured. *Heal him, Lord. Protect him. Mend his body and safeguard his soul.*

So many questions assaulted her, yet she focused on praying as her spirit guided. No, not *her* spirit. The Father's Spirit.

The One who knew, even now, where Micah was and what he needed.

*Bring him back to me, Lord. Safely.*

Micah forced his puffy eyelids open, but all he saw was darkness. He reached out, and his hand brushed the dried underside of an animal skin. No wonder he couldn't even find the stars; he was still in the cocoon of furs he'd made for himself.

When had he finally fallen asleep? It seemed like he'd lain awake for hours, his body convulsing with cold as his mind wandered through his past, sometimes skipping forward to Ingrid. Were she and the others safe? He had to push on today. Had to deliver the vaccines and send people back to help them.

When he peeled the covering off, a blast of cold air hit him, and he pulled the furs tight around his shoulders. He had to force himself. Grit his teeth and push as hard as he had to.

Moving was excruciating. And by the time he rolled his blankets and strapped on his pack, he'd begun sweating, his head lighter than it should be. He reached for a tree to steady himself as the world seemed to sway. He'd have to find a stick to use for support as he walked.

He made it the first hour on the trail by sheer determination. Perhaps he should have tried to eat, but his stomach felt like it would cast back up anything he tried to swallow down. He needed to drink more water, though.

He'd been traveling mostly downhill, and when he reached the valley at the bottom, he allowed himself to stop and rest on a fallen log. He didn't dare drop the pack from his back, because he might not get it back on. But he did scoop snow and press some to his forehead. The rest he stuffed in his mouth for water.

Sweat ran in rivulets down his face, and he could feel more streams inside his coat. They didn't stop the shivers, though. Maybe his convulsions were made even worse by being wet inside. Not that he could do anything about it.

He propped an elbow on his knee and dropped his forehead into his hand. *Oh, God. I can't do this.*

His strength seeped out of him with every passing minute. How would he make it for days more? He had no idea whether it would be one day or five. Or maybe longer. The thought made him want to sink to the ground and curl into a ball.

What were the chances another traveler would come along and find him? Someone with a sled and team? Not as likely as his chance that a mountain lion would track him. Or maybe wolves in need of a fresh meal. Or maybe the smallpox would take over, consume him like it had consumed every good part of his life.

Every part except Ingrid.

He couldn't let that happen. People were counting on him. The town needed the vaccines. And the woman he loved needed him to return for her.

Yes, *loved.* The certainty in his chest flooded a peace through him that eased some of the ache. Faced with the possibility of death, his thoughts were so much clearer now.

He did love Ingrid Chastain. If he recovered and if she'd have him, he'd take care of her for the rest of their days— however long or short they be, whether in Boston, Settler's Fort, or somewhere in between.

*If she'd have him.* When she was back in the safety of her normal life, she might regain her senses.

He pushed to his feet. Still, she was counting on him. And so were the people of Settler's Fort.

He wouldn't let either of them down. Not while there was one ounce of fight left in his body.

# TWENTY-FIVE

By the time darkness fell, Micah's focus had narrowed to his next step and his next breath. Just one more. Then another.

Pain and convulsive shivers flooded his body, but there was no way to escape. Blackness circled his vision, and his body dripped with sweat.

He should stop for the night. Every part of him begged to sink to the ground. But if he did, he may never rise. Could he push on through the night? His body would give out eventually, and he would have less chance of surviving at that point.

*I don't know what to do, God. Help.*

*Help.* He'd offered up that single word to the Lord more times than he could count today. Maybe that's why he was still on his feet. Still able to move one foot, then the next. Pretty sure each step would be the last.

A dark shape appeared at the edge of his focus, just off the side of the road. A shelter? He paused, sucking in another icy breath. A few strides off the road sat a deserted branch lean-to, covered with snow. Yet it'd been built deep enough that a patch of ground inside was dry.

He stumbled toward the structure. Was this God's way of telling him to stop for the night? The shelter was better than he'd expected. A stack of wood sat inside, probably damp from the elements, but at least not covered with snow. He needed a fire desperately to warm himself.

He also needed to get out of these sweat-soaked clothes, but there wasn't much help for it. He'd brought nothing else with him.

After easing the pack to the dry ground, he unrolled his furs and laid them out. Then he took some dried meat from the pack and let himself sink to the bed pallet. He had to eat, no matter how much his body resisted the food. No matter how tired he was.

In truth, he was too weary for anything. As the last of his strength slipped out of him, he curled up on one fur and pulled the others over him.

Was this the same agony Rachel and Ella had suffered? And his other patients? Maybe God had truly made the best choice by taking them on to heaven. Finally bringing them peace from this torment. He could almost imagine Rachel skipping down those streets of gold. Swimming like a beaver in the crystal lakes of heaven. Her red curls drying like a halo as she sat at the Lord's feet. Happy once again.

His throat worked, swallowing down the lump that formed.

God had done what was best for his girls. But he must have something more for Micah here on earth.

He could only pray that included Ingrid by his side. *Lord, protect her and the others. And please make me well so I can help them.*

There was more he wanted to ask. So much more on his heart, but before he could summon the words, exhaustion took over.

"What is it, Ingrid?"

Ingrid pulled her gaze from the fire to look at her friend but tucked her arms tighter around herself. For the second morning in a row, she'd awakened with a knot churning in her middle, a weight on her chest so heavy she had to work to draw breath. "Something's wrong with Micah. I don't know what to do."

Joanna dropped to her knees beside her. "Do you have any idea what's happened?"

Her friend probably thought she'd lost her senses. Or thought she was just worrying overmuch. *Was* this merely lovesick concern?

No, her spirit craved prayer. A sense of danger still lingered from when she'd awakened two nights before. This had to be God's insight.

"I don't know what's happened. I just feel this urgency to pray. Or should we pack up and go to him? Do you think he needs our help?"

Joanna regarded her with the expression she wore when she was thinking deeply. "You think this feeling is from God?"

"I do. I just don't know what to do about it." And the weight of her fears were enough to drive her to distraction.

"If God's leading you to pray for him, then *that's* what you should be doing." She spoke with such a matter-of-fact tone, but the words didn't penetrate Ingrid's muddled thinking at first.

"It seems like I should *do* something. Maybe he needs us to come?" She squeezed her eyes shut against the image that had assaulted her when she awoke that morning. "What if he's lying somewhere in pain? Unable to help himself. Freezing to death."

"Do you think God's directing us to go to him?" Joanna's tone remained so calm.

Ingrid pinched her lips. She couldn't say that urging was from the Lord. It felt too much like her own desperation. She shook her head. "I don't think so. But . . . I don't know." How could she leave Micah to die? Surely God would want her to help him.

"Then let's proceed with what we do know. We'll pray for Micah. Until he returns or God tells us differently, we'll lift him up to God's care. Perhaps there's someone else God wants to send to him." She turned to her son. "Samuel, come pray with us. Mr. Bradley needs God's help."

*Someone else?* The thought slugged Ingrid in her already-queasy middle. But that was fine. However God chose to accomplish the job, she would be thankful.

As long as Micah lived.

"Fella, you need to wake up. I'm not so sure I can hoist ya in the saddle."

Micah struggled to obey the man's words, to push his eyes open. They felt swollen shut. His mouth was as dry as a rock in the summer sun, and he struggled to work up some saliva.

Hands shook his shoulder, making him realize that wasn't the first time they'd jostled him. He had to wake up. Shivers no longer racked his body, but every part of him ached, even his eyelids. Focusing on that pain helped pull himself fully awake.

"There ya are. Fine now. Let's git ya on the mule and on

home. From there, we can take the wagon in to see the doc." The blurry outline of a man hovered over him.

Home. A wagon. *A doctor.* The words settled through him like warm coffee. Did that mean he would live?

The man gripped his arm again and pulled. The movement shifted his muscles, making his body scream.

He gritted his teeth against the agony and forced himself upright. The already fuzzy world spun, sending bright flashes through his vision. He couldn't hold in a groan as he worked to contain his roiling stomach. What little he had left in his belly worked itself up to his throat. He breathed deep to keep it down.

"I know yer awful sick, son. That's why we gotta get movin'."

Squeezing his eyes shut against the spinning, he rolled onto his hands and knees. With the old timer's help, he found his feet, then stumbled forward. His vision didn't spin so much now, and he could make out a chestnut-colored mule.

They reached the animal, and Micah clutched the saddle to keep himself upright. Why was he so weak? And the dizziness still had his world askew.

"Sure wish Isaac was here." The man's mumbled words were almost too low to hear, but his next came out louder. "All right, fella. Let's git you up in the saddle. On the count of three."

While the stranger hoisted, Micah clawed at the leather, fighting to pull himself up.

At last, he draped his right leg over the horse, clutching the saddle to hold himself in place. The spinning resumed with fresh fury, and a dark circle edged his vision. His head seemed to wobble, and he gripped the seat tighter to keep from falling.

"Hold on there, boy." The man seized his arm with a hold firm enough to anchor him. "You are in a mess, aren't ya?"

"I'm fine." He had to speak through gritted teeth, but it was time he recovered himself.

"I reckon' it'll be fine to leave yer pack an' furs here. One of us'll come back for 'em later."

*Pack.* Urgency pressed through him, and he shook his head. They had to bring those vaccines. He was no good without them.

"It'll be fine, son. I'll come back fer the stuff."

The saddle shifted as though the man was about to climb up behind him.

"Wait." The word wasn't much more than a grunt, but the movement beside him stilled.

"What is it?" The man's voice seemed friendly, curious.

"The pack. We have to bring it."

The saddle shifted again, this time like the man was letting loose of it.

"Let me take a look an' see how we can carry it. Anything in particular you need from it?"

"The box." He should get off and retrieve it himself, but his muscles had lost most of their strength.

"Stay put, then." The sounds of crunching snow signaled the man's departure, and Micah let his eyes drift shut again.

He could relax a little now without feeling like he would topple over. Good thing this mule wasn't the nervous sort.

"You think you can sit up there without fallin' off?"

The old-timer's voice jerked Micah from a fog, and he clutched the saddle tighter as his body shook. He must have started to doze.

"I can stay up." Despite his actions thus far, he'd make sure he didn't come off this animal. Even if he had to lash himself to it.

The man was quiet for a minute, then he said, "I guess I'll have to take your word for it, if'n yer set on bringin' this pack."

Micah forced a nod. "Yes."

The man hoisted the bundle up behind the saddle and tied it on. "All right, then. Hold on tight."

The mule started forward, and Micah gritted his teeth as he clung to the saddle. The natural rocking of the animal made him feel like he was pitching side to side, a sensation that might actually make him topple. He forced his eyes open to make sure he stayed upright.

After a few minutes, his vision settled a bit, and he took the chance to study the man who led the mule. He couldn't see much, just the back of his buckskin coat and fur cap. A queue of brown hair hung below the fur, mixed with enough gray to prove he wasn't a youth, but not as much as Micah expected from the gravel in his voice. Pipe tobacco may have added the extra sludge in his tone.

He had so many questions for the man, but his fading strength only allowed for one. "How far to town?"

The fellow turned and sent him a glance without breaking stride. "About half a day's ride at this speed. To our place, that is. Then a little over an hour to the settlement."

*Today.* They'd be there today. Then he could hand over the vaccines and get help for Ingrid and the others.

*Thank you, God.* Against all odds, the Lord had brought him to the end. A miracle as sure as Gideon defeating an army with three hundred men.

Strong hands gripped his arms, pulling him sideways.

Micah clutched at the saddle, powerless to resist the grasp. The shivers had taken over again, convulsing his body and stealing his strength.

"Careful there. He's awful weak."

Arms hoisted him, dangled him. He forced his eyes open, struggled to work his mouth, but his jaw trembled so much he couldn't get words to form.

They swung him onto something hard. Wood. A floor? It must have been a wagon, because it surged forward, landing him against his side so hard he couldn't contain a moan.

The bouncing seemed to last for hours, agony surged through him in wave after wave. Death would be a welcome relief from the torture raging inside him.

Except he couldn't leave Ingrid. Her face appeared in his mind, and he clung to it. Her gentle expression. Those caramel eyes. Every part of her so beautiful it made him ache—the kind of ache he longed for. That ache could swallow him whole, stilling the torment inside.

*Keep her, Lord. Save her, and give her the wonderful life you're preparing for her.* He wanted to be part of it, more than his body wanted relief from this inferno. But a coolness settled in his chest, easing the blaze inside him, settling a bit of peace over the misery coursing through his body.

Even if that wasn't God's plan . . . if He meant only for Micah to deliver these life-saving vaccines, then slip away, so be it. *I'll do what you want, Lord. My life is in your hands.* He'd meant those words from that night before the fever took hold of him. Live or die, God could take the lead.

*Take me, Lord. Do with me what you will.*

# TWENTY-SIX

The hum of voices called to Micah, pulling him from the fog. Tugging him back to awareness. Back to the misery that leeched his strength.

But those voices. The low timbre of men. He had to know who they were.

His eyelids felt so puffy, he struggled to push them open. Finally, he forced a slit, then cringed against the blinding light. He turned away from the glare, groaning as he raised his hand to shield his eyes.

"Looks like he's awake." One of the voices moved closer.

The light was still too bright to focus on the man, but he opened his mouth to ask who the fellow was. Where they'd brought him. But so dry was the inside of his mouth that his tongue wouldn't move the way he told it.

"Here's a sip of water. I'm gonna raise your head so you can drink."

A strong hand gripped the back of his scalp, lifting him. Cool tin touched his mouth. The man didn't seem to have harmful intentions, so Micah sipped the liquid.

Water slid over his tongue, cooling the parched areas,

clearing away the cobwebs. He drank more, letting the liquid soothe him all the way down.

"That's probably enough for now. Don't want it to come back up." The man lowered his head back to the bed.

Micah lifted his hand away from his eyes, still holding it overhead like a shield from the light. He could make out the man's form now.

He worked his mouth to form words, and this time his tongue cooperated. "Who are you?" His voice rasped as though his throat was clogged with sand.

"Name's Isaac Bowen. My pa found you on the road, and we brought you into town for the doc."

The words pulled a memory of him huddling in his furs, racking chills tormenting his body so much he felt halfway to the grave.

But he was alive. And a glance around showed he was in some kind of bedchamber, nicer than any doctor's clinic he'd seen. "Where am I now?"

"The doctor's place. He put you in one of his private rooms to keep you away from the smallpox patients. They're lined up all over his clinic. Pa went to let Doc Stanley know you're awake, but I'm not sure when the doc will be free to come."

A flood of thoughts surged through him with the man's words. Did the doctor not think he was a victim of smallpox, too? The man must have been certain if he put him in private quarters. He brushed the side of his tongue against his gums. Where was the sore he'd felt before?

But that wasn't the pressing concern. The doctor needed the vaccines. They had to set to work inoculating the people in town who hadn't yet contracted the disease. He pushed upright, sucking in a harsh breath against the pain in every part of him.

"Ho, there. Doc said not to let you up until he gave the word."

The room spun, and Micah pressed his fingers against his forehead to make the whirling stop. A hand gripped his shoulder, pushing him backward. "Wait. I have something the doctor needs right away. That's why I'm here."

"Lay back, then, and you can tell him about it as soon as he comes."

He let himself be pushed back against the pillow, mostly because he couldn't believe how weak he still felt. He forced himself to focus on the man's face, keeping his voice steady. "Dr. Stanley requested the smallpox vaccines that are in the box I brought. He needs them right away. Can you please let him know the vaccines from Dr. Chastain have arrived?"

The other man looked to the corner of the room, where the box must be. Then back to Micah. "I guess I can take them to him. I suppose it's urgent, what with all the people who've taken sick."

A reaction in his chest made him want to jump up and grab the box himself. He'd walked for weeks, toting and protecting that crate with every step. The contents could save countless lives. Did he dare trust it into this man's care?

He studied Isaac Bowen again. About his own age. Sturdy lines like any man who worked hard to survive the rigors of life in these mountains. Bearded face, but not unkempt. He was probably both decent and capable.

Through gritted teeth he forced out his words. "Please be careful with it. The vials inside are fragile. Make sure you tell him they're the vaccines from Dr. Chastain in Boston."

He lifted the box and turned back to Micah. "You're from Boston?" His skepticism was plain in his tone and raised brows.

In this bedraggled state with filthy buckskins, Micah certainly didn't look like a dandy from back east—or even a doctor for that matter. "I'm not Dr. Chastain; I'm only the one delivering the parcel."

Bowen nodded, then turned toward the door. "You make sure you stay put."

Minutes seemed to drag by before footsteps finally sounded in the hall. The first man to step in must be the doctor, for he didn't look like Isaac or his father. As the man approached his bed, weary lines marred his face, accenting the dark hollows under his eyes.

Micah knew that look well. He'd seen it in the mirror during the smallpox outbreak in Landsburg all those years ago.

Before saying a word, he pressed a solid hand to Micah's brow. "Fever's gone, that's good." Then he stepped back to level his gaze on Micah's face. "My good friend William Chastain sent you? How is he?"

*No.* He didn't want to have to share the sad news. But there was no choice for it. "He's . . . um, not well, sir. He died . . . on the way here." His voice strained to force out the words. "Wagon wreck."

"No." The doctor took a step back, the lines on his face sagging as though he was losing all strength. "How do you know?"

"I found them—him and his daughter with two others—on a mountain. Ingrid has a broken leg and ribs, but she's recovering."

"Where is she now?" Alarm strengthened Dr. Stanley's words.

"Three days back." At least, that's how long he thought he'd traveled. "With another woman and boy. She sent me on to deliver the vaccines and bring back help to carry her and the others the rest of the way."

Shuffling sounded as Isaac stepped forward. "We'll go for them. Can you tell us where?"

"I'll show you." Now that his fever was gone, he should be able to travel. Especially if they had animals to ride. He saw no scabs on his hands, so maybe his sickness had been influenza or the like. Or maybe God, in His great mercy, had healed Micah from the pit of his misery. *Thank you, Lord, for another chance.*

He needed to get to Ingrid and the others. To see them to safety and tell her everything that had changed inside him. But first he needed to make sure Dr. Stanley had help to begin inoculations. He turned his focus back to him. But the doctor's face had grown three shades paler, and one of his hands pressed against his chest.

"Sit down, Doctor." Micah motioned toward the edge of the bed.

The man obeyed, and his gaze landed on the bedside table, his thoughts clearly far away. "When I sent word of our outbreak, asking for vaccines, I thought he'd hire a courier. I never dreamed he'd try to bring them himself. And with his daughter."

Funny how one decision—or a string of small choices—had the power to change lives forever. Both for the bad, and for the good. Even in the midst of the tragedy of lost lives on that mountainside, as well as Ingrid's horrible injuries, he'd have never met her had their wagon not crashed. He'd have never come to know the brave, strong woman he'd traveled with these past weeks.

She may wish she never came into these mountains, but he couldn't bring himself to feel the same. Albeit, he did wish her father, maid, and driver still lived.

Dr. Stanley straightened and looked back at Micah. "We need to get Miss Chastain here. Is she in danger out there in the wilderness?"

Urgency pressed anew on Micah's chest. "They have a good campsite, but I need to get back to them." He looked up to Isaac. "Can we leave now?"

The man cleared his throat, then shot a look at the doctor. "It's already midafternoon. We could leave in the morning if Doc says it's all right."

The doctor scrubbed a hand over his face. "I've a dozen people in the clinic in various stages of the disease, and I need to get the people around here vaccinated. But it sounds like I also need to go along to treat her wounds."

Micah shook his head. "I set the leg and splinted it. She's healing." The man's heavy brows sunk low, giving evidence of his doubt. He forced out a better explanation. "I'm a doctor." Those words were still so hard to say.

Those brows surged upward. "You are?" His tone belied the doubt still on his face.

He needed to say more so the man would focus on the vaccinations. "I had a clinic in Landsburg, Indiana, for seven years before a smallpox epidemic killed my wife and daughter. I left doctoring and came to this territory." He struggled to meet the man's eyes. "Please. Stay here and vaccinate these people. That's why Ingrid sent me ahead to bring the box to you. When I come back, I'll help with what I can."

Dr. Stanley stroked his beard for a long moment, then released a sigh. "I'm sorry to hear about your family. And you're right. This town needs to be protected against that vicious disease. My own wife died from it several years back. The things she suffered"—his voice took on sad bitterness—"no one should ever have to endure such."

*Exactly.* Micah nodded.

The doctor turned to Isaac. "If his fever doesn't come back and he can keep food down, I think he'll be able to leave tomorrow." He looked back at Micah. "I'll send something for your pain."

As the men filed out of the room, Micah finally gave in to the tug of his eyelids, allowing them to drift shut. *Keep Ingrid and the others safe, Lord. They're in your hands.*

The next morning, he set off with Isaac Bowen and his father in the same wagon he'd ridden to town in, the wheels replaced with sleigh runners, as many people did in the winter. Randolph pointed out the road to their own log home about an hour outside of town. Then, a few hours farther, he turned his mule toward a brush shelter on the right. "We should stop and get yer things from here. This is where I found ye. Nigh on yer last breath, I think. Only by the Lord's mercy did ye come back to life."

Amen to those words. God had saved him through much these past years. Looking back over every snowstorm, every time of famine, every lonely day spent in despair and guilt, perhaps the Lord was saving him for a reason. Was that too much to hope?

He couldn't fathom what purpose, but the idea sent a thrill through his weary body. What if the best part of his life was still to come?

They slept on the trail that night, and with two hale and hearty men helping, setting up camp was easier than he ever remembered the task, even with the three mules to tend.

As best he could tell, they had a few more hours on the Mullan Road before they'd need to leave the trail to travel over-mountain. They'd park the wagon beside the road and ride the mules the rest of the journey.

Only a couple more days, and he'd be with Ingrid again.

Her image stayed constantly in his mind, whether he lay in the back of the wagon while they traveled or slept on his stack of furs by the fire. When he awoke the next morning, he glanced across the dancing flames of the campfire, searching for Ingrid.

Instead, his focus landed on a grizzled face, complete with scratchy gray beard, parted at the mouth to let out a steady stream of snores. He blinked as his mind scrambled to recall the man and the setting. To his right, Isaac sat on his sleeping pallet, a mug of coffee in his hand.

The man nodded at him, raising his cup in greeting. "Morning." A hint of a smile danced in his dark eyes. Almost as though he could read Micah's thoughts and well understood the dismay in finding his father in place of the lovely Ingrid Chastain.

"G'morning." Micah let his eyes drift shut again. If only he could sink back into the dream of her. But the sooner they set out today, the sooner he'd be able to see her in the flesh. To hold her. And, if the Lord allowed, to never part from her again.

Randolph didn't awaken easily, and once he stirred, he sat like a curmudgeon on his sleeping pallet, hair poking in every direction. Isaac appeared to know the magic to bring his father back to life, and after the older man downed two cups of coffee sludge and a bowl of beans, they set about packing camp.

The weariness weighting Micah's bones slowed him to half the speed of the other men, but at least he was up and moving. No fever, although he felt weak as a newborn chick.

As they started out, he sat upright in the back of the wagon so he wouldn't miss the turnoff from the trail. The gentle rocking of the sleigh made his eyes grow so heavy, he almost missed the cluster of trees that marked the spot where he'd found the road days before.

He sat up straight. "There. We turn off at those pines we just passed."

"Ho, there." Isaac reined in the team. "That's a spot we can leave the wagon. Shouldn't have much traffic through here, so I suspect it'll be safe enough."

Within a quarter hour, they were mounted on the mules and turning away from the road. Micah found himself riding an animal the men had borrowed from the livery in Settler's Fort, and the beast seemed to have earned its reputation for stubbornness honestly.

They rode until dusk settled over the landscape, and despite his exhaustion, the thought of stopping edged his nerves.

"How long did you say it took you to walk from their camp to the road?" Randolph asked as they sat around the campfire, eating beans once more.

"Almost three days. I'm hoping with the animals we can cut that in half. Get there tomorrow by dark." The notion of another night on the trail away from Ingrid made his insides clench.

The older man nodded. "Hope so."

Within a few minutes, Micah succumbed to his exhaustion, burrowing deep in his furs. *Be with Ingrid, Lord. Keep her safe until I see her again.*

It was his last coherent thought.

# TWENTY-SEVEN

*I*ngrid pressed the marker into place in Papa's Bible, then closed it, rubbing the leather binding with her gloved hands. His fingers had once gripped this same book, cradling it with the respect and devotion he'd taught her from her earliest memories.

Would Micah ever come to feel the same way? *Lord, be his strength. Show him that he can have a whole life again in you.*

Only Micah could make that choice, and she could never profess her love until he took that step, but every part of her longed for it. Not only for them to be together in this life, but for all eternity, too.

She tucked the book in its special place in her pack, then glanced around the camp. As soon as Joanna and Samuel returned from walking little Handsome, they could all snuggle under blankets out of the cold. This icy breeze slid relentless fingers under the edge of her coat, making the frigid night even more miserable.

Where were her friends, anyway? Joanna had said they might move Jackson's tether rope to fresh grazing, but they'd been gone for at least a half hour and the dark of night now draped the land like a thick shroud.

The crunch of footsteps on snow sounded from the trees, and she eased out a breath of relief. Within a moment, Joanna emerged into the glow of the firelight.

"There you are. I was wondering if you were lost in the woods." She added a teasing tone to her voice.

Joanna stepped close to the fire, reaching out to warm her hands near the blaze. "That wind blows right through my coat. It must be colder tonight than in weeks." She glanced up, then around the camp. "Where's Samuel?"

Ingrid sat straighter. "He's with you. Isn't he following you with Handsome?"

Joanna whirled, peering into the darkness behind her. "He was cold, so I sent him and the dog back to camp." She strode toward the trees, raising her voice to a yell. "Samuel!"

As panic surged in her own chest, Ingrid reached for her walking sticks and worked herself up to her feet. She couldn't help but wince at all the aching parts of her. The broken leg had resigned itself to a dull ache, and her other hip had joined the chorus, probably from all the extra work required with being up on the walking sticks so much.

And her arms. All the tender flesh stung where it had been rubbed raw. But still she limped forward, hobbling after Joanna as fast as she could move. From the sound of her calls, Joanna was quickly outpacing her.

Maybe the boy and dog were with Jackson. That was one of Samuel's favorite places, so perhaps he was snuggling against the donkey's coat.

She followed Joanna's calls to the new place she'd staked the donkey, but Joanna was just moving into the trees on the other side when Ingrid arrived. "Joanna, wait."

Her friend spun. "Did you find him?" The hope in her

question made Ingrid's chest squeeze. They had to find the pair—and quick. With this icy wind, the boy would be frozen before long.

She summoned a breath to think. "No. How long since you last saw him?"

Joanna wrapped her arms around herself. "I don't know, a quarter hour at least."

"And where was he?"

"Right here." Joanna motioned to the donkey. "I was tying Jackson." She spun back around. "I'm going to look near those boulders across the valley. He always wants to go play there."

Ingrid started after her. Should she follow in case Joanna needed help when she found her son? Or search in a different place?

She limped beside Joanna's tracks to the edge of the trees. Through the thick darkness, she could just see the swish of her brown skirt in the distance. Ingrid would never be able to keep up with her.

Scanning the area around them was almost impossible in this overcast sky, but she remembered most of the terrain. A mountain rose up to their right, dipping to a narrow valley before rising into the row of peaks opposite them where Joanna had gone. Maybe she should search along this nearest mountain. Micah had taken the boy there once or twice. Perhaps Samuel had wandered that way now. *What do I do, Lord?*

She felt no stirring in her spirit, but it seemed useless to follow Joanna, so she turned right and started hobbling forward. "Samuel! Handsome!" Her voice seemed to carry little farther than she could see in this murky blackness.

She reached the base of the mountain and paused to call again, then stilled as she listened for a response.

A sound gripped her attention. Was that a whimper?

"Samuel! Handsome!" She adjusted her hands on the walking sticks and limped toward the noise.

If only she had a lantern, or even a torch. But she had neither, nor the extra hand to hold such. The ground moved up into the base of the mountain, a place she'd not explored yet. Snow still covered much of this area, with bumps in the white blanket that might cover rocks or brush—or nothing at all.

There, along one side of the hill, a trail of prints marred the white. She moved toward them, ducking against the icy assault of the wind. There actually seemed to be three sets of marks. The short, sloppy lunges of a dog who hated snow. The other spaced farther apart with longer feet. Maybe a rabbit? And tracking on top of both of those sets were the tiny boot prints of a five-year-old boy.

Her heart quickened. She'd found them—at least the direction they'd gone.

Turning to face the opposite mountain where Joanna was searching, she raised her voice into the wind. "Joanna! I found their tracks! Come this way!" She'd keep calling every few minutes to guide her friend.

Heading up the same path the boy and animals had taken, she called the lad as she went. Her feet had gone numb, and it was so much effort to trudge through the thick snow. Her left pole slipped on a rock under the snow's surface, and she barely caught herself with the other stick and her splinted leg.

A spasm shot up from the bone. Micah had told her not to use that leg, and she'd been doing her best to obey. Mostly because when she did put weight on the limb, the pain returned, just like now. It was a wonder how long bones took to heal.

But it was a wonder they knit together at all. And a little gratitude was certainly in order. *Thank you for healing me, Lord.*

Another whine sounded in the distance. A little louder.

"I'm coming. Samuel, can you hear me?" The cry sounded like Handsome's, but why wouldn't Samuel answer, too? She positioned the walking sticks in a secure perch in the snow and limped forward.

Each step took her higher, the wrapped ends of the poles pressing deep into the flesh under her arms. Rocks poked above the snow like tombstones on a hillside cemetery.

Except not all graves were visible on this incline. Some lay just under the surface, knocking her unsteady supports from under her. Should she stop and wait for Joanna?

Her heart ached at the thought. She must be close to them now. And Samuel's lack of response concerned her more than she wanted to contemplate.

She stopped and called to Joanna again, then continued forward.

The animal tracks split around a crop of rocks stacked high on the edge of the mountain, as though remnants from a landslide. The prints that she assumed belonged to a hare turned right, veering higher up the mountain so they didn't scale the rocks. Handsome's and Samuel's marks bounded straight ahead, from one stone to the next, as far as she could see toward the top of the huge mound. She guessed they probably came down on the other side.

She'd be hard-pressed to scale the rocks piled before her, unless she crawled on her hands and dragged her braced leg behind her. If she tried that, though, she may well have frost-bite before she found the missing pair and returned to camp.

She could probably get herself up the hill where the hare had bounded, then once she was past the heap of stones, she could move back downhill to find the boy and dog.

The mountainside was steep, and she had to pull her right walking stick out from under her arm to use it as a staff. The position didn't support her injured left side very well, and pain shot through her leg and hip with each step.

She was sweating by the time she spanned the distance she'd been able to see from the place where the trails split, even though the glacial wind stung her face with each gust. Why had they wandered so far? Samuel knew better than to leave their camp area on his own, especially after dark.

Had Handsome run away to chase the rabbit and the boy followed after? That was so out of character for her little pup, who never willingly left her. Not since she'd nursed him with a pap feeder as a tiny pup, small enough to nestle in her hand. The knot in her stomach pulled tighter the farther she trekked. She had to find her little friend—both of them.

At last, she paused to catch her breath, then raised her face and called again. "Samuel! Handsome!"

The dog's cry came once more, definitely closer. Maybe only twenty strides or so into the darkness—normal strides, not her slow creeping ones.

"Come, boy." She made the kissing sound she sometimes used to call him.

The whine sounded again, but not any closer. Was he stuck somewhere that he couldn't come to her? Or was Samuel hurt and he wouldn't leave the boy's side? The tension across her shoulders pulled tighter.

*Lord, let him be all right.* Micah wasn't here to tend him.

She started forward again. Her foot hit a mound of snow that didn't give way under her step, sending her toppling forward onto her good knee. Her skirts softened the blow, but as she pulled herself back to standing, she could feel the icy wet through her stockings.

*Freezing.*

She had no choice but to hobble on, her teeth shivering in quick staccato. Over the mound of snow, over the hidden rocks. When she made it a dozen painful steps, she stopped to call them again.

The pup's whine was louder, more pitiful. She must be close. The pulse in her throat thumped harder, driving her onward.

Another few steps and she could hear the steady whimper of her faithful companion. She was close, almost near enough to see him through the darkness.

She strained for a glimpse, finally making out a massive form ahead of her. Her heart froze for an instant, until she realized the shape was a ledge, jutting out from the side of the mountain. Perhaps this was left over from the landslide; it was hard to tell in the snow and darkness.

Handsome loosed a yap, but the sound was coming from lower, just down the mountain.

She limped that direction, her poles slipping on the steep mountainside. "I'm coming, boy."

The slope was almost vertical, and with the splint on her right leg she couldn't bend the limb at all, which meant she had to walk sideways.

Without warning, a hole gaped in front of her, and she nearly slid over the edge. She screamed as she sat hard, digging her poles into the snow to stop herself from sliding down. Her pulse hammered in her throat as she came to a stop, her breath pumping hard at the close call.

Handsome's whine sounded again—from down in the hole. And this time another sound drifted up.

A little boy's moan.

"Samuel?" She scrambled around, shifting onto her belly and turning so she could see into the chasm.

Darkness yawned below, and it took a moment for her to make out a form. Samuel lay sprawled in the snow. Her throat squeezed tight.

A movement beside the boy caught her focus. A tiny black form jumping. Yapping.

"I'm coming. Keep him warm, boy." *Lord, don't let him be dead.*

She twisted back around so she could sit upright. Every movement was a monumental effort now that her entire body trembled from the cold. Samuel and Handsome must be near-frozen, too. They had to get back to the protection of camp and the heat of the fire.

Cupping her hands around her mouth, she screamed with every ounce of strength she had left. "Joanna! I've found them! Come quick!"

She still hadn't heard any response from her friend, but surely Joanna heard a cry that loud. She would come.

Until then, Ingrid had to get Samuel to wake up. If he lay in that icy snow much longer, the cold might be the death of him.

She leaned forward, trying to see down into the hole from her sitting position. She couldn't quite make out the boy. "Samuel. Can you hear me? Wake up, honey."

Without seeing his form, she couldn't tell if he stirred or not.

She propped her good foot on a bank of snow near the edge and used it to brace herself as she leaned farther forward. The muscles in her broken leg burned at the awkward angle, but she ignored the pain. Nothing mattered except saving those two. "Samuel, wake up. You have to get up."

A moan rose from below.

Her heart beat faster. "Samuel, can you hear me? That's right, wake up. You have to wake up."

She pressed her hands into the snow at the edge of the drop-off and peered into the darkness. Was he moving? Yes, his hand moved in the snow.

"Samuel, wake up. You can do this. Wake up." She infused every bit of urgency she could into her voice. If she could get him moving, he'd have a chance of staying alive until Joanna could help get him out. "Get up, honey. Get up." Every part of her strained toward the boy, as though she could lift him up by sheer force of will.

The snow bracing her foot gave way. She slid forward, and her hands grappled for purchase. Her fingers were numb from pressing in the snow, and nothing she gripped held firm.

Her splinted leg slid over the edge, the heavy wood dragging her forward. "No!" She clawed at the snow, grabbing a walking stick as she tried to keep from slipping farther. But the weight of her useless limb was too much.

She skidded downward, her attempts to stop herself as futile as her waning strength.

A scream slipped out as she dropped into empty air.

# TWENTY-EIGHT

*M*icah struggled to see through the frigid darkness, nudging his mule faster. He didn't dare push any harder in this rough terrain, but every instinct pressed him onward.

Randolph had wanted to stop at dusk, but they'd only had another hour or two before they should reach the women. Now, the trees lay just ahead that shielded him from the camp. Just down this slope and around the copse of woods.

Then he'd see Ingrid.

They reached the edge of the trees, and he reined his mount left to skirt the thick growth. This would be longer, but they could move faster if they weren't winding through low branches.

"Ingrid." He was close enough; she may be able to hear. And he didn't want to surprise her. The last thing they needed was to get shot by a nervous woman. "It's Micah. I've brought help." His breath formed an icy cloud around him.

No answer that he could hear. He kicked the mule harder.

As they rounded the edge of the woods, the brush shelter came into view ahead, outlined by the orange glow of a campfire. "Ingrid. Mrs. Watson." No figures moved around, but they were likely asleep. Safe.

The thought should ease the clamp of fear pressing on his chest. But it didn't.

He reined in his mule at the edge of camp, jumping down before the animal came to a stop. "Ingrid!" His bellow carried through the clearing, radiating into the trees.

He strode forward, scanning the campsite. No bodies curled up in the blankets. He pushed aside the furs that were piled under the shelter, just in case.

No one. The place was empty.

He turned, desperation welling inside him. "Ingrid! Mrs. Watson! Samuel!" Where would they have gone in the thick of night? With this bitter cold freezing everything, surely they hadn't been gone long.

His heart thudded in his chest as he strode toward the woods. Maybe they'd gone to the donkey. "Ingrid!" Every part of him longed to hear her sweet voice call back to him. He could imagine the sound of his name on her lips, wrapped in joyful wonder at his return.

A sound drifted from the trees, freezing him in his tracks. A woman's voice? He strained to hear and was preparing to call again when the voice sounded a second time.

"Mr. Bradley!"

He started into the woods, following the sound of Mrs. Watson's distant voice. Every few minutes he stopped to call, listening for the direction of her response.

She must be running. Something was wrong. The dread in his soul spread further through his limbs.

At last he saw a flicker of movement in the dark woods. "Mrs. Watson. Where are the others?"

She was breathing hard as she drew near, close enough to grab his arm. But it took a moment before she caught her breath enough to speak.

He clutched her elbow, every nerve inside him tensing to run. To help. "Where's Ingrid? And Samuel?"

She pointed back the way she'd come, panting. "They fell . . . in a ravine. Hurt . . . need rope."

*Dear Lord.*

He turned to find Isaac and Randolph behind him. The younger man spoke. "I'll get rope. Anything else?"

"Blankets. And a light, if you have one." Mrs. Watson was finally regaining her power to speak.

Isaac spun and ran back toward camp.

Micah gripped her arm. "Where are they? I'll see if I can start pulling them out."

She pointed the way she'd come. "Straight to the edge of the trees, then you'll see the tracks at the base of the mountain."

That was all he needed to know. He released her arm. "Make sure he gets what you need." Then he sprinted the way she'd pointed, dodging trees as he ran.

*Lord, save them. Don't let us be too late.*

When he emerged from the woods, it wasn't hard to find Mrs. Watson's tracks. At least one other person had walked this path, but the prints were going the other direction, away from the trees. And it wasn't hard to see the drag marks from walking poles and a splinted leg.

His heart surged in his chest. Ingrid had walked this way.

He took the path as fast as he dared, falling twice on the icy rocks buried just under the snow. As the mountainside grew steeper, it was a wonder Ingrid could have maneuvered this terrain. Had she hurt herself again? Reinjured the healing bones?

He pushed on, trying not to imagine what could happen to a woman with a broken leg on the side of this mountain. In the dark. With temperatures plummeting.

*Lord, please protect her.*

The trail neared a mound of stones, covered mostly by snow, but with enough of the rock face peeking out that it was clear these were remnants of a landslide. Ingrid's tracks veered up the mountain. How had she ever made her way up that incline?

He trekked upward, coming upon a spot where the snow was stirred, as if she'd either sat to rest or fallen—the second being more likely. A fresh batch of fear welled in his chest, making it hard to draw breath. How badly was she injured?

Through the darkness, he could see a dark mass, a bulk of snow that protruded differently than the rest of the mountainside. The tracks led him right up to the jut in the rock, and as he glanced down at the snow, a churned spot down the hillside stirred his gut into a full roil.

"Ingrid!" He screamed her name. His gaze followed the marks in the snow down the mountainside. The slope grew steeper as it faded into darkness.

She was down there. And Samuel, too.

"Here." Her voice sounded so much weaker than before. Yet she wasn't far away.

"I'm coming. Hold on." He half-slid down the gradient, bracing himself against the snowy ground as it steepened.

He skidded down part of the slope and barely caught himself at the edge of a steep drop-off. Sitting hard to keep from toppling, he landed in a heap in the icy snow, with something hard poking under him. He shifted to pull it out.

A long, straight pole. Ingrid's walking stick. This must be the ravine she was in.

"Micah?" Ingrid's muffled tone called up from below.

"Ingrid." He leaned forward, as far as he dared, peering through the murky darkness. "Where are you?"

"At the bottom of the mountain. I fell trying to get Samuel." Her words drained from her like the last few drops of oil from a jar. Slow and weary.

"How badly are you hurt?" His heart clutched his throat, nearly strangling him with his need to get down to her. To hold her. To make her well again.

"I . . . don't know. I'm cold. My leg hurts. But it did before, too."

"Is it rebroken?" He strained to hear the true answer in her breathing and moans. The words she wasn't saying.

"I'm not sure."

Which meant it might be. He scrubbed a hand over his face. "And the boy, how is he?"

"I can't get him to wake up. He just groans. I'm trying to keep him warm."

He had to get them both out of there. "Are the boards in your splint still intact? Or did they crack in the fall?" Getting her up would be no easy task, but worse if they had to worry about the broken bones moving, too.

"No. It doesn't feel like they broke."

"How far down are you?" He couldn't see anything in the murky darkness below.

She was quiet for a moment. "Maybe twice as tall as I am."

He eased up to his knees. "Mrs. Watson and the men

traveling with me are coming with rope and blankets. I'm going to see if there's a spot that isn't so deep."

"Hurry." Her voice seemed to be growing weaker.

*Dear Lord. Help us. Please.* Only God could bring both of them out of this alive.

# TWENTY-NINE

Ingrid fought the shaking that consumed her body, clutching tighter to Samuel's little body. Every part of her ached from the cold, and her mind felt buried in snow.

"Ingrid, is the dog down with you?"

Her hand went to the ball of fluff huddled into her side. He was shaking almost as badly as she was. "Yes."

"How did you get all the way out here?" Micah's voice wrapped around her, soft and gentle like a blanket, tugging her further into the fog.

"I don't . . ." How had she gotten here? Handsome licked her chin, nudging a bit of memory through her dulled mind. "Samuel and Handsome were missing. I found them in this hole."

"Is the dog hurt?"

Had she checked that? She couldn't force the icy fog in her brain to clear enough to remember. She raised her head from the bed of snow to look at him. But she couldn't get a good angle, so she worked her elbow underneath her. Her back ached all the way down to her hips, and a dull pain stabbed her thigh.

She gritted her teeth and rubbed the dog. Her fingers couldn't feel the fur that should be soft against her skin. Then she realized she wore gloves. She couldn't feel the sensation of the leather, either.

Handsome didn't have blood anywhere, and he didn't act in pain, except for the shivering.

She sank back against the snow, letting her head loll and her eyes drift shut. She was so tired. More than she could ever remember being. Ever.

"Ingrid?"

Micah's voice pulled her eyes open. Had she dreamed it?

"Ingrid, are you there? Speak to me."

Not a dream. She tried to answer, but her mouth wouldn't move the way she intended. Finally, she forced her lips open. "I'm . . . here." The words sounded so garbled, she tried again. "I'm here." That was better.

"And the dog? Is he hurt?"

She glanced at the pup. She'd checked him, hadn't she? If only she could make her thoughts move through the sludge in her mind. "I don't think . . . I don't think he's hurt. He's shaking."

"All right, love. We're going to get you up from there. The others should be here soon with rope to pull you out. Keep talking to me."

Micah. Hearing him again was like drinking tea with sweet cream—soothing and warm and so delicious. She let her eyes drift shut, soaking in the melody of his voice.

"Ingrid!" He was yelling at her.

"What?" Why was he angry?

"I asked how long you've been down there. Do you remember?"

How long? She looked around, trying to make sense of the snow and darkness around her. Nothing seemed right.

She let her head fall back and her eyes close again. "I don't know." All she knew was she'd like to sleep for days.

Every part of Micah wanted to climb down the cliff and take Ingrid in his arms. Something was wrong with her. Very wrong.

Her words slurred like a man on a three-day bender, and she seemed to have trouble remembering. Had she hit her head in the fall? Or had she lain there so long she was freezing into unconsciousness? How frozen was Samuel if he'd been there even longer?

He squeezed his fists to keep from doing something that would make the situation worse. But if Isaac didn't come soon, he'd have to do something. Maybe he could lower himself over the edge and drop the last few feet. As long as he made sure she wasn't beneath him, that should work fine. Then he could assess her injuries and keep her warm.

A distant thumping stilled his thoughts. Footsteps.

*Thank you, Lord.* He leaned over the side and called to Ingrid again. "Ingrid, help is here. We're going to pull you up. Can you tie a rope around you?" He might need to jump down after all, to get her strapped tightly enough to hoist. Would Isaac be strong enough to pull them up? Maybe with his father's help. It wouldn't be easy with nothing to brace against.

The man appeared through the darkness, clutching an armful of harness and blankets. "There wasn't a long enough rope, so we brought the donkey harness."

"That should work. Ingrid's barely awake, and the boy's not conscious at all. I need to go down to strap them in the leather." Should he throw a cover down? Might be best to focus on the harness first. The blankets wouldn't be as helpful if they became wet.

"Ingrid?" She hadn't answered his last question.

Silence drifted up from below.

Fear clutched at his throat. "Ingrid!" He barked the word so it would penetrate her fog. And because his emotions were running rampant. She couldn't let herself fade away. She couldn't leave him.

"What?" The soft voice below sounded sleepy. Almost comatose.

"I'm coming down to tie the harness around you." He glanced at Isaac.

The man nodded, his mouth set in a grim line.

They set to work untangling the lines and shifting over so he didn't drop down on Ingrid. Mrs. Watson and Randolph came panting down the slope, and he relayed their plan in a few quick statements.

"Talk to them. Keep Ingrid talking back." He motioned Mrs. Watson to a safe place by the edge.

She dropped to her knees and called down. "Ingrid, how are you both?"

Within moments, he was dangling over the edge of the cliff, hanging by his elbows dug into the snowy surface above. *Lord, don't let me fall on a rock. Keep me safe so I can help Ingrid.*

With the prayer on his lips, he loosed his hold and dropped.

The fall lasted longer than he expected, and his feet hit the ground with a force that sent shooting pain through his ankles. He tumbled onto his side, pausing only long enough to make sure nothing was broken. His legs felt intact.

"Ingrid." He pushed to his feet and turned to search for her in the darkness.

The dog whined, drawing his focus to a dark mound. He sprinted to her side.

"Ingrid." It felt like his heart cried out as he found her face. He pulled a glove off so he could check her temperature. Her skin felt nearly icy.

She opened her eyes, a groggy frown contorting her features. "Micah?"

"We have to get you warm, love. And out of this cold place." He reached for the boy she was curled around. The lad's skin was icy, but the pulse at his neck still thumped. Micah ran his hand quickly around the boy's skull. A good-sized bump stood out above his temple. That might explain at least some of the reason he wouldn't wake up. But the cold was likely the bigger culprit at this point.

Every minute mattered for these two.

The dog nudged him, drawing Micah's focus. "Hey, boy. We're going to get you all out of here." He stroked the pup as he moved down to Ingrid's injured leg. The wood did seem intact, which would make it much easier to lift her out.

"I'm dropping the harness down." Isaac's voice sounded from above.

"Good." When the leather tumbled to the snow, he grabbed it and straightened the pieces he'd be using.

Samuel should go up first. He was by far the colder of the two.

Micah lifted the lad from his nest at Ingrid's side, then laid him on the harness and tied knots in the leather to hold him secure.

Then he looked upward. "Ready to lift Samuel up."

"Lifting him now," Isaac's voice called from above, steady and sure.

"Be careful." Mrs. Watson's tone strained. He couldn't imagine what torment she must be enduring.

Or rather, he *could* imagine. And his heart broke again as he lifted the boy.

*Keep him alive, Lord. Don't let her lose him. Please.*

As Samuel was lifted over the ledge, Micah turned back to Ingrid. "Are you awake, love?" He dropped down beside her and reached for her hand to rub it. She may still lose an appendage to frostbite, but he'd do everything he could to keep from it.

A moment later, Isaac's voice sounded again. "Dropping the harness back down."

When the leather piled nearby, Micah reached to untangle the straps and position them. Now to get Ingrid moved.

He shifted back to her side. "I'm going to lift you up for a minute to get you strapped in the harness."

"Mmm . . ." She didn't open her eyes, but at least she responded.

Slipping his hands under her the way he had so many times to lift her from the cart, he couldn't help taking a moment to hold her close, breathing in her sweet scent.

She snuggled into him, releasing a soft sigh. A sound that sent a surge of warmth through his chest.

A warmth that reignited his urgency. He had to get her back to camp where he could care for her. He would not lose this woman who had become his heart.

*Lord, please don't take her away.* But God had once taken

away the family that meant everything to him. Who was to say He wouldn't think it best to take Ingrid, too?

A paralyzing fear gripped him, turning his chest as cold as ice. *No.* He'd put his trust in the Lord. Given his entire life to Him. Promised to be content without Ingrid, if that be His will. But in his moment of surrender, he'd only thought of Ingrid walking away, going back to her old life and choosing a man better suited for her.

He'd not planned for Ingrid to die.

He dropped to his knees in the icy wetness, her snow-covered body still clutched in his arms. *I don't think I can handle this if you let her die. Not Ingrid, too.*

Tears burned his eyes, and he squeezed them shut. *Please, Lord. Don't do this.*

*Trust me. My plan for you is good.* The words whispered through his mind, impressing on his heart.

Trust God. What if that plan included Ingrid's death? How could that be good? He clung to her, warring inside himself. He needed to keep moving, to get her back to camp.

But why would it matter what he did? God had control over whether Ingrid lived or died. If the Almighty wanted to take her, nothing Micah did could stop Him.

A sob surged to his throat, squeezing out his breath, spiraling from the pain pressing hard on his chest. "I don't think I can do this, God. Not again."

*Trust me.*

"I want to. I do. But I can't do it without help." Could he truly release Ingrid into God's hands? Accept that whatever God chose would really be best? For her? For him?

Tears flowed freely down his face, freezing his cheeks as the wind whipped around them.

He had to do this. Had to release everything to the Lord. He'd never have peace if he held back.

"She's yours, Lord." He raised his face to the heavens, Ingrid cradled in his arms—an offering. "If you want to take her away, she's yours. And I am, too."

A breeze swept over him, not as frigid as before. Drying his tears, purging the pain from his heart. Leaving behind a certainty.

A fragile healing.

Not as strong as he'd need to be to withstand the tempests in life, but a start.

He inhaled a long breath, taking in as much of the Father's strength as he could. "All right, then."

He dropped his gaze back to Ingrid's face, her lovely, delicate features. He could see the strength in them now, a strength he'd missed in those early days. A strength she'd need in order to come back from this frozen condition.

"Let's get you back to camp." He wanted to press a kiss to those lips, but there would be a better time later.

He laid her on top of the harness, then worked to fasten some of the buckles and tie a knot in another section to create a sling for her. Her head would dangle if she didn't hold it up.

Taking hold of her shoulders, he gave them a little shake. "Ingrid. I need you to wake and hold on to this strap." Maybe that would help her stay alert.

Her eyelids rose slowly, flickering. She gave him a groggy stare.

"Hold on to this strap and keep your head up." He placed her hands on the leather.

She nodded and seemed to be trying to close her fingers around the rein—a good sign.

The dog waited patiently beside them, and Micah reached for him next. "I'm going to put the little shadow in your lap to ride up with you." The pup tucked himself in where Micah placed him. Ingrid didn't seem to be in a condition to hold the dog, but he should be fine as long as he didn't try to jump.

He straightened and looked up. "She's ready, Isaac. Hoist her up while I lift."

When the man pulled the leathers tight, he slipped his hands under Ingrid to assist with the effort. The distance up was at least twice his height, maybe farther.

*Lord, only you can make this happen without more injury. Don't let the straps break. Give Isaac and Randolph strength. Keep their footing secure.* Because if either of the men on the ledge above lost his footing and slipped over the edge, they'd all be in more trouble than they could handle.

But God could handle it. He had to believe that.

His pulse raced in his throat—a hundred beats for every handbreadth they raised her. At least it seemed that way.

She looked to be struggling to keep her head raised, and she mostly accomplished the feat as she was lifted higher and higher. Past the reach of his hold.

Out of his hands.

*Dear God, keep her safe.*

Isaac grunted with each heave as he bore the full weight of her. And Micah didn't breathe again until the man gripped Ingrid's arm, rolling her up and over the edge of the cliff.

Only Isaac's leg could be seen from below, as he must have collapsed beside her. His ragged breathing rang loud in the darkness.

Next would be Micah's turn. He stepped close to the rock wall, touching the stone and as he peered at it, searching for footholds. The side was vertical, or at least mostly so. There were a few places he could hook a toe into, but most of the way he would have to be lifted by Isaac. Could the man do it?

He was no stranger to physical activity; one look at him made that obvious. But Micah wasn't scrawny himself, and Isaac would only be as strong as his footing in the ice and snow above.

*You're going to have to handle this one, too, Lord.* But in truth, didn't God handle every step? Every breath. Every moment they lived.

He inhaled a deep, steadying lungful of air, then released it. And when Isaac lowered the harness again, Micah was ready.

# THIRTY

*I*ngrid was barely aware of the jarring through her body as someone carried her. Strong arms, moving swiftly.

She couldn't seem to break through the shroud around her mind. And she was cold. So frigid her body had stopped shaking. Was she frozen solid?

Moving took too much effort. Thinking was too hard. She'd rather sleep, but the jarring footsteps underneath her wouldn't let her rest.

Voices drifted around her. Calling. The deep intonation of a man. Then a woman. A child? She was lowered to the ground—a hard ground, unforgiving. But maybe now she could sleep.

Then people were all around her. Tugging at her arms, her hands, her feet. A shot of pain seared up her leg, almost jerking her eyes open.

The voices continued, flowing around her, melting together. One alone stood out. A low murmur. An earnest tone.

Micah. His voice called to her, pulling her from the haze. She struggled to make out his words.

"Gentle with her hands. When the blood flow is coming

back, it's easy to damage the skin. That's right. Warm water works well, too. But not hot. When those rocks are ready, we'll wrap her feet up before we put the stones in."

Not all his words made sense, but she could gradually feel a burning sensation in her feet. Or perhaps more like the stinging of a dozen wasps.

She winced and tried to pull her feet back, away from the pain. Fire shot through her left thigh, bringing the clarity of mind she'd been searching for.

"She's awake." A man's voice spoke, just above her. A gravelly voice she didn't recognize. An older fellow, maybe.

Ingrid focused her gaze and found a lined face that matched the voice, but she'd never seen him before. Where was she?

She tried to speak, but her face felt too stiff to move. After working to loosen her mouth, she tried again. "Who?"

Another face appeared in her vision. Nearer, and so wonderfully familiar the burn of tears stung her eyes. "Micah." When had he returned? She barely remembered the dream where he'd talked to her from a cliff on the side of a mountain. She squinted at him, trying to remember. "What happened?"

"You and Samuel fell down a hole in the mountain and nearly froze to death. Thank God Mrs. Watson found you in time and we were able to pull you both out."

*Samuel.* She remembered his quiet, still body as she did her best to warm him. The snow had been so very cold. The memory of it made her shiver, even now. "How is he?" She almost couldn't bring herself to look at Micah's face. Could the boy survive all his body endured?

"Warming up and finally awake." He glanced over to where the boy must be. "His mother and Isaac are working on him."

"Isaac?" She looked that direction for the older man she'd first seen.

"Isaac Bowen and his pa, Randolph, came with me to bring you all to town. I'm more thankful than I can say they were here to help."

"Me too." Ingrid winced as the wasp stings began in her fingers. The pain intensified in her feet, and she had to grit her teeth to keep from crying out.

"I know your limbs are aching now. The pain may get worse over the next hour before it gets better, but the hurting is actually a good thing." Micah shifted down to her feet, where he worked gentle fingers over her toes.

She'd seen him in this position before as he'd rubbed her feet, kneading them to help her blood flow with the broken leg. He'd never shied away from anything that would help her, even if it caused momentary pain.

The sight of him broke through her defenses, and tears slipped down her cheeks, trailing into her ears.

He saw them, special man that he was, and moved to her side. "Oh, Ingrid." Her name had never been cherished so much as the way he spoke it. His hands moved to her face, his thumbs stroking away the tears. She couldn't seem to stop them, though, even when they blurred her vision of his wonderful face. Those piercing eyes.

He lowered his face, and for a second she thought he would bring his lips to hers, even with people all around. Her mouth watered at the thought, her own lips coming alive. But he pressed a kiss to her forehead, his breath bringing a blessed warmth.

When he pulled back, he didn't raise all the way up. Just far enough so he could look in her eyes. "God kept you alive for me." She could see his gaze now, the way it shimmered. Was that grief? Wonder? She couldn't tell for sure, but it looked more like love with every passing moment.

The same feeling that dwelled inside her.

The tears started afresh. She wanted to touch him. To hold him. To be held by him, cradled in his arms.

Though her fingers resisted, she made them curl. Brought her hands up to touch his chest, but his coat seemed an impenetrable barrier between them.

Micah closed his hand over hers, his strength covering her.

She needed to say something. To let him know how much she'd missed him. How thankful she was that he'd returned.

Sniffing away the tears again, she worked her mouth to speak. "Micah." It was the only word she could get out before another rush of emotion swarmed her.

"What is it, love?" He stroked her tears away again with the hand that cupped her face.

Did he truly love her? The thought seemed too much. *You are so good to me, Father.* As the tears flowed freely, a smile took over her face, bending and freeing the muscles. Despite the pain, she wanted to laugh. To sing and dance and fling her arms around him.

Instead, she settled for squeezing his hand that held hers, and telling him what she could no longer hold back. "I love you, Micah. I love you."

As exhausted as he was, Micah slept in bits and pieces, rising every hour or so to replace the hot stones under Samuel's and Ingrid's furs. Both appeared to have warmed finally, but they had to be kept toasty for their bodies to recover fully.

Mrs. Watson slept with her son tucked against her, and the connection probably did him more good than anything.

Micah turned away from the sight. It was impossible to express how thankful he was the boy had survived, but it resurrected the ache in his chest once again. He could still remember seeing Ella curl around Rachel in that same way.

He looked at Ingrid, focusing once again on the steady rise and fall of her blankets as she breathed. So beautiful she was, even with only the top of her face peeking out from under the blankets and furs.

He must have fallen asleep, sitting there against the corner of her shelter, for he woke upright, a sharp pain in his neck. The little pup lay stretched out beside his leg, the position the dog usually claimed beside Ingrid. He rubbed a hand along the animal's back. He didn't seem injured from the ordeal the night before—another miracle.

Daylight was creeping over their camp, but none of the others had stirred, except Isaac. The man sat by the fire, a cup in his hand that must contain coffee. He watched Micah through eyes that gave no evidence of their adventure in the night. Just his typical relaxed pose.

Micah straightened and tried to unfold himself. Every muscle and nerve in his body protested the movement. When he finally worked himself to standing, the dog rose, too, and stretched, then moved toward Ingrid to collapse again in the furs.

Isaac held a cup out to him. "Coffee?"

The word alone made his mouth salivate for the rich brew. A drink he'd not had in years, except for these past few days with the Bowen men. "Thanks." He took the cup and bent to pull the carafe from the coals. Isaac must have added more wood to the fire, for the flames leapt in a healthy blaze.

He settled in across from the man to drink. There was much he should be doing, but there would be time for it once his body came fully awake. Besides, he needed to say a few things.

He sipped a burning swallow of the bitter brew, working to keep a grimace from his face. At last, he eased out a long breath, letting the drink work its magic inside him.

Then he turned to the man across the fire. "I appreciate your help last night. This entire trip."

Isaac only nodded, his gaze wandering around the camp. "It's a wonder they've survived so well here on their own."

Did he think Micah had been imprudent to leave them? Possibly, but they'd weighed the options, and no choice had been without danger. "Perhaps I shouldn't have left them, but Mrs. Watson was still recovering from an illness and wasn't ready to travel yet. The vaccines had to get to Settler's Fort, and this was the best camp we'd found for a while."

Isaac studied him. "Didn't say I faulted you. Just that they've done well to come through."

His manner was hard to read. He seemed so matter of fact. Maybe his words held no deeper meaning. Micah should just take them as simple fact.

He took another sip of coffee and nodded. "You're right."

Isaac was quiet for a few minutes, but then he broke the silence. "Think they'll be able to leave out this morning, or will they need a day?" He nodded toward the brush shelter and its inhabitants.

"If you don't mind waiting a few hours 'til the sun comes out and they all get a warm meal, I think we could leave today. The sooner we get them to a warm building, the better." Samuel needed rest, which he could get in the wagon for now, and Ingrid needed to be in a cozy house with her leg properly cared for.

The other man nodded, then stood in an easy motion. "Let us know when you're ready. I'm off to tend the animals."

As silence settled back over the camp, he looked to the brush shelter, finding Ingrid with practiced ease. Her eyes were open, watching him with those big brown orbs.

The pulse inside him quickened, and he couldn't help the smile that tugged his mouth. "How do you feel this morning?"

Her own mouth softened into that wispy smile that made his heart squeeze. "Better, I think."

She pushed the blankets back to sit upright, and it was impossible to miss the grimace on her face, though she tried to hide it.

Micah stood and moved to her side, kneeling so he could face her. "I haven't heard how things went the rest of the time I was gone."

A bit of color slipped into her face, and she glanced at the other woman and boy, who were still sleeping. The dog must be buried in the furs somewhere. "Nothing so exciting as last night." Then she looked back at him, concern welling in her eyes as she reached out to touch his arm. "What of you?"

"I made it." He closed his hand over hers. "A little fever along the way, but God brought me through."

Twin lines furrowed her brow. "Was that your second night out? After the snow?"

He worked the days in his mind, just to make sure. "That's when it started. How did you know?"

Her eyes drifted shut as she breathed in what sounded like a steadying breath. Then she opened her eyes and searched him with her gaze. "The Lord pressed me with a burden for you, even more than normal. He woke me in the night to pray for you. I didn't know why or what exactly I was praying for, but I knew it involved your healing."

Her words penetrated him like an arrow, working through to his core. Had her prayers been what delivered him? It was God who delivered him, he knew that without a doubt now. But why had the Almighty needed Ingrid's prayers? Unless the Lord was knitting the two of them together, even through illness.

He moved her hand to his lap and fingered the fabric wrapping with both his thumbs. Then he told her the details of that night, the following day of walking, falling exhausted in the brush shelter the Lord provided. Randolph finding him and the feverish haze of riding into town. Then finally waking from the fever in the doctor's home.

Urgent excitement replaced the worry on her face as he mentioned Dr. Stanley. "Did you give him the vaccines? Were we in time?"

Love for this woman swelled in his chest. Her first thought was always of others. "I gave him the vaccines. He had a clinic full of people suffering from the disease." His chest ached at the memory of the rows of people lying on bed pallets, lesions marking their faces and hands. He scrubbed a hand through his hair. "He needs help."

She let out a long breath, as though she'd been holding it all these weeks they'd been traveling. "I'll help him." Her gaze dropped to their hands, but her eyes seemed distant, as though her thoughts were a hundred miles away. Or maybe a few days' ride away, in a little town called Settler's Fort.

# THIRTY-ONE

*I*ngrid." Micah reached for her other hand, too. "I plan to help him, too."

She raised her eyes to his, searching. She must have heard the weight in his tone, or maybe she knew what a difficult step this would be for him.

Swallowing to summon moisture into his suddenly dry mouth, he searched for the right words to begin.

He cleared his throat. "I've had a lot of time to think during these last few days. The times I wasn't delirious with fever, that is." Her cautious gaze softened at his light words. Good.

"There are two things I've come to a clear understanding about: things I want and things God seems to be calling me to. The first is more the Almighty's pushing than my desire." He let a grin touch his mouth before he forced out the words that were harder than any he had to say. Almost any. "I think it's time I resume doctoring. Officially."

The joy spreading over her face made his decision worth every moment of angst. "That's wonderful, Micah. God's given you such a talent; I'm grateful you're going to use it." In the midst of the happiness in her expression, there was still something like longing. At least, he hoped that's what she felt.

A longing to match his own.

Cradling her hands in his, he looked into her fathomless brown eyes. "The other thing I want even more than that, Ingrid, is to be your husband. To have you by my side, come what may. Whether in Settler's Fort assisting Dr. Stanley, or in Boston, or any place you wish to go."

He swallowed as emotion clogged his throat. "I never thought I'd love again. . . . I didn't want to. But then God brought me to that wagon wreck on the side of the mountain. And what I thought was one more curse from the Almighty was actually His way of blessing me . . . so much more than I deserve." His eyes burned as the depth of that truth swept through him.

And even if God deemed it best for Ingrid's path to separate from his, he would always be thankful for the way the Lord used this courageous woman to bring him back to life.

Tears pooled in Ingrid's eyes, magnifying their depths. "Micah." She seemed to struggle with the word. Was she trying to find a kind way to send him away?

But her lips formed a tremulous smile, lighting her face so she almost glowed. "I prayed you felt that way. But I'm not sure I really thought it would happen."

She looked so beautiful, every part of her, with that smile accenting her delicate features—and those eyes. They soaked him in, capturing him so he'd be happy never looking away.

They drew him nearer, and he felt the warmth of her breath before even realizing he'd moved closer. Close enough to kiss.

Her eyelids dropped closed, and he narrowed the distance, touching his mouth to hers in a contact that sent shivers all the way through him.

*This woman* wanted to marry him. At least, that's what she'd been saying, right?

He pulled away just enough to ask, "That was a yes to wedding me, right?"

She giggled against his lips. "Yes."

He closed her in again, letting his kiss share the joy that word inspired.

The sounds of whispering broke through his fervor, pulling him back. Ingrid seemed to catch the sound, as well, and they both turned to see Mrs. Watson still tucked under the blankets with little Samuel. She held one hand out like a shield to keep her son from seeing their kiss.

Mother and lad were clearly awake and whispering behind that shielding palm.

"Oh, Joanna. I'm sorry." Ingrid's face reddened all the way to her forehead, and she ducked away from him.

He couldn't help a chuckle. "Yes, we do apologize." But he couldn't be the least bit sorry about what had just transpired. "Have you been awake long enough to hear the news, or should we repeat it?"

Ingrid's gaze jerked to him, eyes widening as though she couldn't believe what he'd just said.

Mrs. Watson lowered her hand enough to peer over it— as if to make sure the view was safe—then dropped her arm and sat upright. "We're happy for you both. It's the perfect match."

As she pulled Ingrid into a hug, he pushed to his feet. Best get food started so they could head out. The sooner they reached Settler's Fort, the sooner their new life could begin.

⋅‹─◦═◦─›⋅

Once again, Ingrid was riding in the little cart, pulled by the ever-faithful Jackson. Samuel lay in her lap, covered in blankets and furs, still exhausted from his harrowing adventure.

Even though she was in the same position as all those weeks they'd traveled before, this stretch of the journey felt so different, with three mules plodding in front of them. Joanna sat atop one and the two Mr. Bowens rode the others.

Micah strode beside Jackson, looking back every few minutes to make sure she was comfortable. Ever her champion.

And soon to be her husband.

The thought sent giddy shivers through her anew each time she let the words slip into her mind. How long would they need to wait? She had no idea what the situation would be like in Settler's Fort.

Micah said the doctor had at least a dozen people suffering from the disease in his clinic. Were those the only people ill? Had the doctor quarantined them in time to keep the disease from spreading?

So much she didn't know.

And when the outbreak was over, would they need to build a home? He likely wouldn't have an excess of funds, since he'd lived in the wilderness for so long. But they had Papa's money, so that wouldn't be a concern. Getting the money to this territory might be. As best as she could remember, Dr. Stanley had to send his request by messenger to Helena, where it could be telegraphed to them in Boston. Money would need to be sent that same way. Could they get to Helena in the winter? She had no idea the distance.

*So much she didn't know.*

She breathed in a long breath and with her exhale sent up a prayer for patience. *Help me wait on you, Lord.*

For three days they traversed the mountains, covering terrain every bit as treacherous as any they'd traveled thus far. Ingrid clung to the boy with one hand and the side of the cart with her other as the donkey trudged forward.

When they stopped to eat midway through the third day, an icy wind swept across the mountainside, chilling the air more with each minute. Gray clouds hung low in the sky, the same clouds she'd seen every other time it had snowed on this journey.

Micah pointed out across the valley below them. "See the patch of trees on the far hill? The Mullan Road runs through them. The wagon is parked just off the trail. Hope we make it there before the snow hits."

"Is Jackson gonna ride in the wagon with us?" Samuel piped up from his seat on a rock beside the younger Mr. Bowen. The boy seemed to have found a new hero in the man and didn't often leave his side. "His legs are so little, he won't be able to keep up with the big donkeys."

"You better not let Dandy hear you call him a donkey." Mr. Bowen bent close to the boy, as if sharing a secret. "He thinks he's special 'cause he's a mule." That last bit was spoken in a stage whisper.

The lad wrinkled his nose. "I didn't think he mattered about stuff like that. Don't tell him I said it."

Ingrid slid a glance at Joanna to see if she caught the interchange. She was watching her son with such a soft expression on her face, it made Ingrid's chest constrict. Would she and Micah one day have a babe to love as much as Joanna cherished her boy?

She couldn't stop her focus from sliding to that man, who

sat beside her, listening to the elder Mr. Bowen relay a tale about a fierce winter he'd experienced years back. She had the perfect view of Micah's profile, the strong contours of his face so beautiful in their perfection. So ruggedly handsome, just looking at him made it hard to breathe.

*Lord, if it's not too much to ask, I'd love to have a son who looks exactly like him.* Those dark eyes would be as striking on their boy as they were heart-stopping on this man.

As though he could read her thoughts, he turned to her. Gazing into her soul with those piercing eyes. The corners of them crinkled in a gentle smile. She could never get enough of his smiles.

In fact, that just may be her new goal in life—to draw out as many of his smiles as she could.

He raised a brow. "You look like you're thinking mischievous thoughts."

She almost laughed as she slipped her hand in his. "Perhaps. But nothing you need to worry about." Loving this man would be pure pleasure.

"Are you sure you folks don't wanna stop off and rest a spell? We can take you into town come mornin'."

Randolph made the thought sound so tempting, Micah shot a glance at Ingrid before answering. With a light snow still falling, maybe they'd be content to stay the night at the Bowen cabin where they could all get warm and dry.

But she was already shaking her head. Of course she'd feel an urgency to see how the people fared in Settler's Fort.

He turned back to Randolph. "We appreciate the offer, but I

think we need to push on tonight." He looked to Mrs. Watson and the boy to make sure he hadn't spoken too hastily.

She nodded her agreement. It seemed they were all ready to settle into a permanent place. At least, something that felt more permanent than a campsite.

"Alrighty then." Randolph raised a hand in farewell as the wagon rolled forward, leaving him and the donkey and cart at the Bowen's home outside of town.

Samuel clambered to the back edge of the wagon, waving his good arm. "Bye, Jackson. We'll see you in a few days."

"Careful, son. Don't fall out." Joanna gripped the boy's shoulder just as the wagon hit a bump that would have knocked him sideways.

As Isaac drove the wagon on, Micah settled back against the creaking side. With Ingrid nestled into him, the feeling that swept through him was better than a warm cabin in a snowstorm.

As the buildings of Settler's Fort appeared in the distance, he could feel her shoulders begin to stiffen. Was she worried about what they'd find? Or meeting Dr. Stanley?

He tightened his hold around her—not much, just enough for her to feel his presence. His support.

She looked up at him, eyes searching. She didn't speak, though, and he craved to know what concerned her. Wanted to slay whatever she feared.

"Do you want to go straight to the doctor's clinic? Or find lodging first?" His voice rumbled between them.

"I'd like to see Dr. Stanley first. I want to know what's happening."

She must be worried about the people. He met her look, letting her see his own resolve. "Whatever we find, we'll face it together."

Her chin bobbed and she looked away. "I just hope we're in time. I don't want Papa's sacrifice to be in vain."

His chest ached for her. For the loss she'd endured. For the price she'd had to pay in all this. He couldn't take it away. Couldn't change the past. All he could do was be there for her in the future.

He lifted her chin with his finger so she looked at him again. "God has a plan in this. He didn't take your father in vain, and He's guiding us even now. We need only to make sure we follow His leading."

A tender smile brushed her face, softening her eyes. "When did you become so wise?"

He returned her smile, the love in her expression making him sure of what he already knew—there wasn't much he wouldn't do for this woman. "I think it was somewhere between the fever on the trail and thinking I might lose you in the bottom of that ravine."

She reached for his free hand and slipped her fingers through his, then laid her head on his shoulder. "You're God's way of showing His love for me."

Her words brought a lump to his throat, and he tucked her more closely into his side. It was almost too much to fathom how God had worked in their lives to bring them to this point.

*Thank you, Lord. For everything.*

And for the first time in his life, he meant those words with every part of his being.

# THIRTY-TWO

*D*r. Stanley was just like Papa described him—a big man and an easy friend. Papa hadn't mentioned the heavy graying in his beard or the fact he walked with a limp as he stepped out of his front door to greet them. Were those more recent occurrences?

Ingrid handed Handsome down to Samuel, then worked to climb down from the wagon herself—with Micah's help.

The doctor moved close and took her hand. "Miss Chastain?" He spoke the words with a depth of emotion that brought on the same in her own chest.

"Yes." She met his gaze and her heart ached at the sadness there.

"I'm so sorry to hear about your father's passing. The news grieves me more than I can express." He closed his other hand over hers.

"Thank you. He is missed, but I know he wouldn't count it a loss if the vaccinations have helped the people here." She studied his face for an answer to the question she hadn't quite asked.

He nodded. "It's been a rough outbreak, but I think we're on the tail end of it. With the vaccines your father sent, I pray we can keep any more from falling to the disease. We've lost twelve, with two more who may leave us still. But the rest are recovering. I've vaccinated most of the people in town, but I'm still working to reach those in the outlying areas." He raised her hand, his eyes carrying an endless depth of sadness. "Your father's sacrifice will save many lives."

She nearly slumped with the weight of the news. So much pain and sadness. Yet, there was hope amidst it all.

"Here, let's get you inside. Do we need to take a look at that leg?" He looked at Micah.

Then suddenly, she could feel the heat of both men eyeing her. Her mind scrambled to replay the doctor's last words. Was he questioning whether she trusted Micah's doctoring skills?

She sent a look to the man whom she'd come to trust in full. "Only if Micah thinks there's something that still needs doing, now that he has access to more supplies."

His gaze caressed her, sending a *thank-you* she could feel down to her innermost being.

He turned back to Dr. Stanley. "We should remove the splint and take a look at it, but it will be fine to wait until morning. I think they'll all be better off with a nice meal and a good night's sleep. Is there a place in town we can lodge?"

The man stepped back, sweeping his hand toward the two-story building behind him. "Right here. I have a few rooms in my living quarters you're welcome to. And my housekeeper will be happy to have people to dote on. Come in."

Micah offered to carry her inside, but she shook her head as she put her new walking sticks under her arms. These fit

304

a little better than the pair she'd lost when she fell down the mountain, though she'd still be happy if she never saw them again after today.

But they allowed her to move on her own, and for that she was thankful.

Micah stood close as she mounted the steps into the building, and it was nice to have him there to help. He finally eased his hovering as they stepped down the wide hallway that passed through the center of the house.

"This is where I usually see patients." The doctor motioned to an open door on the right. "But you can see we've run out of room in there." Two people lay on pallets in the hallway, pocks marking their faces. The man looked up at them as they passed but didn't make an effort to speak. The woman, however, pushed herself upright, her thin, blond hair falling over the shoulders of her nightdress.

Ingrid moved toward her, wishing she could kneel beside the woman to be at the same level. "Hello. I'm Ingrid Chastain, come to help Doctor Stanley. How are you feeling today?"

Dark shadows ringed the woman's eyes, but her face softened. "Better." Her voice rasped, probably from lesions in her mouth and throat. Talking had to be painful for her.

Ingrid offered her brightest smile. "Rest now. I'll be back soon to see how I can help."

As she turned on her walking sticks to rejoin the rest of the group, she caught Micah's expression. His face had paled, and his jaw formed a hard line as he stared at the patients. *O, Lord. Wrap him in your love. This won't be easy for him.* She moved toward him and slid her hand into his.

The contact seemed to pull him from his thoughts with effort, but he turned to her and looked like he was working to soften the tightness in his jaw. She leaned into him and rested her head on his shoulder.

The others had already moved on, heading toward an open doorway near the end of the hall.

Micah squeezed her fingers with his gentle touch. "Let's get you settled." His voice was tender, with a trace of sadness lingering. But that was to be expected.

She straightened and looked into his eyes, letting her gaze tell him everything she wanted to say. They would work through this together. With God's strength, they would help these people.

No matter what, she'd be by Micah's side every step of the way.

*My Darling Rachel,*

*Do you remember how you always wanted a pet? You brought home injured birds and frogs and even a prairie dog one time. Mama and I never let you keep them because wild things might sometimes need our care, but eventually they must go back to the place where God created them to live. That's where they'll be happiest.*

*I still believe that, my little Ducky, but I'm only now discovering the entire truth of it.*

*I've met a little dog you would love. His name is Handsome, and his hair is almost as curly as yours, although the color is so black I sometimes call him Shadow.*

*He traveled with me to a nice town called Settler's Fort, and I think we might stay here for a while. At least until God says He has a better place for us.*

*I still miss you, my girl, but I now realize you're in the home where God created you to live. Someday I'll join you in heaven, and we'll skip rocks across the crystal lakes together.*

*Until then, I'll be working hard to do the things God has planned for me, living in freedom, just like those wild animals were after we let them go.*

*Always remember how much I love you.*

*Papa*

◆⊱━⊰◆⊱━⊰◆

Micah stared out the hall window, nerves churning in his gut. When would Ingrid stir from her room?

After eight days working in tandem, he and Dr. Stanley had finally finished the vaccinations that morning on everyone who would agree to receive them. It was a relief to have that done, but the work had been a good chance to meet many of the townspeople.

And a good opportunity to know Dr. Stanley better. He couldn't deny he liked the older man. Weary and overworked, to be sure, but he truly cared about his patients. Cleanliness seemed important to him, too—something frontier doctors didn't always worry with.

Both of those were strong considerations for what he had to discuss with Ingrid.

"Micah?" Ingrid's soft voice made him spin away from the window.

She stood in the doorway of her room, the little dog at her side, soft light framing her slim figure. Wisps of hair hung around her face, accentuating her beauty in a way that took his breath away.

307

He ached to stride to her, take her in his arms, breathe her elegant scent. To relish her, see that soft smile that played across her features, feel the smoothness of her lips with his.

For a long moment, he just stood there, drinking her in. Letting the sight of her fill him.

When she moved, slipping the walking sticks under her arms, his mind finally remembered the thoughts that had been swirling through him.

He stepped forward. "Do you feel better after a rest?"

She slid him a guilty look. "I shouldn't be sleeping when there's still so much to do in the clinic."

He tipped her chin up so he could see those beautiful eyes. "I hear you've been tending patients all morning. And you're still a patient yourself. The doctor ordered you to stay in bed several hours each day to let your leg heal."

In truth, rest was what her weary body needed. He'd never seen her features so relaxed as they were now. A faint line creased her cheek, like the seam of a pillow, making her look more adorable than ever. Warmth slid through him at the thought of her nestled under the covers. One day he'd be there with her. Hopefully soon.

But first, they needed to work out some details. His chest tightened at the reminder of the conversation to come.

"What is it? What's wrong?"

He brought his focus back to her now-worried gaze. Not the feeling he'd wanted to give her. He forced himself to relax as he touched her forearm, sliding his hand down the length of it. "Nothing's wrong. I had a chance to speak with Dr. Stanley, and I'd like to tell you what he said if you have time."

"Of course." The worry in her gaze only intensified. She

turned her wrist so his hand slipped into hers and clung to him. "Tell me."

He'd not meant to worry her. He ran his thumb over the back of her hand. "It's not bad. I mean—it's good." He motioned toward the two chairs by the window. "Can we sit?"

She limped forward, determination marking her stride, even with her shoulders hunched over the walking sticks. After sinking into the chair and adjusting her blue skirt over her splinted leg, she turned resolutely toward him. "What is it?"

He wanted to chuckle at the picture she made. Despite the fragile appearance her refined features and lean build gave her, this woman was no wilting flower. She could face up under any blow, no doubt about it. That was one of the things he loved about her—one of the many.

Her pretty brows drew low and she tilted her chin. "Now you're laughing?"

He leaned forward, reaching for her hands, no longer holding back his grin. "I just love how you don't shy away from a challenge." His thumbs stroked the backs of her fingers as he struggled to gather his scattered thoughts. "I asked Dr. Stanley if there was room in his practice for another. An assistant or . . . fellow doctor."

For some reason, he couldn't bring himself to look at her. Saying the words aloud seemed so pretentious. Sure, he'd finished formal training to be a physician and been Landsburg's only doctor for seven years. But he'd been out of the work almost as long. Why should he be allowed to just step back in, as though he'd never stopped?

"What did he say?" Her words drew his focus back up, and he drew strength from the encouragement in her eyes.

"He said he's been praying for help for over a year now.

He'd like to make me his full partner . . . with the thought of his leaving the area eventually. He'd like to move back to Kansas where his children and grandchildren live. But he wants to wait a few years." He watched her as he spoke, searching for horror or fear or anything else she might try to smother in an effort to make him happy.

Her eyes rounded, not in fear but in . . . wonder? Then definite joy as she squeezed his hands. "Oh, Micah. That's wonderful." She searched him, as though trying to read him, too. "Do you want to join his work?"

They were a pair, weren't they? Neither one of them quite sure what to think about this sudden gift. "I want to know where you want to live—Settler's Fort, or back in Boston, or another place altogether? If God is truly calling me back to doctoring, He'll have work for me wherever He leads us."

Her eyes shimmered, illuminating them from inside. The delicate lines of her throat worked, and she released a breathy laugh as a smile lit her face. "Oh, Micah. I'm so thankful." She pulled one of her hands away to dab her eyes. "I'd be happy anywhere with you, but I do like the idea of staying here."

After a delicate sniff, she took his hand again. "This feels like a blessing from the Father, but I suppose we should pray about it to make sure. Would we need to build a house?"

"Well, Dr. Stanley offered to have us move in here. I don't know how I feel about that permanently, but at least it gives us shelter for a little while." He couldn't help adding the next part. "Once we have children coming, it might be nice to have our own place."

She leaned back in her seat with a chuckle, crimson stealing into her cheeks. "Well."

For a long moment, the two of them sat, looking at each

other, silently taking in the possibilities laid before them. The decisions they made would affect them in ways he didn't even want to consider.

*Give me wisdom, Lord. And courage.* He couldn't let this fear back in. Couldn't pass up the gifts God was giving him just because he wasn't worthy of them. *I need your strength, too, Lord. That inner strength Ingrid talks about. You made Gideon strong when he asked, and I've seen you do it with this remarkable woman beside me. Now I'm asking, too.*

Because God had been good enough to give him this second chance. Loved him enough to give him the best, even when he didn't deserve it.

And now only the Almighty's strength could accomplish the work ahead.

# Epilogue

*T*his day seemed surreal.

Though Ingrid had mostly focused on Papa's work through her growing-up years, she'd occasionally let herself dream of what her wedding day might be like. Not once in all her imaginings had she ever thought she would be in a rustic house in this tiny town in the Montana Territory.

Yet as she stared out the window at the majestic mountain peaks rising as far as she could see, their snow-covered grandeur surging inside her to awaken the sleeping parts, she couldn't imagine being this happy anywhere else.

She hadn't forgotten the treacherous climbs that tested the fortitude of both man and beast, nor the frigid nights unable to feel her toes, nor the view from the top of a cliff, staring down its steep descent. Still, she'd be willing to face any of those trials again—and more—as long as Micah traveled with her.

Micah and the Lord who'd brought them together.

Now, her husband-to-be waited for her in the hallway. The

time had come. Inhaling a deep breath, she turned away from the window.

Joanna stood by the door, a gentle smile softening her face. "Ready?"

She let the joy welling inside her spread onto her face. "More than ready." She'd have married Micah when they first arrived in Settler's Fort, had she been given the chance. But at least this extra time had allowed her leg more time to heal so she only needed a single walking stick. And she'd finally talked Dr. Stanley into removing the splint that morning. Everything had come together for the perfect day.

If only Papa could be here.

Her chest clenched, and she willed the wave of sadness away. Papa was here in spirit, and he'd be happy she found a man like Micah. She had to focus on the good so she didn't dampen the day's joy.

Joanna opened the door and stepped aside as Ingrid limped forward.

A man stood in the open frame, his figure stealing her breath. His blue cotton shirt stretched across his broad shoulders and tapered to a lean waist at the band of his trousers. It might take some time to get used to seeing Micah—her strong, capable mountain man—in such civilized clothing.

Yet he could wear a woolen shroud and her heart would still race at the sight of him, at the love flowing from his dark eyes. The smile creases around them made her yearn to step closer. To place her hands on either side of his handsome face and reach her lips to his.

"Ready?" He raised his dark brows, a twinkle sparkling in his gaze.

Had he read her mind? She fought the heat rising to her

face and nodded. She stepped forward, working to rein her thoughts back to the ceremony before them.

He took her hand but didn't immediately turn to walk her to the minister. Instead he stood, watching her. She met his intense gaze, falling into the love there.

She couldn't have pulled her focus away if she wanted to as he moved in, lowering his mouth to hers. Her eyes drifted shut and every part of her concentrated on him, inhaling his love, melting into his touch.

This man had been created for her. She'd never been so sure of anything in her life.

*Thank you, Father.*

Micah eased away, and under her palm on his chest, his heart pulsed a rapid beat. He pulled back just far enough to study her face, his expression earnest, searching. "I wish your father could be here. He'd be so proud of the woman you are."

Hot tears sprang to her eyes. How had Micah known the one thing that kept this day from perfection?

His thumb brushed her cheek, wiping away the drop that slipped past her defenses.

She sniffed. "I know he'd love you. He's finally getting that son he always wanted, and he'd be so proud you're a doctor."

Something in his face shifted, an ache or maybe a yearning. His Adam's apple bobbed. "I've never had a father I knew. Not an earthly one, anyway."

"Oh, Micah." She moved into him, letting him slip his arms around her. She pressed herself into his chest, absorbing his strength, giving what comfort she had.

Together. They would move forward, taking life in stride . . . together.

After long moments wrapped in his security, renewed by

his love, she pulled back. "Now I'm ready." Her smile felt so much lighter, the weight lifted from her chest.

He slid his fingers down her arm, taking her hand in his, then raised it to his lips. As he pressed a kiss to her fingers, his eyes never left hers. "Me too."

And with her hand tucked safely in his, they turned and moved toward the group clustered at the end of the wide hall. With this man by her side and the Almighty leading the way, they could accomplish whatever lay before them.

And she had a feeling the excitement had only just begun.

*USA Today* bestselling author **Misty M. Beller** writes romantic mountain stories set on the 1800s frontier and woven with the truth of God's love.

She was raised on a farm in South Carolina, so her Southern roots run deep. Growing up, her family was close, and they continue to maintain those ties today. Her husband and children now add another dimension to her life, keeping her both grounded and crazy.

God has placed a desire in Misty's heart to combine her love for Christian fiction and the simpler ranch life, writing historical novels that display God's abundant love through the twists and turns in the lives of her characters. Learn more and see Misty's other books at www.MistyMBeller.com.

# Sign Up for Misty's Newsletter!

Keep up to date with Misty's news on book releases and events by signing up for her email list at mistymbeller.com.

# You May Also Like . . .

Only while trick riding can Ella Fleming forget the truth about who she really is—the daughter of a murderer. Phillip DeShazer buries the guilt he feels for his father's death in work and drink, and his guilt continues to grow the more Ella Fleming comes to his rescue. Will they be able to overcome their pasts and trust God to guide their futures?

*What Comes My Way* by Tracie Peterson, BROOKSTONE BRIDES #3
traciepeterson.com

## BETHANYHOUSE

# More Historical Fiction from Bethany House

Growing up in Colorado, Josephine Madson has been fascinated by but has shied away from the outside world—one she's been raised to believe killed her parents. When Dave Warden, a rancher, shows up to their secret home with his wounded father, will Josephine and her sisters risk stepping into the world to help or remain separated but safe on Hope Mountain?

*Aiming for Love* by Mary Connealy, BRIDES OF HOPE MOUNTAIN #1
maryconnealy.com

Gray Delacroix has dedicated his life to building a successful global spice empire, but it has come at a cost. Tasked with gaining access to the private Delacroix plant collection, Smithsonian botanist Annabelle Larkin unwittingly steps into a web of dangerous political intrigue and will be forced to choose between her heart and her loyalty to her country.

*The Spice King* by Elizabeth Camden, HOPE AND GLORY #1
elizabethcamden.com

As part of a bargain with her wealthy grandmother, Poppy Garrison accepts an unusual proposition to participate in the New York social Season. Forced to travel to America to help his cousin find an heiress to wed, bachelor Reginald Blackburn is asked to give Poppy etiquette lessons, and he swiftly discovers he may be in for much more than he bargained for.

*Diamond in the Rough* by Jen Turano, AMERICAN HEIRESSES #2
jenturano.com

**❖ BETHANYHOUSE**